ALEC

A BROKEN HORN RANCH NOVEL

R.M. NEILL

CONTENTS

Author's Note

CW: amateur light bondage

I wanted to let you know there's rodeo talk in this book. Now if you're not familiar with anything rodeo you'll likely not notice or care, but some of you likely know a thing a two about rodeo.

Hunter and Alec are team ropers. This sport uses a steer, and neither party leaves their horse. Alec, though, he also does tie-down roping, also called calf roping. This event involves him getting off the horse to tie a calf's legs together.

A steer and a calf are two different animals, with the calf being smaller and easier to handle. I've done my best to use the right term in the right places, but if I missed one, please forgive me.

And if you've never heard of mutton busting, it's a kid's event where they hold on to the back of a sheep and hope they don't fall off as it runs across the dirt arena to another sheep.

I initially planned for this book to begin the series. Zane appears in Drawn In By You, the last book of the Sheltered Connections Series. I had huge plans for him to lead this series with a bang, but his voice disappeared when I presented him with Alec. Instead, I carried on with the other couples and hoped Zane would work with me later. Which is how he came to be the final book instead of the first.

But the cool thing is, when I postponed Zane the first time, it was because I wasn't listening to him. I wanted him in a box of my choosing and, as you'll soon read, that's not Zane. I'm glad I waited until it felt right for him because while this is Alec's story, it's also Zane's.

And they both get their happily ever after.

Thank you for sticking with me to get both their stories. I hope you enjoy the eclectic rodeo.

Chapter 1

Alec

"So, will you do it?"

Jacob chews his thumb, eyes scanning my face with hopeful brown eyes as I read the flyer once again.

Bloomburg's First Annual Rodeo

"What exactly do you need me to do? It's been a long time since I've done anything rodeo."

"Not true!" Zane sings from behind the bar, and I roll my eyes.

He places a tray of glasses on the counter haphazardly and leans in closer as the glasses teeter on the tray as if they're unsure about toppling to the floor or not. His green eyes glow with mischief, and I sigh inwardly. Zane is always up for rattling my chain.

"Alec, you rope all the time on the ranch and ride your horse. Same. Thing."

He flashes his charming smile and I shake my head, suppressing the small smile Zane always pulls from me.

"Rodeo is more than roping and riding a horse, Zane. We've been over this."

"Don't listen to him." Jacob says. "It's for charity and I only need someone competent to run a mutton busting competition for the kids. Dan said he'd let us use the sheep from the ranch and you've been in a rodeo. I don't know what the hell I'm doing." He bats his pretty, long eyelashes. "Puh-leeze?"

Pretty boys of all kinds have always been my weakness. Even though Jacob is in a relationship and a friend, I can't say no to those damn doe eyes and lashes.

"Fine. Just tell me what you need and I'll do it."

"Thank you, thank you!" Jacob hugs me and steps back quickly. "Uh, since you already said yes, and offered so kindly, I'd love to add a roping demo. I used to do 4-H, and I found a farmer who said I could borrow a few steers." He swallows hard, straightening his shoulders. "I have an idea."

Zane cackles from behind the bar, and I glare at him.

"I swear to god, Zane. If you did something…"

I let the words die because he knows I'd let him get away with anything. Including making me dress up on Halloween as a bull so he could be a bullfighter. Which worked because I was mad as hell he'd entered us in a contest without asking. Charging was going to happen. But also, he'd rocked that matador outfit. It was worth it in the end. Even if it meant I went home frustrated with my dick in my hand.

"I only mentioned to Jake that you were good at roping. That's all. Then his eyes lit up like a slot machine with triple sevens. Whatever he has planned is on him."

"It's not bad, Alec. I swear." Jake laughs and I sit at the bar, motioning to Zane that I'll have my usual. Since I moved here and took the position as foreman at the Broken Horn Ranch, I've been coming here most evenings. The pub-style restaurant and bar attached to the brewery that Zane co-owns is like a second home. I met Jacob here with his partner, who is also a co-owner, and the men at the brewery became an extended family. My ranch people are too, but this is my place to socialize. Which I don't do as much as I used to while in rodeo. I loved my rodeo days, but it was exhausting hiding all the time.

The homophobia I encountered almost daily wasn't worth it. I loved my sport and the horses, but it was time for me to be me. Especially once I punched the last guy for his ignorant slurs on what was supposed to be a night out with a friend. He lost a tooth that night. And a '*friend*'. I don't regret the punch, but the fine from the rodeo association hit my wallet hard. And my partner at the time didn't like it either.

Zane places a coaster in front of me with a flourish and sets a chilled glass of draft beer on top. I know from the lighter colour that it's not my usual. He quickly turns and does the same for Jake, only Jake drinks *Coke*. And Zane knows I have to say something.

"What the fuck is this, Zane? You know I hate it when you make me a guinea pig all the time."

His lips fight to stay neutral and not give away his amusement with my protest.

"You'll like it. Just try it. Broaden your horizons!"

He spreads his hands in the air in an arch and cracks his usual easygoing smile. The one that makes me forget I'm miffed I didn't get my usual draft. The same smile that drew me to him like a moth to a flame and still does every damn time I see him.

"It's a pale ale with honey. It's not going to kill you. Locally sourced honey, even. Try it." His voice softens as I raise the glass to my lips. "You like honey."

Because I trust Zane–except when it comes to picking Halloween costumes–and I do like honey, I take a sip.

"Mmm, that's really good."

Zane slaps a hand on the bar. "Told you!" He wags a finger at me. "I never steer you wrong with food or beer, my friend. Trust me."

He's not wrong. Doesn't mean I have to give him the satisfaction of being right though.

"So, roping." Jake taps my arm for attention and I can't help but smile. I know I'll say yes to whatever he asks because he's too excited about the event. Besides, the ranch works closely with the brewery and the men here are friends. It's just what you do. You help a friend and, in turn, the town that supports both of your enterprises. I'd be a total jackass to say no.

"What's this idea of yours?"

"I was thinking we would sell tickets to have people's names drawn. Maybe six. We'd have six steers numbered and each steer would be a different prize for the winner. Like, roping steer number five would have the winner get whatever is in box number five. You'd rope them for the winners, and the fastest one roped will win the jackpot."

"What's the jackpot?"

"I don't know. Blaze said he's taking care of it and it would be worth it. I just need you to show up."

"So are we talking tie-down roping, too? You want me to do the whole bit?"

"Uh, yes? Whatever cowboys do when they swing the cool rope and then tie the calf's feet."

There's a slight flush to his cheeks and if I didn't know better, I'd think Jake has a thing for cowboys.

"And jump off my horse, run to him after roping and then get back on my horse and do it how many times in a row?"

God, my body aches just thinking about it. Sure, the ranch work keeps me fit, but it's not so easy for me anymore, dismounting and doing the tie-down part. It's been years. And my injury doesn't help either.

But it's also a small town rodeo. They won't even know if I screw up. They'd just know I'm slow.

I have to admit I'm excited because I've always loved rodeo, but... I'm out of practice and this could hurt.

"What if instead of doing tie-down with the actual steers–and me being lame for a week after–we use something else?"

Jacob nods along. "Okay, like what?"

"Well, if you just want me to '*swing a cool rope*', as you put it, I could aim for a target. Like a set of horns or even a teddy bear on a barrel or something. Anything to keep me from the constant off and on the horse."

"Oh! I like that idea! I wouldn't need to worry about trailering steers either. Set up would be stuffed animals on barrels and maybe the prize would be inside! That's a better idea, Alec."

Thank god. I love roping. But even I know my hip would be killing me after that. I won't be telling him team roping is an option, either. My partner ditched me the same night I threw a punch, standing up for myself. I never rode with another roping partner after that.

"Okay, so when is this event planned for? Soon, right?"

"You have two weeks to practice, and I, ah, Blaze said he knows some guys from the Prairies who sort of do other events on the side. If you wanted to, we could do a mini rodeo. Like a skills competition, he said!"

Fucking Blaze. Leave it to him to make a bigger deal out of this for the town. I should've known all his questions over the last month weren't just innocent curiosity. He's a sly one, pretending to ask me where I first started and getting my rodeo life story.

"Looks like I need to have a discussion with my so-called friend. But don't worry, I'll do what you need me to."

"Uh…" Jacob clears his throat and I raise an eyebrow.

"What?"

"Don't get mad."

"That's never a good way to lead with a question, Jake. Spill it."

"A cowboy auction," he blurts and grins so wide it might be painful. Zane was right, his eyes do light up like he hit the jackpot on the nickel slots.

"Explain, please."

I gulp a mouthful of the honey ale I'm too stubborn to tell Zane is really freaking good, and wait for Jacob to give me the story.

"It's like a bachelor auction, but with cowboys? Instead of fancy tuxedos, you'll wear those amazing wranglers and boots and *ohmygod*, one of those huge belt buckles if you have any!" He blushes when my eyebrows shoot up. "And, uh, we would auction you for a date."

Jacob runs a finger through the condensation on his glass. "So...do you have one of those belt buckles, by chance? I mean, I'm just curious."

"I have several." I lean closer, lowering my voice. "One even has diamonds on it because the rodeo was called the Diamond Rodeo. It sparkles."

I chuckle as Jake sucks in a breath.

"So, what's the big idea Jake had? I missed it because, unlike you two, I work here."

"A cowboy auction!" Jake blurts again and this time I can't hold the laugh in. I think this might be some long-repressed fantasy he has. I should let his partner, Matts, borrow a belt buckle.

"Ohhh, very cool." Zane nods as he slides a glass of water over when Jacob empties his *Coke*. "I think that would bring in a crap load of money for the shelters. Are you bringing in any celebrity cowboys? Is that a thing?"

"You'd have to talk to Blaze about that, but I think a few models from my brother-in-law, Logan's, agency are coming. I think they just want to meet the cowboys, but it means famous names on the poster."

Jacob's NHL star older brother married a supermodel, and that's the whole reason he organizes these events; to raise money for the animal shelter and LGBTQ youth shelter in town. I know nothing about models, but another pretty face in town for a few days wouldn't be a hardship.

"Jacob, it's a good thing I like you. I thought I was only agreeing to a rodeo demo. Now I'm doing a skills competition and auctioning myself."

"Yeah, I'm sort of sorry about that? But Zane wasn't really sure what you might agree to and neither was Dan. But when I asked Blaze he got really excited and said I should, *'not be immediately transparent'*, so I figured I'd err on the side of caution, just in case."

Zane delivers my favourite mushroom and swiss burger with caesar salad—croutons on the side.

"Thanks, Zane. Are you joining me, Jake, or do you have what you need?"

He checks his phone before standing.

"I'll take a raincheck and we'll catch up over dinner once I get to the final details. Thanks again, Alec. It's all for a good cause, remember."

He pats me on the back as he heads toward the offices, likely to find Matts and go home for the night. When I open my burger to add my usual condiments, Zane places a hand over mine.

"I did it for you already."

"Did you sneak something new in there?"

"I promise you'll like it."

"Tell me what it is and pray you didn't fuck up my burger. I'm really hungry, Zane."

"You'll like it, I promise. It's a new mushroom and onion combo. Red onions with sliced portobello steak mushrooms and a tangy mustard."

When I make a face, he laughs at me again. "Just eat it, Alec. It'll be good."

The thing with Zane is that I trust him more than anyone. He's never been wrong about what I like and don't. But change is hard for me sometimes. Even if it's only a new kind of mushroom.

But when I taste the burger and sigh at the flavours that burst onto my tongue, Zane grins.

"Told ya."

"Stop being right, it's annoying."

"Stop being so grumpy and eat. Are you still coming over tonight to watch the next episode of the *Mandalorian* with me?"

"Of course I am. We always watch it on Tuesdays."

And because it's more time alone with Zane where I can just be with him and all his... *Zaneness.*

"Cool. I was just checking. I know you've been busy at the ranch, so I didn't want to assume."

Nodding as I chew and swallow the amazing burger I'm loathe to admit he made better, I agree.

"We have been busy, but I'm not missing this. I'll follow you home as soon as you're done here."

As Zane moves off to help a new table that was seated for dinner, he calls out.

"As long as following me home doesn't mean I have to ask my mother to keep you."

He laughs and again I shake my head.

Zane. Two people more opposite than us shouldn't exist so well together. And yet, we fit so easily, balancing each other.

His over-the-top to my reasonable. His blond to my dark. His bravery to try new adventures and food to my preference for staying with the tried and true.

He's been my best friend for the last three years and is my ride or die.

He feeds me even when I say I don't like it. He shows up at my house and takes care of my plants without me asking, and he's the only friend I've ever had who pushes me to try things, not because he wants me to, but just because he knows I'll like it.

Except that Halloween costume. I'm still not over that.

"Hey, Alec. I hear you said yes to Jacob. He just talked my ear off for ten minutes. You've made his day."

Dylan, one of the brewery owners and Zane's best friend since high school, pulls out the barstool next to me.

"Hi, Dylan. Yeah, it appears he was coached on how to ask me so I'd not say no." Wiping my chin, I laugh. "I wouldn't have said no anyway. I knew he was planning another event and I know they're always for charity, so...not much to consider, you know?"

"Dylan! You staying?"

Zane knocks on the bar in front of Dylan with his knuckles and lifts an empty glass.

"Nah. I need to get home. Nell and Travis are cooking for me tonight. I cashed in a Father's Day coupon and I'm a little nervous about it."

"Yikes. I don't blame you. Well, the diner is open if it's horrible." Zane jokes and returns the glass to the tray. He steals a crouton off my plate and I roll my eyes.

"I just wanted to say hi to Alec and tell him how thrilled Jake is." He pauses. "And something about belt buckles?"

I snort. "I'm pretty sure there's a story there, but I don't want to ask."

"Fair enough. Okay, have a great night and I'll see you tomorrow, Zane."

I've finished my burger and Zane makes sure the night staff is set before he signals he's ready to leave. I toss a twenty-dollar bill on the bar and he stuffs it in the tip jar. If he never wants to charge me, I just leave the money for the staff. I would never feel right leaving here without paying in some way. Zane knows not to fight me on it. So that's our compromise.

"Do you really think Jacob has a fetish for belt buckles? Is he a secret...what do you call them? Buckle bunny?"

Laughter bursts from my mouth.

"Yeah, that's what we call them. And I don't want to know."

"He's going to ask you for a buckle you know."

We both slide into our vehicles. Like I always do, I parked next to him in the spot he had made for me in the staff parking area.

"Okay, cowboy. Try not to follow too close on the way home."

He closes the door to his BMW and I climb into the pickup truck I've owned for far too long.

I always follow him at a safe distance.

That's how you don't get hurt.

Everyone knows that.

Chapter 2

Zane

The end credits begin rolling with the theme music and I glance over to find Alec with his chin to his chest, lightly snoring.

I knew he'd likely fall asleep. I just lost track of when he did because I was too into the episode. I don't even like this kind of show as a rule, but ever since Alec turned it on one night, I've been hooked and it's kind of our thing now.

Easing off the couch so I don't disturb him, I pad down the hall to my linen closet and gather the spare blanket and pillow in my arms. I know I could wake him up and he'd likely get home just fine, but... I never allow him to do that. Not that I make the choice for him, but I think he appreciates that I don't force him off my couch, and he has the option to stay.

He raises his head when I return to the living room. Groggy blue eyes blink at me before a slow smile appears.

"I didn't think I'd fall asleep."

I laugh softly.

"Alec, you've been working hard, and it's a late night. It catches up to you."

"I remember *Mando* telling the kid to go for help. Then I fell asleep. Something good happened, didn't it?"

He unbuckles his pants as he stands and I sort of smile, since he never wears the giant belt buckles Jake is so hot for. He'll take his jeans and t-shirt off and sleep on my couch. He'll wake up before me and put the coffee on. We'll share our morning coffee before we go our separate ways.

Just like we've done so many times before over the years.

"Yeah, something really good. We'll have to restart there next Tuesday."

His jeans thump on the floor, the belt jingling, and his shirt gets thrown to the pile.

Taking the blanket I hand him, he snuggles down onto my oversized sofa and under the fuzzy blanket with a sigh.

"Thanks, buddy. I'll see you in the morning for our coffee."

Soft snores already sound from the couch before I can answer.

"See you in the morning, cowboy."

On the way to my room, I check that the nightlight in the bathroom is on so he can find his way. Sometimes he's so sleepy he walks past it to my room and then mutters before turning around and heading back to the bathroom.

I quickly strip to my boxers and slide into bed.

Smiling to myself in the dark, I'm grateful Alec decided we could be friends. Which is sort of what happened. Since my best friend, Dylan, found his match with Travis, he's not always available to hang out. And not everyone accepts my caretaking ways. It's not like I don't have other friends, they just don't understand me like Alec does.

From the moment he showed up at the brewery with Dan to help with our grand opening of the restaurant, we hit it off, and we've been almost inseparable.

And these nights he sleeps over? They're the best because he makes amazing coffee the next morning. It's the only time I ever drink coffee since I prefer tea. Just another thing Alec had me try, and now I can't live without. I suppose we balance each other well, since I'm always shoving food down his throat to try. He never complains and I'm usually right that he'll like it.

Except for that time I thought for sure he'd like the pumpkin spice in his beer.

Spoiler alert - he didn't.

Sometimes I wonder if I should look into adopting a pet to dote on, but Alec assures me my friends appreciate all my food and caregiving. So I've listened and haven't rescued a cat from the shelter. Besides, he said I could go to the ranch whenever I want and help with any of the animals.

And his plants. I really like taking care of his plants, too. That reminds me, one of his violets needs a bigger pot. Before I drift off, I make a note on my phone to buy one... with soil, because he probably doesn't have that either.

With a yawn, I finally roll over and fall asleep.

The bed dips next to me and for a moment I'm disoriented. But then I hear Alec's low chuckle and the scent of coffee at my nose.

Blinking my eyes open, Alec smiles next to me, holding a mug of morning nectar.

"*Ohmygod* you're a prince. Gimme."

He lets me take the steaming mug, but I hand it back to him immediately.

"I can't drink laying down." I grumble before pushing myself up and taking the mug again.

After a sip, I close my eyes with a sigh.

"Fuck, you make good coffee. I don't even like it anywhere else. Only yours."

"Years of practice. I better be good at it."

He picks up his own mug from my nightstand and I hide a smile at the pillow line on his face. Good thing he's working with animals who won't laugh.

"Can you do me a favour today?"

"Of course. As long as it's nothing illegal, I can do what you need."

"Can you buy me a few different types and sizes of teddy bears for the thing Jacob has planned? I'd like to practice on them and see what will work best."

"It won't be a chore to shop for teddy bears. I have to get a new pot for your violet, anyway. How many teddies would you like?"

He shrugs, running a hand through his messy hair.

"Just pick some of varying shapes and sizes. Nothing too small, but it still needs to be a challenge. And make sure some have long legs."

He stands gently so I don't slosh my coffee.

"I trust you to pick something reasonable. I've gotta get going. We have a load of hay arriving and I think I need to fix some of the stalls in the barn for a few of the boarders. I'll talk to you tonight?"

"Of course. Have a good day."

He smiles as he leaves my room, knocking on the door frame as he walks through.

Sitting up, I drain my coffee before pulling on a pair of sleep pants and wandering to the kitchen for a refill. Alec left his folded up blanket on the couch next to the pillow and as I reach the kitchen, he pops back through the back door.

"That raccoon was in the garbage again, Zane. You really need to be careful with him and lock up your garbage. Do you have time to clean it up?"

With a sigh, I nod.

"Yeah, I do. I'll get new garbage cans today, too, and try that."

"Wear gloves and be careful."

Alec disappears again and once the crunching gravel under his tires fades away, I pull out a pair of rubber gloves and a garbage bag to clean up the mess.

At least the raccoon raided the trash cans before I had a shower. Gotta look on the bright side, right?

It wasn't as bad as the previous messes, at least. I had it all cleaned up and was out of the shower thirty minutes later, just in time to see my phone light up with an incoming call from my ex-girlfriend.

With a sigh, I answer.

"Hey, Marla."

"Hi Zane. Is this a good time?"

"I have a few minutes."

Which is not a lie. While I don't hate talking to her when she calls, sometimes I feel bad because I can't say what she wants to hear.

"I found one of your t-shirts here. Would you like me to drop it off?"

Ugh. I wish she'd stop doing this.

"Marla...listen. If I left anything there, just get rid of it, okay? There's a better person for you out there."

She sniffles and I wish I hadn't been the one to make her sad. But I couldn't stick around and pretend. She's a nice person. She's just not *my* person.

"I miss you. I know I forced you into things you didn't want, but I can accept that you don't want what I do, Zane. We can try your way."

"That's not how it works. We've been over this. You didn't force me, okay? I just don't feel the same as you."

More sniffles fill my ear, and I don't know what else to say. I don't love her. I never did. We had sex a few times and dated a few months. I left not because I was afraid of commitment, but because we had no connection other than what was on the surface. A walk in the park, a talk about current events, but nothing that made me want to love her that way.

"I'm sorry, Zane, but you're really hard to get over, and the fact you keep being nice about it makes it worse. I can't even be mad at you."

"I feel like I should be flattered, but Marla, I just couldn't stay when you felt that way and I didn't. Promise me you'll stop calling, please? It's not good for you."

I know she's crying, and it breaks my heart because I'm the reason.

"Goodbye, Zane. I'm sorry and I hope you find someone to love, too."

After she ends the call, I sit on my couch, spinning the phone in my hand. Marla doesn't need to know, but her declaration of love and the discussion that followed between us opened my eyes.

I spent a lot of time analyzing my past relationships and questioning things I thought I knew about myself. I still am, because it's a hell of a revelation to have. Learning you aren't in one specifically labelled sexuality box makes the whole dating thing more challenging than it was before.

I found Marla very attractive, and we did sleep together. She thinks she forced me into it, but I did it willingly. It wasn't a bad experience. It was just... hard to describe because it left me not caring if we did it again. I cared about her as a person, but not as a romantic partner.

I didn't love her and I never would.

And now that I've worked that little bit out with the help of a therapist, there's another part I need to work out still.

My gaze lands on the folded blanket Alec left behind.

I just hope I don't break my own heart in the process.

Chapter 3

Alec

There's nothing quite like a long day of physical labour to remind you of your age. One day I'll stop putting my body through this, but it's not anytime soon. As much as my hip aches, I'm too stubborn to quit. I love what I do and I can't envision a future without my work.

The horses, the ranch, and the labour that comes with it are what I love.

And aside from my time in the rodeo, it's all I know.

The steaming water of my hot tub hits my exposed flesh and I groan as I settle in. There's nothing like a little hydrotherapy at the end of a hard day. I called Zane like I promised and told him I'd not be by the bar tonight. I didn't tell him it was because I was in pain, because that would only make him worry. Although I do love it when he goes all mother hen on me. He brought me soup when I had a cold once. He's left me dinner in the fridge a few times when we spent long days in the fields, and he knew I'd be collapsing into bed instead of my nightly bar visit.

But tonight I want to just be.

I'm in a mood.

Loneliness and a bit of pity crept in when I wasn't paying attention.

A hairline fracture, initially thought to only be a deep bruise from being kicked by a horse, had morphed into a bone spur over the past several years. Some days it feels like one wrong step will have me tumble to the ground in a mass of twisted limbs. Other days I chew on ibuprofen like they're candy and get by. Barely.

No matter what the pain level of the day is, the hot tub always helps. Once I'm in position in front of the massaging jets I allow the tension and discomfort of the day to float away with the bubbles on the water's surface.

The only thing to make my busted up body feel better, next to the hot tub, would be having Zane massage my CBD lotion across my back and hip. The cream lasts longer than pills and is an amazing pain relief. Having my best friend's hands on me in intimate areas, though, was something I couldn't keep doing.

Not when I'm already desperately in love with him.

Rather than lay my heart bare for him and see if the affection could be returned, I choose to live with it in silence. Burying it like a treasure I try not to look at every day because it's too beautiful. I'm too much of a coward to open the box and show Zane.

"Alec? You back there?"

Blaze's voice booms in my tiny yard, and I sigh.

"Yep. Come around if you want to?"

Blaze's footsteps come closer as he walks along the tiny brick path beside my house leading to my deck. His smiling face comes into view when he bounces up the steps and drops his ass on a patio chair.

"Are you mad at me?"

There's a genuine concern in his voice, and I shake my head.

"Not overly. I know you mean well. I just wish you didn't hide what you wanted all the information for. I would've told you, anyway."

"Yeah. I thought of that after and I figured you would, but then I didn't want to say in case Jake had a plan. Anyway, I'm sorry. I just wanted to say that. Since you know about the rodeo and auction and stuff now."

"It's fine. Although I do want a heads up on who you've contacted to come here. Not all the people I spoke about are friendly. What are you doing here so late, anyway?"

Blaze sets his *Stetson* on my small patio table, running his hand through his hair.

"Dan and I had a meetin' about expandin' the ranch and staff. It's stretchin' us all a little thin right now. I'm sure you wouldn't mind havin' a little more free time."

I shrug and shift under the water to reposition myself in front of the jets.

"It's not like I have family to visit or anything. Or someone to take a vacation with."

Blaze is the only one I confessed my feelings to about Zane. He's listened to my heartache over far too many coffees and sunrises. His current look of sadness doesn't help.

"You still don't want to tell him, do you?"

"Blaze, I can't do that. It would change everything, and I don't think I'd survive it if he told me to fuck off."

"He would never do that."

"But you don't know that!"

He jerks back at my sudden shout, eyes wide, and I breathe a heavy sigh.

"Blaze, I know you're a huge romantic, but my life has never gone like the script of a *Hallmark* movie. I'd rather suffer quietly and keep him close."

He knows not to mention it anymore and shifts to the topic he came here for.

"I've invited three guys to come for this rodeo skills comp Jacob is all horny to put on. Jimmy Collins, who does bronc ridin', Mike McCaw, the bull rider, and Hunter Sotherby, another roper you said you know well."

Oh no.

Swallowing, I figure it's a good time to tell Blaze how I know Hunter so well.

"I do know Hunter. He was my closeted partner for two years before I punched someone and he left me in case he was found out. So I have mixed feelings about Hunter."

"Shit. Why didn't you tell me that part? I wouldn't have invited him."

I wave my hand at him to be quiet.

"It's fine. We parted on good enough terms. It was just painful because he wasn't willing to be out with me. I...yeah, it's okay. Really."

Time has allowed me to get over the blip of reality that not everyone chooses to fight for the same cause. He had a lot at stake, and I understood why he left. Mostly. Didn't make it hurt less when he did. But he's a great roper and even went on to win a few awards after I left the rodeo circuit. I was happy for him.

"As long as you're okay with those three and you aren't just sayin' so."

"I'm fine."

He stands and places his hat back on his head.

"I'm lookin' forward to the auction part myself. If you need help with a wardrobe, you let me know."

He winks at me as I shake my head with a laugh and he leaves the way he came in.

Stepping out of the hot tub, I grab a towel from the rack, drop my swim trunks, and pat myself dry before wrapping it around my waist. I close up the hot tub and go back inside, grabbing the tube of CBD cream out of the bathroom.

Sitting on the side of the bed, I rub it into the sore spot. Even if I did tell Zane how I feel, what would he want with me? I'm a forty-something ranch foreman with an arthritic hip. As part of my salary, I live on the ranch in this tiny house I adore. I don't want to move or change a thing. My time in rodeo earned me some big money that I've invested, but never touched. I'm just a simple guy who talks to his plants and loves to be on a horse as often as possible.

Zane could do better than a damaged cowboy. Besides, he's straight anyway, so either way you look at it, I'm living with this bullshit of unrequited love forever.

Wiping my hands on my towel, I throw it in the hamper and stand naked in front of the mirror behind my bedroom door.

I'm in decent shape. Turning sideways, I suck in my belly. My body isn't as defined as it once was, likely from drinking all the beer the guys at the brewery make. And maybe from the stuff Zane always feeds me.

He's an amazing cook. And person.

I do love my eyes, though. So there's that. But blue eyes aren't enough to win an auction. I could find my chaps, maybe. I hear that's a kink for cowboy lovers.

Maybe the models coming will be into me and I can lose myself in a few days of naked fun and forget this mess I've made in my heart.

With a sigh I let my shoulders sag.

"What am I getting myself into? Rodeo and a cowboy auction? It's been ten years since I've played the cowboy part. And an auction like I'm a side of beef?"

Zane's words from a prior conversation still cling to my brain, though.

You're a catch.

Surely if he thinks that someone else must, too.

Sliding under my covers, I close my eyes and wait for the fatigue to take me to sleep.

Whistling a command to Dan's sheepdog, Daisy, I watch as she burns away to the side, herding the sheep down the field toward the chute where they can cross the road into the next pasture.

My horse, Domino, a gorgeous black-and-white quarter-horse I've owned for almost fifteen years, twitches her ears and snorts as I lead her in the opposite direction of Daisy. Domino picks up her pace with no coaxing. She knows what she needs to do. I'm just on board for the ride. I love herding the sheep with these two. It's so peaceful and, with Domino and Daisy, it's easy.

Domino and I move as one. She allows me to stop thinking and live in the moment. Just a man on his horse in the open field, grateful for another day above ground with the blue sky. Daisy is well-trained, and it's an absolute joy to watch her work needing only a short whistle or wave of my hand. The soft bleats of the sheep and the gentle thumping of the herd's feet over the grass are my favourite melody. It's accompanied by Domino's periodic snorts and the squeak of the leather saddle, and my heart fills with the contentment that can only be found out here.

You can't take the cowboy out of the man. No matter where I live and what I do, I'll always feel most comfortable on the back of a horse. The rope around the saddle horn is something I was also comfortable with once. Zane thinks I use it every day. Which I do when I need to perform fast rope ties when halters break or a gate needs extra latching. But that's not the same as swinging a lasso over your head and timing it just right to land around a calf's neck to lead it out of harm's way.

A few sheep try to break in a new direction, but I whistle the command and Daisy zooms after the breakaways, herding them back to the flock.

"C'mon girl." I click my tongue and nudge Domino with my heels, and she breaks into a smooth run. I guide us towards the gate we're steering the flock to and lean over to unlatch it. It swings out into the small country road to block any traffic that might happen by while we're changing fields. In all the times we've done this, I've yet to see even a tractor putter by, but it does help the crossing go smoothly.

I quickly secure the open gate across the road by attaching it to a fence post on the other side. I repeat the process for the second swing gate. Once finished, it's a direct chute across the road and into the next field. Domino waits for me to remount and when I do, I step us out of the way and command Daisy to move the flock forward. As the sheep stream by, I glance down at my tying rope and lasso.

No time like the present to practice, right?

Once all the sheep have crossed the road, I dismount and put the gates back to unblock the roadway. Daisy pants at my feet.

"Good work, Daisy. Let's get you some water."

Pulling a dish and a canteen of water from a saddlebag, I let Daisy drink from the bowl while I watch the sheep spread out to graze in the new pasture. Domino grazes near me, knowing she can have a long drink once we hit the creek on the way back.

My long range walkie talkie crackles to life with Dan's voice.

"Alec? Where you at?"

Pressing the talk button, I answer.

"I just crossed to the new pasture and I'm about to head back. What do you need?"

"Heath's car broke down and Dante needed him to help load goods for the llama thing he's doing. Can you help him when you get back? I'd do it, but I'm about to head out to pick up a pair of donkeys that have nowhere to go."

"Sure, no problem, boss. Did you already get a stall ready for the donkeys?"

"I did. The isolation barn is set up, but feel free to have a look when you're back to make sure I didn't forget anything."

He doesn't forget things, but I'll check, anyway.

"Tell Dante I'm about an hour away."

Dan acknowledges, and I mount Domino after repacking Daisy's dish. My rope practice will have to wait.

CHAPTER 4

ZANE

"I sent you a proof of the new pride can label. Did you get it?"

Martin's voice pulls me away from the text Alec just sent.

"Uh, yeah. I think so. I'll check again."

"Is everything okay?"

Martin's sharp gaze misses nothing and it cuts into my concentration as I search for his email.

"It's fine. Alec was supposed to come over tonight, but he has to help Dante with something." I shift my focus to Martin. "I was going to make his favourite pizza, but now that he can't make it, my evening is free. Do you want to hang out tonight?"

Martin laughs with mock insult.

"You're inviting me out because your first choice bailed. Flattering."

"Sorry, you know it's not like that. But honestly, it's been a long time since we caught up and had a guys' night. You've been just as busy as me."

"That's true. Since Dan isn't back until late tonight, I'm free. I think it's a great idea. I need to wrap up a few things and we can leave in about half an hour, if that's okay?"

I nod, relieved in a weird way to spend time with Martin. We used to go out together a lot when we were the only two single guys in the group. Back when Dylan still had a wife and both Martin and I weren't really looking for love. Now he's found happiness with Dan and I'm still the single guy.

Finding the email Martin sent, I open the artwork for the label he designed. We wanted something special to celebrate the diversity of sexualities. An inclusive design to show our patrons what we stand for, and a portion of sales will go to not just the local LGBTQ youth shelter, but other worthy organizations province-wide.

Now that we were a stable company, we decided as a group to step up our brand and make a larger effort for charitable causes. Including sustained visibility. The can wouldn't just be for Pride Month, but all year round. Two of my business partners are gay and one is bisexual in a same-sex relationship. Those things don't change the other eleven months of the year. I support them three-hundred-and-sixty-five days a year, not just the thirty days of Pride. If our extended efforts can help even one person, it's a success.

For some reason, a wave of emotion washes over me and my chest tightens as I stare at the beautiful design on my computer screen. A rainbow ribbon wraps around a bouquet of various flags of the LGBTQ community. I don't know all of them, but one flag in particular stands out to me because it's one I've been thinking about a lot recently.

"This is beautiful, Marty. How did you choose which flags to put on? Last I read, there were over fifty different flags for all the sexual diversities."

He leans back in his chair with a sigh.

"I wanted to use them all, but I couldn't make a design that worked where they all got the attention they deserve. I'm thinking of creating a few designs similar to that one and showcasing a few at a time. It's important to me for us to be completely inclusive and not come across as rainbow washers."

His jaw tightens with his statement. We've seen other companies be outed for that and there's no way we want to be lumped into the same category. This label rebrand needs to be well-thought-out and we want our message heard.

And if someone stops drinking our beer because of it? Well, that says more about them and we're not changing a thing.

"Rotating designs is a good idea."

My gaze shifts back to the image on the screen. Hands of all shapes and colours hold the flag bouquet. It's simple yet powerful. Our logo sits underneath the bouquet and in a delicate font it reads, '*We stand for everyone*'.

"Do you want to go to the steakhouse tonight? I feel like a glass of wine, otherwise I'd suggest the diner."

I laugh. Martin loves his fine dining with wine.

"Sure. I could go for a giant hunk of meat."

He snorts. "Careful what you say, Zane. I might think you don't mean steak." He closes his laptop and stands, a teasing grin on his face. "If so, I need the deets."

I shut down my computer and laugh, hoping it sounds normal because he's too close to what's been on my mind.

"Oh, shut it. I just want something big and juicy." He laughs again, lifting an eyebrow at me. "Oh, for god's sake, I want a piece of steak. Stop making everything dirty."

He shrugs into his suit jacket. "I can't help it. Blame Dan."

Martin spins his phone on his desk before snatching it mid spin and placing it in his pocket.

"You drive. I might drink a bottle if it tastes good."

"Still the same bossy guy who used to make me fetch him drinks from the bar, I see."

We leave the building together, waving at the bar staff as we leave. My kitchen manager is top-notch, and that allows me to leave worry free.

As we drive to the restaurant, we chat about the weather and the recent increase in costs for our packaging. I ask Martin about his family and he tells me how they're on his back about making an honest man out of Dan.

"Your parents want you to get married?" I laugh because Martin's parents are the most liberal people I know. His older sister wasn't married before she had a baby and it was never an issue. Actually, I think she's *still* unmarried *and* living with the guy. But they're on Martin's case?

"Yeah. They tell me my sister will never do it and they want to see one of their kids get married before they die. Then my dad will dramatically clutch at his heart to lay on the guilt. No pressure there, right?"

"I'm sorry, man."

I park the car out front of the steakhouse, and he surprises me as we walk inside.

"Don't be. I was already thinking about it before they brought it up."

"Really!? Shit, are you going to propose?"

A small grin plays on his lips. "Maybe."

Opening the door for us, he lets me go in first. The hostess greets us, and it's not until we're settled in our booth that I press for more details.

"Marty, you can't bring that kind of thing up and not tell me more. Spill it."

He's about to, but the server shows up and Martin asks a million questions about the wine list before finally ordering something I can't even pronounce.

"First of all, I trust you to not say anything." Martin leans across the table, excitement dancing in his eyes.

"You know I wouldn't. I've still never told your parents it was you who puked in the flower bushes that one night. Your mom was pissed, and I took her wrath for you, my friend."

He barks a laugh.

"You did, and I still thank you. She always mentions how her rose bush died because of you and I have to change the subject."

I snort. "I hope that makes you feel guilty every time."

Martin's face grows serious and his voice drops to a whisper.

"I never believed in real love until I met Dan. Nobody could be more perfect for me." He sucks in a breath. "I bought a ring."

"Oh my god, Marty. I'm so happy for you. When are you going to ask him?"

"I don't know." He chuckles a nervous laugh and pulls a small box from his coat pocket. "I've been carrying it around every day thinking I'd surprise him. I'm a creature of habit, as you know. He reads me so well, and *just once* I want to get a step ahead of him and ask when he doesn't expect it. So I've been carrying it around for the last two weeks."

He flips open the lid and inside the box is a simple metal band. Platinum, if I had to guess, because Martin does nothing lowbrow.

"I also have a silicon one, since I'm not sure if he'd wear something this fancy every day. He works with his hands so much and I know they'd cut it off if he were to get hurt. He'd hate that. So I wanted to give him options. Options to wear, not to answer. Because no isn't an option."

He spews all that out on a single breath and there's a slight shake to his hands.

"Marty, take a breath. He won't say no."

He snaps the box closed and slides it back in his pocket right as the server arrives with our drinks. After placing our dinner orders, I raise my glass to my long-time friend.

"Here's to you and the next step in your life. Dan is a wonderful man and you deserve happiness forever."

Martin places his wine down after a long, and maybe not so gracious, chug from the glass.

"Thanks, Zane. I've missed our outings. How are things with you? I know you've been working a lot and, since Marla, you don't seem to talk about dating much anymore. Are you even getting out?"

"Some, but it hasn't been going well."

Martin raises an eyebrow. "You're striking out?"

A nervous laugh bubbles out. "Something like that. More like I can't be bothered to lift the bat these days."

Martin cocks his head and peers over his wine at me. I feel like I'm trapped in *Superman's X-ray vision* and he knows everything I haven't said.

"I know you won't repeat that."

He shakes his head. "I'd never do that. But...do you want to talk about it?"

Do I?

I don't know. I've been twisting myself up over it and questioning a whole lot of stuff about myself these past few months. I know I can trust Martin, but I'm not ready to talk out loud just yet about something I'm still figuring out about myself.

"I don't think I'm quite ready yet, but thank you for the offer. When I am, I'll be sure to take you up on it."

He nods and eases us back to safer topics when our salad arrives.

"Eww, you don't get your dressing on the side?"

"For a Caesar salad? Why would I do that?" He says around a mouthful of greens.

"So I can eat your croutons. Alec always gets his dressing on the side so I can eat non-soggy croutons."

"Well, I'm not Alec, and I like them *in* my salad. Eat your own."

"Rude."

He laughs and I eat my spinach and goat cheese salad without croutons, thanks to Martin.

Our evening is amazing. We talk and laugh like two long-lost friends catching up. Even though we work together and see each other every day, we've been missing each other's company.

Martin made the right call with me driving. He did drink the entire bottle of wine and he's now very drunk.

And chatty. Extra chatty.

"Zane, you know I love you, right?"

His voice slurs as he smiles at me all crooked in the darkness of the car.

"Yeah, I know Marty. I love you, too."

Thank god he's a loveable drunk and not an angry one.

"You need to be happy. Have you noticed how much you laugh with Alec? He's so great." He sighs with a giggle. "I love him. Like, not '*in love*' with him, of course, but if I was single I'd look twice, you know?"

He hiccups and laughs while I shake my head.

"He's funny, yes. We laugh together a lot."

"He's into you. That doesn't bother you?"

I snap my eyes away from the road to stare at my friend in the passenger seat.

"What? No he's not."

Martin snorts and slaps his thigh.

"*Zaaanne*," he drawls with an exaggerated eye roll. "You are so oblivious."

My heart races with Martin's words.

"You're drunk and being silly. I'm not oblivious. He's a friend, just like Dylan."

When Martin suddenly goes silent, I risk a glance his way and immediately pull over.

"Don't puke in my car, Martin. Open the door."

Thankfully he does, and stumbles out onto the shoulder. Leaning against my car, he inhales deep breaths as I hover close by in case he needs help.

"I'm okay. I don't drink wine much anymore. It sort of snuck up on me."

"Well, you're almost home at least, and I can hand you off to Dan."

He smiles again and looks up into the clear night sky.

"Home. It still sounds weird. My home on a ranch. The bed I share with a rancher. Home, home, on the range," he sings with a snort. "His half of the closet is practically empty and mine is bursting with suits and designer clothes." He's still leaning his body against the car while it idles, the headlights cutting a path along the quiet dirt road.

"You've never been happier than when you're there, though, Martin. I remember how you hated spending the night at Dan's at first. The early hours. The smell of the barn."

He wrinkles his nose and gags. Maybe I shouldn't have brought up the smells.

"I...fuck, Zane. I'm so gone for him." He laughs, but it's a strangled sound on the verge of tears. I forgot what it's like with a drunk Martin. Along with his talkative streak, he's hyper-emotional when he drinks.

"I know you are, Marty. Now why don't you get back inside the car and I'll take you to him? If I know Dan, he's probably waiting up for you."

Another loopy smile as he wobbles towards the car door.

"I bet he is, too. Fuck, I love him. Maybe I should propose tonight?"

He buckles himself in and fishes the engagement ring from his pocket.

"I say this as your closest friend, Martin. *Don't*. You're drunk. You can do better and he deserves better."

He sighs. "You're right. I need to do something special. But I love him."

"You've mentioned that several times. I know."

"I could just blow him instead. Drunk sex is the best sex." With a sigh, I put the car in gear and pull away from the shoulder.

"Please don't tell me about your sex life, Martin. It will only remind me I don't have anything to share in return."

"Zane!"

He shouts so loud my ears ring in the confined space and I swivel my head to stare at him.

"What the hell are you yelling for? You scared the shit out of me!"

"Sorry. Zane," he whispers, or tries to because it's still loud, but better. "You can share if you date Alec. I bet he gives great bjs."

"Jesus Christ, Martin. Stop talking about him like that." Thankfully, the arch for the ranch comes into view and in a few more minutes I'll hand Martin off to Dan for his sloppy, drunk blowjob I didn't need to know about. "He's my friend, so let it drop, please."

Parking in front of the farmhouse, the porch light is on and the front door opens before Martin even steps out of the car. Dan smiles as Martin, still in his full suit, stumbles up the stairs and falls into his arms.

"I missed you. Have I told you I love you today?"

Dan laughs softly as Martin's hands roam to the front of his sleep pants.

"You have, but I never get tired of hearing it, baby." He grabs Martin's wrists to stop them from doing anything else and nods his head towards me.

"Thanks for getting him home safe. I hope you both had a good night."

"We did. He's all yours now. He might need some meds in the morning. He drank the whole bottle."

Dan winces. "Red or white?"

"Red. The one with the fancy name he likes."

"Ouch. Well, tonight should be interesting then." He steers Martin towards the door. "Thanks again, Zane. Good night."

After Dan corrals Martin into the house, I pause at my car. The lights are still on at Alec's place.

Before I can talk myself out of it, I walk up the front steps and knock.

Chapter 5

Alec

Who knew llamas could be so strong and stubborn? What I hoped would be an easy task helping Dante turned into something... not so easy. We moved the llamas to another barn so we could fix two stalls. One llama freaked out, body checking me into the wall while we moved them.

Dante said it was Hawkeye, and it wasn't intentional because her eyesight's compromised. Of course, it wasn't intentional. She was merely reacting to something that frightened her and I was an innocent bystander. She was quite sweet to me when we brought them back in afterward. It was hard to stay mad at her when she went to great lengths to poke her nose in my pocket for treats. Once she found them, she crunched away and glued herself to my side.

After the unplanned stall maintenance, we loaded forty-three boxes of product. Yes, forty-three boxes of anything from balls of wool, to llama's milk soap, and stickers of each individual llama. Dante has been busy. Once loaded, we drove an hour away to an outdoor vendor market, who will sell the items on Dante's behalf as he tests the market for his products.

We unloaded, unboxed and set up displays. Dante went through his price sheets and answered any questions the vendor had. While we were there, a woman stopped and asked about the logo on the side of the ranch truck and wondered if we could take in her aunt's peacock while we were there.

So we made an unscheduled visit and placed a peacock in the empty truck bed with a borrowed dog crate. I wasn't sure if it should go with the chickens or not, so I quickly threw together a mesh covering to toss over a horse stall so the bird had a place to go while we figured out what to do with it.

I really, *really* just want to soak in my hot tub and order take-out. The extra delivery fee for a rural address would be worth it. Zane was going to make my favourite pizza tonight and I'm disappointed I had to miss it. It was all I could think about until I had to cancel on him. I love his homemade pizza.

If I called him, he'd probably bring me some, but I don't want to be that friend. Instead, I forget about ordering take out or calling him for food, and grab a box of *Ritz Crackers* and a block of cheese. I'm about to head to my hot tub with my meagre dinner when there's a knock on my door.

I'd know that silhouette through the glass anywhere.

"Hey, I was just dropping Martin off and saw your light on. You're usually asleep by now. Is everything okay?"

Zane waits for my reply, and I step aside to let him in.

"You don't normally knock."

"I know, but it's late and just in case you were..." He clears his throat and looks away. "If you were with someone, I didn't want to barge in."

It takes a moment for me to realize he meant in case I was here with another man. I almost want to blurt out that it won't ever happen because he's the only one I want. But instead, I choose a far more eloquent sentence.

"Nope. Just me and some crackers."

His brow creases. "Is that your supper?"

"Yeah, it was a long day, and I was about to have a soak before bed."

Closing the door behind him as he kicks off his shoes, he doesn't even ask, just heads to the kitchen to rummage through my fridge.

"You go get in the tub. I'll cook something better for you. You've got stuff for a veggie stir fry. It won't take me long."

I stare at Zane's back, with his head in my fridge as he loads up his arms, and the cracker box dangling from my hand next to me. He's been here so many times, and so many nights, it's like his second home. As he bends to get the wok out from the lower cupboard, I'm rewarded with his shirt riding up his back to reveal a strip of white skin.

I'll store that for later. Just like everything else.

He hums as he gathers everything he needs, and it's *this* that I want. Maybe moving to stand beside him as he teaches me how to cook. Or maybe him in those low-hanging lounge pants he sometimes wears at the end of the day while we watch *The Mandalorian.*

"Why are you still here?" He shoos me away with his hands. "Go, I know you need it. I'll take care of you." He smiles, but it doesn't reach his eyes like it usually does. "Of this, I mean. I'll take care of this."

"You don't have to cook for me. It's late."

He bites his lip before turning his attention to the pile of vegetables.

"I know. I want to, Alec. Please? Just go have your soak."

Placing the box of crackers and my cheese on the table, I leave Zane as he asked. With my heart trying to claw its way out of my chest to stay with him, I exit through the door off my mudroom, and out onto the small deck.

When I moved in here, I built the deck with Dan's permission, because a hot tub had become a lifeline for me. The old farmhouse had been updated throughout before I came here, and I was more than happy to live on the ranch. I loved it here. It was a pocket away from the prying eyes of the world, and I hid my pain under the bubbles of the jets. Well, my physical pain, anyway.

Nothing takes away the scars on my heart. When I left rodeo and my relationship–if you want to call it that–with Hunter, I vowed to never put myself out there again. I'd never be kept a secret or allow myself to be that vulnerable with someone. Promises were nothing. I needed more.

Mistakes were made, and I learned from them. I'd occasionally had lovers over the years, when I needed the warmth of another body next to me, but it's been a long time since I've felt the allure of something else. That magnetic pull, the magical feeling of that special something you can't quite put your finger on. To touch someone and feel their presence in that visceral way that's like an empty cavern when they aren't around.

The jets bubble as I shift in the tub, and behind closed eyes, my thoughts turn to the man in my kitchen. The one who's pulled all those feelings from me without even trying. Or even knowing.

Somehow, Zane slid behind my defenses. Undetected, he made himself at home in my life and my heart, and I noticed too late. By the time I worked out what was going on, I'd already fallen ass over Stetson in love with my best friend. My *straight* best friend.

Talk about a fucking cliché of a love life. Gay cowboy falls for his straight friend. Leave it to me to walk another path of heartbreak after vowing to never go there again.

"Hey, dinner is ready."

Zane appears with a tray and a steaming plate of food.

"It's a nice night, so I thought you might want to eat out here. I know you like to watch the fireflies."

He settles the tray on the small table and pulls a chair out for himself.

"Thanks, Z. That smells amazing."

Pulling myself out of the hot tub, I step over to the towel rack. Without thinking, I do what I always do. I strip off my trunks and wrap a towel around my waist. I do it almost daily as part of my routine; the wet shorts hang on the little clothesline to dry, and I towel myself off before returning to the house. That way, I don't track water everywhere. For three years I've done this, but the moment my shorts hit the deck with a splat, a squeak sounds from the corner.

Sure, Zane has rubbed ointment on for me before, but I've always been wearing shorts or boxers. I just flashed a full moon at him, and my entire body burns with embarrassment.

"Sorry. It's a habit, and I didn't think."

Zane stares at the plate in front of him.

"It's fine. Totally fine. We're friends. I've now seen your ass. It's not weird. Do you think it's weird?"

Taking the seat across from him, I pick up the fork and shovel food in my mouth so I don't have to answer him. I don't think it's weird, but his reaction is.

"This is delicious. I can't thank you enough for this, Zane. You're a lifesaver."

As I chew, I scan the field for fireflies and smile when I see a few. It's still early in the summer. In another month there will be a lot more out there, blinking sporadically, like they're sending me a coded message.

"That's what friends are for. You know I like to cook."

"I'm sorry I couldn't make it over tonight. I really want to watch that episode I fell asleep watching. Should we try again tomorrow?"

Zane returns to his normal sunshine self and the tightness in my shoulders loosens.

"Yeah, we can do that. I'll make your pizza for you then."

"You spoil me." I laugh, but I mean it.

He shrugs, suddenly shy again. "I like to. You're a good friend, Alec."

I nod, smiling to acknowledge his sentiment, but I'm afraid to speak. What the hell is going on that I'm so tied up all of a sudden? So I dropped my swim shorts. No big deal.

"So, what did you and Martin do tonight?" I ask instead, to get us back to some kind of normality.

Zane laughs, and my smile lifts. He shifts forward, green eyes sparkling as he tells me about his night with a friend.

"We had dinner at his favourite steak place. He got shitfaced on wine, and waxed poetic about how in love he is with Dan. I drove him home, but stopped once when he thought he might throw up." He places his hand on his chest. "He didn't, thank god. He'd have been pissed if he messed up his suit or wasted the wine he drank. I wasn't ready to listen to that kind of moaning tonight. But we had a great time. I'm glad we caught up."

"How long have you known him? I feel like I know this, but I don't remember."

He settles back again. The comfortable ease we have together falling back into place.

"Dylan the longest, since we were seventeen. I met Martin at our former place of work, so I'd guess about ten years now. Matts I've only known since we opened the brewery."

"Oh, right, I remember now. It's cool that you all know each other and work so well together."

"Didn't you have friends you worked well with on the rodeo circuit?"

"True, I did. Those weren't friendships that spanned decades, though. Mostly just seasons. Friendships to achieve goals."

"Were any of them…more than friends?" He rushes on. "Sorry if I overstepped, I was just curious. You've never really talked about that time."

I guess this is as good a time as any to tell him about Hunter.

"One. His name is Hunter. Blaze invited him for the rodeo thing. He was my roping partner for a while."

Zane stares at my empty plate, nodding. "So he was a friend that became more, but it didn't work out?"

"Something like that, yeah. We didn't keep in touch after I left."

"Well, that's too bad for him. He should have kept in touch." He clears his throat and stands. "Let's get this inside. You likely need to get some sleep soon. The ranch still wakes up with the sun."

"Before the sun, actually."

"Fucking early is what it is."

Zane at least understands how it is on the ranch and fills the tray with my empty plate and cutlery. When I move to join him, I hiss with pain. It's a doozy tonight.

"Alec? You okay?"

Wincing, I limp gingerly into the house with him.

"One of the llamas body checked me today, and I think that bone spur in my hip was aggravated. It hurts like a bastard tonight."

Setting the tray on the counter once we're inside, he spins right back to face me.

"Go lie down. I'll get your pain cream. You should have said something earlier."

His brow knits with concern, and suddenly that feverish flutter takes hold of me again. The one that only happens with Zane. Without a word, I walk down the hall to my bedroom and ease myself onto the bed, facedown. I'm torturing myself by letting him do this, but I'm powerless to deny him.

His footsteps enter my room, and the bed jostles slightly as he sits on the edge near my hip that's still covered with the towel. There's only a towel between us, and it takes all my effort to maintain calm, steady breaths. But the air escapes my lungs, sucked from the room with an invisible vacuum, as he gently pulls the towel away, exposing my right ass cheek.

The bottle cap clicks, and the cool lotion hits my heated skin along with Zane's fingers. Goosebumps race up my body despite the inferno raging within. Zane's firm, but gentle hands spread the lotion into my ass cheek, my lower back, and as much of my thigh he can reach. There's no way in hell I'm shifting my body to give him more room. This alone has my dick aching. It's one thing to explain dropping my swim shorts, but how do I explain an erection after touching me?

But it feels amazing and a small moan escapes my lips.

"Is that a good sound or a bad one?" he whispers.

"Good." I grunt. "So good."

Zane's hands stop moving for a beat and he presses harder into the flesh of my ass at the top of my hip.

"You have a big knot here. Probably from limping so much the past few days." He murmurs.

The tight ball of muscle moves under his fingertips, rolling back and forth like a marble, as he digs in deeper, and I cry out.

"Sorry, but if we get this knot out, you won't strain your hip so much, and hopefully you'll get some relief since the spur won't be so painful."

"When did you become a doctor?" I rasp. But he's likely right. I should have just gone with the surgery when it happened, but I was too stubborn at the time.

After a pause, he says, "Since I researched this kind of injury, and know what to look for."

I don't know what to say to that. He's researched my injury? I will not allow my mind to make more out of that than what it is. He's just my friend who wants the best for me. Nothing else.

The bed jostles as he stands, and before he pulls my towel back over my ass, a single fingertip drags across the swell of my ass cheek and down my thigh. It's almost too light to notice, but when it's Zane I feel everything, magnified a thousand times. The single touch is like a brand to my skin, and I bite my lip to stay silent.

With the towel back over me, he says goodnight and his feet stop at my bedroom door for a beat before continuing on the way out.

It's not until I hear the front door close behind him that I finally allow myself to release the broken cry I've been holding.

Chapter 6

Zane

Oh my god, what have I done?

I just groped my best friend... and I liked it.

Thank god Alec stayed facedown because I don't know how I would have first explained the tent in my pants or, second, how I caressed his ass before leaving. What the hell was I thinking?

The damn raccoon raided the garbage again while I was gone, but I'm not even stopping to pick it up tonight. I can't. My brain *should* be able to concentrate on something as simple as cleaning up trash. Somewhere between touching Alec's glorious nakedness and the drive home, all functioning brain cells have become obsessed with one thing and one thing only.

Rushing by the mess and straight into the house, I collapse against the door behind me.

"Okay, Zane. Be cool. You can figure this out. It's fine."

It's not fine.

Flipping open my phone, I consider calling Dylan, but it's late. I don't want to wake him and what if Nell has something going on tomorrow he needs to be at his best for? I can't call Martin; he's passed out drunk. Or having drunk sex, according to him.

That leaves one other person, aside from Alec, who will answer my call anytime.

My sister, Zen.

I pace the living room while I wait for her to answer.

"Hey, baby brother."

"Hey, Zen. Thanks for answering."

There's a click and a rustling noise. "Let me get the light on and sit up. This sounds like you're gonna hit me with something heavy."

I laugh. She's not wrong. Thank god for sibling intuition.

"I'm sorry for calling so late, but I need to talk to someone I can trust."

"Oh? Is everything okay?"

'Okay' is such an odd word.

I've been in a car accident, but I'm okay.

I fell on the ice, but I'm okay.

I'm confused about thoughts I'm having over another man, but I'm okay*!*

Puffing out a breath, I put my sister on speaker phone and start talking.

"God, I don't even know where to start." A sigh laden with all the tension over this conversation passes my lips. Shaky. Breathless. I plop on the sofa in the darkened room and pull the pillow Alec used onto my lap. "You remember, Alec, right?"

"Yes. He's your friend who helps on the ranch, right? The guy you always cook for and water his plants."

"Yeah, him. He's a good friend. He always leaves his croutons on the side of his plate for me. Unlike Martin, who doesn't care and just bathes them in salad dressing without asking first."

"Uh, but it's his salad? And I'm confused. You're calling about someone's preference to eat croutons?"

"No, sorry. I'm all over the place right now. That's why I needed to call you."

"Well, I'm still listening, Zane. Take your time."

I've been thinking about this for a while, and until tonight I thought maybe it was just me being weird. Me being lonely and just wanting a partner. Maybe I developed feelings for someone I see all the time, some kind of delusion of the brain. It happens right?

"I think I have a crush on someone. Do people still use that word? I don't know what else to call it, but recently they're all I can think about."

"Sure, you can say crush. Tell me about them. What are they like?"

Her question immediately brings an image of Alec and his warm smile as he laughs at something I've said or done. Or the way he speaks to the horses when he thinks nobody can hear him. And the way he named his violets after people and animals he's loved. Followed now by the new sensation of flutters after seeing his wet, naked ass earlier tonight.

"Uh, about the same height as me. Really large, gentle hands. Great laugh. Killer smile. Kinda can't stop thinking about the way one side of his mouth tilts up higher when he smiles."

The silence hangs and now I wish I'd video called to see her expression. I just admitted to my sister that I have a crush on a guy.

And yet I rush on.

"He always comes when I need him. He loves animals and has a soft heart, even though he tries to hide it. He hates it when I change up his food, because he likes things to always be the same, but he still tries them for me." Playing through my brain like a stuttering film reel are memories. His scowls that I turn into smiles. The way he sits his Stetson on his head that he wears everywhere just so. His naked body tonight, with the water running down his muscled back and the tiny scar on his hip where a bull's horn grazed him. "His hands are so gentle," I whisper. A final admission to this new thing that I don't know what to call. I know I said that twice, but it's something I've been fixated on. How he can switch from capably using his hands to tie a knot to restrain an animal, to placing his hand on my back in a crowd so I know he's there.

Jesus Christ.

I do have feelings for him. Big ones.

"That's some heavy info you just dropped on me, bro."

"I'm sorry. I just...I had to talk to someone about it. You always steer me straight." I laugh at my word choice. "Or maybe not-so-straight, I guess."

"Do you...are you sure about this?"

My hands pull at my hair and the same loop runs over and over in my mind. The way I feel at ease with Alec and how I look forward to seeing him every day. The way he's so quietly confident, even when he's arguing with me about my choice in garbage cans and how it's not critter proofed enough. I noticed how his lips tick up a little more on one side, for fuck's sake. And that weird, hot and fluttery feeling I got when he flashed his ass by accident. That's new... and not unwelcome.

I can't forget how it felt so different to have his skin under my hands tonight...and the sounds he made. I've put his medication on before, but it was never, ever anything like tonight. Something's changed.

"I think so, Zen. I haven't told you this, but the last two women I was with, I left because I had no interest in sex. Sorry if that's TMI."

She huffs a tiny laugh and I wish she was here so I could hug her.

"Just a little, but it's still important. Don't worry, I'm not judging you. Do you know why?"

"Not a clue. They were both attractive. Like, model-beautiful, and I was physically attracted to them, but the sex just wasn't a priority. With the first girl, we didn't even make it to sex. It's hard to explain. I liked them both, but I wasn't interested in anything sexual after the first few dates."

"Relationships can change like that over time, Zane. Even sexuality. I have a friend who went through something similar. She couldn't understand why she was so drawn to one of her work colleagues of the same sex. She finally said screw it and asked the other woman out. After a lot of talking and dates, they accepted they weren't so straight and just followed their hearts. Maybe you should do the same."

I finally release the death grip I have on my hair and stare at my phone. I knew my sister wouldn't judge me, but it's scary. I'd hate to lose Alec as a friend or make anything awkward.

"Zen, until a few months ago, I didn't even know there were so many different sexual identities. I've been doing a lot of reading. I plan to talk to Dylan about it too, since he kind of went through this with Travis, but he already knew he was bisexual when we were in college. I've never been attracted to a man before. I thought for sure it was just me being weird and it would pass. But it explains a lot of things."

There's a clatter of dishes as my sister likely rattles around her kitchen making hot chocolate, but she keeps talking.

"It's been a long time since you've talked about someone like this. I can hear it in your voice. Sure, you're confused because it's new, but you're also excited. You like someone. You feel a connection that's not just *'wow, you're really pretty'*. You have history. You've already had some epic moments together, and it's genuine. No matter what gender or identity the other person is, it's real. Those are the little things that build into bigger, beautiful things, Zane."

I let her words settle over me. She could be right. Maybe I've been going about things all wrong my whole life. I admit to being a sort of player in my younger days. Relationships never interested me. It was all about the sex and the chase of someone new. We'd date—and that's a very loose term for it—for a few months and one of us would part ways with the other. It wasn't always me who left, either. When I was the one dumped, I never dwelled on it.

The more I think about it, there were never any feelings involved. Not once did I think I loved any of those women, or was really heartbroken over a break-up.

I cared, but I was never in love.

Holy shit. Isn't that another revelation? Have I really been that detached from these people all my life?

"You don't think it's weird then? That I might be, like, into a guy?"

"I wasn't expecting it, but it's not weird. How are you going to handle it?"

"I don't know. What if he's not interested? I'd hate to make the friendship awkward."

More silence settles and I check to make sure she didn't hang up.

"I'm going to be honest, Zane. I've met Alec. I feel like I know Alec because you always talk about him, and I'd like to point out a few things to you." There's a rustle again and I think she's back in bed. Likely with her hot chocolate to go back to sleep.

"Here's what I know about Alec based on our conversations since you've met him. He's gay, and he hasn't dated anyone since arriving to work on the ranch. You two go out together often, and when you take someone home, he prefers to go home by himself, but only after he knows you made it somewhere safely. He leaves his croutons on the side for you to eat. Every single day, he shows up at your house or the bar to spend time with you. You have a key to his house you never need to use because he leaves the door open for you. He doesn't laugh when you talk to his plants because he does it, too."

"Okay, that's a lot, but what's the point you're trying to make? Any friend would do that."

"Zane." Her voice takes on an edge, forcing me to listen. "What happened tonight to make you call me? What made you finally need to snap and talk about this when you've clearly been thinking about it for a while?"

"You don't need to take the 'big sister voice' with me."

"I do when you're being obtuse. What happened?"

Swallowing hard, I recall how the goosebumps ran up Alec's back when I boldly squeezed his ass.

"Sometimes his hip hurts, and he has a medicated lotion he puts on the area. I saw his light on when I was dropping Martin off, so I went over to say hi. He's usually not up this late. I guess I wanted to be sure he was okay. He was about to have a soak in his hot tub, but he does that most days because it's good for the arthritis around the joint."

My sister chuckles and I bristle.

"Why are you laughing?"

"Because I've never heard you sound like this. You're like a mother hen. It's adorable."

"Whatever," I grumble. "Do you want to hear the rest or not?"

"Of course I do."

"Anyway, I'll cut it short for you. I put the lotion on for him while he was mostly naked and...I maybe strayed away from the target area and groped his ass."

"And what did Alec do?"

"He didn't say a word. I left right away and said goodnight because while I was touching him, everything seemed different. It was…I liked it. Not just in a sexual way."

"Does he let anyone else help him like you do?"

"Not that I know of. He doesn't like people to know about the pain sometimes. He prefers to go about things like nothing is wrong."

"Zane, little brother, listen to me, your wise sibling."

Zen's tone is serious, even if her words aren't.

"Alec obviously trusts you and I wouldn't be surprised one bit if he has feelings for you, too. If I'm wrong, I'll give up coffee."

I laugh at her comment, but my heart speeds up with her statement, too.

"You think so?"

"Call it a hunch, but Zane, if you think you're attracted to him for real, and it's not some kind of experiment or one off night of feelings, I think you should talk to him. If he feels the same way, you could have something great."

"But if he doesn't, I could lose my best friend."

"If he's worth his salt as a friend, he wouldn't leave."

A yawn comes across the line, and I'm hit with a pang of guilt for keeping her up so long.

"Thanks for this, Zen. I'll let you go to sleep. I love you, sis."

"Anytime, Zane. You know this. Please keep me posted and if you need me, please call again. I love you, too."

After ending the call with my sister, I remain sitting in the dark, holding the pillow that smells like Alec. A little bit like grass and leather with the faded scent of fabric softener. I don't know how to approach this with him, but Zen's words echo in my head.

Martin's words yesterday as well. He thinks Alec is into me, but not once has Alec ever hinted that was the case. He's never, ever crossed the line like I just did.

What do I do now? He didn't freak out on me for touching him tonight, so that has to be a good sign. Maybe he'll never mention it.

We can just go about as we usually do and everything will be fine. Totally fine.

CHAPTER 7

ALEC

You know how it feels when you're so tired you want to sleep, but you can't because you passed the point of sleep, and now you're so awake it feels like you've mainlined caffeine for days?

That's me this morning.

After Zane left, I was afraid to move.

I wanted to burn the feeling of that single caress against my flesh into my memory forever. And the sound of his breath catching in his throat when he did it? I didn't want to forget a single beat of it.

I laid awake wondering if it was just my mind playing tricks or maybe Zane was having thoughts of the bisexual kind.

We should probably discuss it like any normal adult would. But how the hell do you bring that up?

Hey, Zane. When you touched my ass, I almost shot my load. Are you into guys now?

Are you into me?

I want you to bend me over and crack me in two.

Can we still be friends if you don't like dick?

With a sigh, I lean on the barn stall, and stare at my scuffed cowboy boots. Why does shit like this have to be so hard? I've never been one to shy away from difficult conversations, but this one is... potentially life changing.

"Are you an ass man, Alec?"

For a moment I'm frozen, mortified that someone else peeped into my thoughts. But then I remember where I am and laugh as Blaze joins me in the isolation barn with the two donkeys Dan brought home.

"Real original, Blaze."

"I don't claim to be a comedian, but I couldn't resist."

"The vet will be here soon to check them out. I don't see any outward issues and will probably get them out to pasture today and into a permanent stall tonight."

Blaze reaches over and scratches the ears of the older female.

"Do you have a minute to talk about the rodeo stuff?"

"Of course. I'm just in here cleaning up while I wait." And dreading a conversation I need to have later. "What's up?"

"Jacob mentioned you said about just ropin' and not usin' animals for a game instead of his skills competition idea. I think it's a better idea for logistics. Then the guys just need their own horse if they want to bring their own. Which I think they will, because when I invited them, all three said they'll be in the province at other events close by."

"Yeah, I asked Zane to get a variety of stuffed animals so we could rope them. Or tie them. Turn it into a game for him and to sell tickets for, he said?"

I'm not sure what we'll come up with, but I'm sure I can make it better by roping teddy bears rather than steers. And yes, me not jumping on and off a horse repeatedly is appealing. Although I don't know if tying a stuffed animal will be easier than a real one or not. Guess I'll find out soon enough.

Blaze hums under his breath, and I turn to face him.

"What? I hate it when you do that all-knowing smirk thing. How does River put up with that?"

Blazes laughs and steps closer to the donkeys, who watch us closely.

"First off, when I invited them all, I wasn't sure they would come. When three said yes, I wasn't prepared." He reaches into his pocket and feeds the donkey, Mabel, a sugar cube. "Now I need to tell them it's a teddy bear ropin' competition. You think they'll still come if that's the case?"

Reaching over the stall, I pet the other donkey, Marlene. They didn't arrive here due to neglect, which is a pleasant change. The owner was simply tired of them and just wanted them gone. Dan couldn't say no to that, and it's likely why Blaze was showing such an interest in them already. He knows what it feels like to be tossed away and I can relate.

"I think they'd still come. Jimmy and Mike will for sure if you've offered them any kind of appearance fee."

He nods. "I did. And Hunter? What's he goin' to think?"

"I don't know. We never stayed in touch."

Blaze is silent for a minute before he turns towards me. He clears his throat to draw my attention.

"Hunter offered to do it for free. As a kind of payback for you. He said he owed it to you." He rocks back on his heels and I stare above his head. "Is he comin' after you, Alec?"

"What do you mean?"

"Pardon me if I overstep here, but will he cause any problems for you...and Zane?"

"I don't understand how that's even an issue?"

Blaze shifts, a stern look on his face. "He said he looked forward to seein' you again and sounded genuinely excited about it. I know your history with him isn't the best and with Zane now I —"

"What do you mean *'with Zane now'*? I haven't told him anything about how I feel. He's a friend, and for all I know, so is Hunter now."

Blaze says nothing for a long time, which isn't like him. He's always on my case about something. Sometimes serious, but most times joking. Right now, there's no humour in his eyes and there's a tightness to his jaw.

"You know, I've been watchin' you moon over Zane for a year now, Alec. A year. I don't enjoy seein' my friend wastin' his life pinin'."

"You're one to talk." I throw back. He did the same with River, but it worked in the end for him at least.

"I deserved that. But I mean it, Alec. Don't leave it so long you regret never sayin' anythin'. I'd hate if Hunter showed up and it caused problems."

"There's no problem. Hunter and I were a thing years ago. He made his choice then. Zane is...Zane. He's my Zane, is all."

I close my eyes when Blaze cocks his head. I shouldn't have said that.

"He's your Zane, is he? Does he know that?"

Thankfully, my phone chimes with a text and try as I might, I can't hide the smile when I see Zane's name. Or the absolute cold terror of discussing what happened.

"Alec, tell him for god's sake. You two are dancin' around each other like the world's best two-steppers."

Snapping my head up, I focus on Blaze.

"He's not dancing around me."

Blaze is about to say more, but the veterinarian shows up, cutting off our conversation.

"I hear there's a pair of fine asses I need to examine." He snort-laughs and sets his bag on the ground.

"Everyone's a comedian today." I shake his hand as Blaze tips his head at me behind the doctor.

Tell him, he mouths, before slipping out the door.

The veterinarian rambles on and for the first time in my life I tune out at work, distracted by the text still unread on my phone, and the words of Blaze. Excusing myself while he works with his assistant, I step out of the barn and inhale a lung full of fresh air before reading the text message from Zane.

> **Zane:** Just confirming you're still coming over tonight for the missed episode. If you still want pizza, let me know if before or after we watch is better.

Why a simple text makes my hands shake, I don't know, but I send him a reply.

> **Alec:** I'm finishing up with the vet and I'll be there in a few hours. Maybe we can eat after the show?

Zane replies almost immediately.

> **Zane:** That works for me. I'll see you soon!

I reply with a heart to the message, because the thumb is just rude and noncommittal, and pocket my phone.

For the first time in three years, the butterflies in my stomach for seeing Zane aren't for joy, but for nerves. Bulls have charged me, bears have come too close for comfort, horses have kicked me, and once I had to walk through a *Bath and Body Works* store to pick up a package for a friend during a sale day.

None of those scared me.

But the prospect of this conversation with Zane has me on the verge of a panic attack.

I'm going to come home elated or shed tears for the first time in forever.

Heading back into the barn, I pocket my phone and pray tonight doesn't end with my face on a tear-soaked pillow.

Chapter 8

Zane

Alec has been here a million times before. We've hung out. We've watched movies, played cards, and shared dinners I've made.

He has his own pillow and blanket in my linen closet.

Him coming to my house is nothing new.

But I've spent the afternoon cleaning my house like I expect the King for dinner. A million butterflies have danced in my gut all day, and I know this visit is different. I won't lie to myself and try to convince the thoughts in my head it will be fine.

I want to. Very much.

But after a sleepless night, I decided my sister was right. It's the small things that build into something beautiful, and I want to know now if there's a chance for that with us. Needing to know if Alec would be willing to take our relationship further than just friends is not something I can keep under wraps anymore.

Even if Alec didn't notice my wayward caress, I have to tell him about the feelings I've been struggling with. Zen gave me a pep talk via video call this morning and I'm still reeling from all the possible outcomes that lay ahead. He's still my best friend. I trust him to not hurt me, no matter what.

A light knock on the door sends my heart rate soaring, and I answer it with what I hope is my usual smile.

"Hey, you never have to knock. You know that."

I greet Alec, and he ducks his head. He'd only knocked the first time I ever invited him over.

"Yeah, I don't know why I knocked, actually."

Stepping aside, I let him past, and he tugs off his cowboy boots like he usually does, lining them up near the pantry door right off the kitchen.

"I noticed you got new garbage cans. They look like a good choice."

Instead of making himself at home like any other time, he stuffs his hands in his pockets and nods his head like a bobble-head doll on the dashboard of a rally car.

"Uh, yeah. They have critter clips? It's supposed to make it harder for them to get the lids off."

Now *I* stuff my hands in my pants and it's the most awkward encounter I've ever endured. I'm just about to address the elephant in the room when he strides over to the fridge.

"I could go for some iced tea. Do you still have some?"

"Of course. I always have the strong sweet tea that you like."

I notice it then. His hand shakes as he pulls the glass pitcher of tea from the fridge and sets it on the counter. Gripping the edge of the counter, he hangs his head and exhales.

My heart stops because this is it. He's about to tell me to fuck off or we're no longer friends. Something bad. He's too tense.

"Alec?" My voice wavers. "Are you okay?"

The silence stretches and when he finally lifts his head, I bite my lip to keep the pained moan inside. His eyes. The most beautiful blue eyes that smile no matter what look... sad. Broken. And it's my fault.

"Zane, we need to talk."

"About last night," I whisper.

He nods and I motion for us to sit in the living room where I've already cued up–and paused–the episode of *the Mandalorian* he missed.

"Did you clean today? It smells lemony in here."

"I used *Pledge*, if that's what you mean by cleaning."

He snorts, and a tiny smile lifts his lips. Alec takes his spot on the couch and I sit in mine. He always sits on the end cushion, and I sit in the middle, leaving a cushion between us to share snacks.

Alec drops his head back on the couch with a shaky sigh.

"I want to start by telling you I'm not angry. Not even a little. I just...I guess I need to know your thoughts before I can tell you mine."

I mimic him and rest my head back. Neither of us looks at each other, instead talking to the ceiling and it's a little easier this way, I must admit.

"That's fair. I'm happy you're not angry because I'm not sure why I touched you like that. You didn't ask for it and I'm sorry. I feel very guilty for breaking your trust." My breath hitches again. I've never broken a friend's trust before, and while I'm relieved Alec isn't angry, I still feel horrible for doing it.

"But I need to know, Zane...are you just curious? Or is there something more to it? Why?"

I feel my throat work, but no words come out. Even though I practiced what I wanted to say, I can't get the words to cross my lips. Alec slides his large, gentle hand into mine with a squeeze.

"I'm not going anywhere, Z. Maybe that helps. I promise no matter what you say, I'm still here in whatever way you ever need me."

Squeezing his hand back, I turn my head to look at him. This man, who just set me at ease and made a promise before I could spit my thoughts out, has already turned his head my way. The warm eyes of my friend wait patiently for me to explain myself.

"I think I like you, cowboy." I blink back the burn behind my eyes. "It's been a weird few months for me as I've pieced together a few things about myself. There's been a lot of questions, and thank god for my sister." I smile, but my lips tremble and I push through. "My sister said sexuality can change anytime in our life. I know you're gay, but all I've known is being straight. So figuring out I have feelings for you was...a shock."

Squeezing my eyes shut, I keep going. "Until last night, it wasn't a sexual thing. I mean, it was, but it wasn't. I just know that somewhere over the last three years, you've become the first person I think of every day and the last person I think of at night. I look forward to every minute we spend together, and I know people expect sex to be in there somewhere too, but I hadn't thought about it until I saw you like that last night."

Finally, I open my eyes to find Alec's blue ones locked on me.

"Do you want it to be about sex, Zane?"

"I've never been with a man, Alec. I don't know. I just know that I enjoyed touching you last night and maybe I wouldn't mind doing it again."

"Is it more than that, though? Because Zane, I don't want to be an experiment. Not with you. I'll do anything you want. But I can't do that. It would break me."

Alec's voice cracks and I stare at him more closely. Martin and my sister are right. He already cares about me. How have I been so blind?

"I'm willing to make it more. I mean, I don't want to experiment. I want you. With me. I'd like to try."

"I want that more than anything." He swallows. "I have for a very long time, Z."

My heart races so fast it's hard to catch my breath. Alec is still holding my hand, and that whole fluttery feeling runs up and down my body.

"Would you...could you kiss me?"

His eyes drift closed as a shaky sigh escapes his lips. "Zane," he breathes before moving his hand to my neck. "I'd love nothing more than to be your first kiss."

I lean in closer, and his hand squeezes my neck. "You're sure? I can't take this back and it's not going to be easy to forget once we do this."

I huff a small laugh. "I don't ever want to forget. Just shut up and do it."

"Such a romantic."

Alec leans forward to close the final gap between us and his lips slide across mine. Soft at first, until I part my lips and kiss him back. His tongue darts out, gently licking across my lower lip, and sliding next to my tongue.

No alarm bells go off. I don't freak out. It's the opposite, in fact.

Fire licks up my spine as his hand slides into my hair. His fingers curl and tug gently on my hair, and I moan into his mouth.

I pull away, panting, and Alec immediately sits back. A wary look on his face.

"It's okay. I'm just…I wasn't expecting to like it so much. I got scared."

He brings my hand to his lips, kissing my knuckles with those same soft lips and my heart melts at this sweet side of Alec.

"Don't be scared. Never with me, Z."

I just kissed my best friend. I'm still terrified I may have fucked up our friendship, but Alec's eyes never lie.

"Can we watch the episode now?"

He licks his lips, staring at me with eyes so intense it's like he sees my soul.

"We're good?"

I grin. "Yeah, we're good. More than good, I think."

"Then let's watch this show and don't let me fall asleep this time."

He winks, and I think I actually swoon a little.

Alec didn't fall asleep. In fact, we watched two episodes with frequent pauses to discuss it as it played out. He loves this show and I'm oddly happy that he shares this with me. It's like our own little thing.

Somehow, we'd snuck closer together on the couch, and Alec's arm has wrapped around my shoulders while I've slid down to rest my head against his chest. His fingertips brush up and down my arm periodically and he even kissed the top of my head after I fed him a black jelly bean from the bowl. They're his favourite.

I'm comfortable, but there's still this odd pulse inside of me, whispering that this shouldn't be happening. That I'm odd for finding such joy snuggling with my best friend, who happens to be a man. But stronger than that is the feeling of right.

Of a completeness that's just out of reach, but still attainable. Something far greater than my fear of being different lies ahead of me. I feel it inside, fighting with that whisper as it tries to drown out that doubt with a scream of triumph for getting this far.

Alec kissed me tonight.

I want more.

"Would you spend the night? With me?" I blurt it out before I lose my nerve and Alec stills. "Not like sex, but like this? Could you sleep with me like this?"

Alec says nothing. He touches his lips to my head and inhales deeply. Planting my hand on his strong chest–he's got muscles!–I push myself back to look at him.

"Is that a no?" My voice wavers and I hate that I sound so small.

Alec shakes his head.

"It's not a no. I'm just overwhelmed, Z. I don't want you to do anything you might regret later."

"Will you regret it?"

"Not one bit. I'm afraid I'll love it too much and never want to leave. My only regret will be letting you go when you wake up."

Oh, my god. How can he still be so damn sweet to me when this is something he's wanted from me for years?

"I won't regret it, Alec. I just...I think..." I inhale a breath and try to focus on something other than his face. It's so expressive. He's hiding nothing, and it's all there for me to see. The want, the desire, the love. The sacrifice he's willing to make so I can work this out on my own time.

"Please stay with me."

With newfound bravery, I place my palm on his stubbled cheek. His chest fills with a shaky breath.

A single nod. "As long as you want me to. I'll stay."

His words lift the weight from my chest, and I smile. Standing, I hold out my hand to him.

"Then let's try to sleep. Tomorrow you have roping practice."

He takes my hand, and after I turn off the TV, I lead him down the hall to my bedroom. Not that he doesn't know where it is.

"Um, I'll sleep in my boxers tonight." Alec moves to unzip his pants and I don't hide my curiosity as he undresses before me. He's trying to hide it, but he's terrible. That and his body gives him away.

"Does your chest always get flushed like that when you're nervous?"

Alec glances down and sighs.

"No." He lifts his eyes to mine, and a spark runs through my body. "I'm not nervous. I'm just..." He shrugs and I let it go because he'd never lie to me. I know that.

He walks to the side of the bed I don't sleep on and slides underneath the covers. I roll to face him.

"Any preference on spoon positions?"

He fights a laugh. "None. Whatever you need, Z."

"Good. I think I want to be the little spoon tonight." Rolling over, I scoot back until I meet Alec and press back into him as his strong arm loops around my waist and hugs me close.

Running my hand down his arm, I catalogue the coarse hair, the corded muscle, and when my hand reaches his, I thread our fingers together and pull it up to kiss his palm.

"Good night, cowboy."

"Good night, Z."

With Alec's body snuggled up against mine and the weight of his arm over me, I feel like I just placed a missing puzzle piece into my life.

The weird thing is, I didn't think I was missing a piece before.

CHAPTER 9

ALEC

Zane's deep, rhythmic breathing makes me a little envious. He slipped off to sleep so easily while I've been lying here staring at the back of his head with my mind spinning like a top on a freshly waxed floor.

He shifts, pulling my arm into him tighter, and a small, contented sigh crosses his lips. How did we get here? How the fuck did I go from loving him from a distance, to being his first kiss with a man to now, spooning him like we're lovers?

My flushed chest he'd thought was nerves, wasn't that. It was fear. We'd crossed a line, and while I welcomed it, I'm afraid he'll change his mind. Maybe he'll wake up tomorrow and say it was too strange and we should go back to being just friends. Which I would do for him, but it would squeeze all the hope from my life. There's nothing I won't do for him, and that includes standing aside if he thinks this isn't the right thing.

Which is how I found myself in bed with him, my dick smashed against his ass cheeks. Only separated by two thin pairs of boxer shorts. Yep. Not uncomfortable at all. But what he said tonight about his feelings and how it wasn't sexual until now, he'd spoken confidently, like he had just learned something great and new about himself and now he was exploring that.

I wanted to discover it all with him, because Zane already lived inside me. I took him to bed every night in my heart because it was the only place I could have him so close to me. To be here like this with him now is a fantasy come to life.

And a test of patience.

I love the cuddles and the spooning, but it's Zane. I've imagined him bringing me to blissful orgasms in more ways than the Kamasutra has positions. My lips ache with a need to map every inch of his creamy skin and it's a damn miracle I haven't begged him for more after that kiss.

A kiss that has no descriptor in the English language. Because there's no word I know of that packages up years of wanting and wishing, coming true like a gift from heaven.

But this is a start. A start to something new, and while I said I couldn't be an experiment, I can still be his safe place. As long as he doesn't throw me away if he discovers I'm not for him. That's not the same thing as an experiment.

An experiment is mixing known items together to predict how they will react with each other. Will they catch fire? Explode? Or simply remain separate like oil and water, never mixing long enough to sustain excitement? I know without a doubt we'll ignite faster than a house fire. The unknown variable is if he can accept that with me.

I feather a kiss on the back of his neck, inhaling his scent that mixes with a hint of lemon from his dusting earlier, and my eyelids finally droop. I need to sleep, like Zane said. Tomorrow is a big day.

A metallic crash from the kitchen launches me out of my semi-sleep. Lifting my head, I listen for it again. There's more metal scraping along the floor. Another thump as something falls.

Someone is in the kitchen.

Zane still snores softly, oblivious to anything but whatever he's dreaming of. I gently pull my arm away and his eyes immediately snap open.

That's...kinda creepy.

"What's wrong?" He mumbles, trying to pull my arm back and snuggle closer.

"Sweetheart, I think someone is in the kitchen," I whisper, and place my hand over his mouth when he opens it. "Shh, I'll go check it out."

Zane says nothing when I remove my hand, processing what I said as he remains under the blankets. Sliding out of bed, I scan his room for something to use as a weapon.

Nothing.

"You should have brought a lasso." He whisper-shouts and I place a finger over my lips, hoping he gets the message to be quiet.

A snort-laugh somehow sneaks out at how he thinks a lasso with a possible armed intruder is a good idea for self-defense.

"I'm not fucking Wonder Woman, Zane. You should keep a hockey stick or something in here."

"Well, I didn't plan on having someone break in!"

He jumps out of bed and slides up next to me. "I'm coming with you."

Another loud crash sounds and if this really is an attempted robbery, the criminal is the worst in the world at their job.

With Zane plastered against my back, I open the bedroom door, and together we creep towards the kitchen to investigate the ruckus. When we reach the end of the hallway, I slap a hand over my mouth and stare at the scene in front of me.

There's a fucking raccoon in Zane's kitchen.

Not just any raccoon. It's the one that's been getting into his garbage, and I have a strong suspicion Zane has been feeding it on purpose.

The furry intruder has opened all the cupboards in Zane's tiny kitchen and found the jackpot. Boxes of cereal and pasta have been ripped open and litter the floor, discarded like they weren't quite what he was looking for. The critter currently sits shoulders deep in a giant plastic pail with his bushy, ringed tail poking out the top. While I debate how to get this thing out of the house without requiring a rabies shot after, I notice the back door leading to the porch stands wide open. That answers the question about how the damn thing got in here. Zane usually locks the door after I leave, but I didn't leave last night.

I grab a pot lid from the floor, keeping a wary eye on the raccoon as I do so. If I can sneak over and grab the broom from the corner without him noticing, I can push him towards the door and hopefully, he'll run out.

Hopefully.

"Don't hurt him. He's just hungry."

I raise an eyebrow at Zane and he shrugs. "Even animals need full bellies, Alec."

"Zane...just stop talking."

As I inch my way closer to the broom, discarded *Froot Loops* crunch under my feet and I freeze. The raccoon stops rustling in the pail and his tail disappears with a chatter. With a silent prayer on my lips, I launch my attack and hope a trip to the hospital isn't in my future.

I lunge forward to grab the broom while throwing the pot lid towards the masked bandit. It clatters on the floor and the pail spills over, revealing the biggest, fattest raccoon I've ever seen. It screams and chatters, waving its hands at me like I should understand his raccoon language. I can barely master English before coffee some days, so raccoon is way out of my league. Using the broom, I poke it towards the open door. With what I can only describe as a leisurely waddle, he exits through the door and walks towards the side tree line with Froot Loops still stuck to its tail.

In a rush, I slam the door closed in case it suddenly develops ninja moves and makes his way back inside.

"That asshole stole my Froot Loops!"

Zane crunches his way across the floor to the bucket and swears so much the air turns blue.

"I just filled this up."

"Well, I've been telling you for months to deal with this thing. They get bold when they want something."

I survey the mess in the kitchen. There are Froot Loops everywhere. It's like a rainbow shattered into a million pieces on his kitchen floor.

"Ah, Zane, exactly how many packages of Froot Loops did you have here?"

"I don't judge you on your secret stash of jelly beans."

"It's not a secret if you found them, is it? And I'm not judging. I'm just...shocked."

Zane's not a huge guy. Average build in every way, and this can get tacked on to the very short list of things I didn't know about my best friend. I knew he liked Froot Loops. I didn't know he was so obsessed with them he bought them by the bucket full.

"So, this animal just walked up and opened the door? How is that even possible?"

No longer caring about the crunching cereal under my bare feet, I pull the coffee out and start the coffeemaker, like it's the most normal thing to do when one wakes up to find a raccoon foraging in the kitchen pantry.

"Well, they have little hands and they're smart. They can do all kinds of things with them. I've heard of raccoons getting into houses before, but not by opening the back door and just walking in."

"I fed him a few times." Zane blurts, and I have to laugh. That's Zane, always taking care of everyone and everything.

"I figured you did. He's too comfortable around you."

He sighs as he surveys the mess. The sun has barely peeked over the horizon, and we're in our underwear with crushed cereal on the soles of our feet, waiting for coffee to brew. Even in the middle of a raccoon-made hurricane that interrupted my first sleepover with Zane, a smile finds its way to my lips.

"Hey, come here."

The coffee pot gurgles and sputters as Zane takes the few steps over to me. Once within reach, I grab his hand to tug him a little closer. He smiles when he guesses my intentions, and steps into my arms, his chest against mine.

"Don't feel guilty. You were only trying to be helpful. We can replace the cereal."

I settle my hands on his hips, and he licks his lips as he stares at mine.

"I know, but I wanted to...I wanted to spend a little longer in bed with you." He swallows hard before meeting my gaze. "I liked you holding me like that. It's been a long time since I slept that well." He hesitates before lifting his hand and brushing the hair off my forehead. "I like the way you look right out of bed."

Zane trails his fingers down my cheek and across my jaw before letting them rest on my lips. I touch the tip of my tongue to his fingertips and his lips part with a small gasp.

My grip on his hips tightens because, minus the crunched-up cereal and kitchen mess, this is a perfect morning. If Zane looked at me like this every morning, I'd never start the day in a bad mood for the rest of my life.

"Can I kiss you again?" he breathes with a shaky voice and I nod.

"You never have to ask me."

A torturous amount of time seems to pass as he brings his lips to mine. With the softest of brushes, he kisses me, then presses his lips harder against mine. Parting my lips, I let him taste me and meet every tentative touch of his with a sure one of my own. He pulls away and feathers soft kisses down my neck. Trembling hands slide up my naked chest.

It's beautiful torture and there's no way my cock won't respond. Zane is kissing me and touching me. His hands and lips are against my skin. *My Zane.* If it wasn't for the coffee pot beeping to signal the end of the brew, I'd think I was dreaming.

He swallows when he looks down between us, both of us straining in our boxers that only enhance the display, not hide it.

"I guess we both liked that."

"Are you okay with it?"

He nods his head. "Very much, but I'm not ready for...other stuff." He laughs softly and flashes me a shy smile. "I'm sorry. I know it's frustrating but I...I'm not confused. I just..."

He rests his head against my shoulder with a small huff, and I tighten my arms around him.

"You don't have to explain it to me, Z."

"It's just that it's you, Alec. I don't want to screw anything up, because I need you in my life. If not like this, then as we were, because you're my cowboy and I don't want you to be anyone else's."

Kissing his temple, I ease back, missing the feel of his skin next to mine.

"I'll always be in your life. Even to clean up the mess of a raccoon with you."

Stepping around him, I slap his ass as I reach into the cupboard for coffee mugs. He squeaks and smacks my shoulder, which draws a bark of laughter from me.

"We need to deal with this mess first. Then I need to rope up some stuffed animals and report back to Blaze. So let's get this day started."

I hand him a mug of coffee, and he takes it with a scowl.

"Fucking raccoon. We need to go buy more Froot Loops, too. I'll die without them."

"I never had you down as a drama queen." I laugh.

He gives me the finger as he sticks out his tongue and wrangles a vacuum from the closet. I grab the broom again. We tackle the mess together, drinking coffee and grinning at each other like fools, half-dressed as the sun comes up.

If this is what they call domestic bliss, I'll take it.

Even if it involves a raccoon.

Chapter 10

ZANE

After tossing the last oversized, bright-green dinosaur in the backseat, I hop into the passenger side of Alec's 1999 *Chevy Sierra* that he calls Old Green.

He refuses to buy a newer model. He says as long as it runs, there's no reason to abandon his favourite vehicle. But I'm almost certain it's because he's too attached to it. Other than his violets that he's moved around with him for years, Old Green is a comforting presence in his life. I can't fault him for hanging onto a truck for the memories it holds.

"Did you honestly have to buy that many animals? I said four or five."

As he backs out of my driveway, he's not even trying to hide his smile.

"I know. But I took Dylan's daughter Nell, and then we saw the unicorn, which led me to the dinosaurs and well...here we are with nine different animals for you."

And honestly, I just want to see Alec with all these super cute stuffed animals in his hands. He's such a rough and tough cowboy on the outside, but inside he's all mush. It will be fun to see him do this. And cute. I'm a big fan of cute.

Our drive to the ranch is quiet. But the good kind. It's comfortable.

Alec rests his elbow against the window as he rubs his stubbled chin with his hand. His other hand grips the steering wheel and there's nothing extraordinary about it. Just an everyday action that anyone does as they drive. But this whole loopy feeling grips me. It's my *Alec feeling*.

He mouths the words to the song on the radio, oblivious to my roaming gaze. We've done this a million times. Only now I *see* Alec. I see him not just as my closest friend and proverbial partner in crime.

I see a man. An attractive man.

And not for the first time, I wonder how it took me almost forty years to learn this about myself. All this time, dating women and having sex I didn't enjoy seems like a wasted life. It wasn't until I was talking with a group of teenagers at the LGBTQ youth centre that I even learned about such a thing as needing an emotional connection before sex. They were throwing around labels and terms I'd never even heard of... but they were describing so many of my experiences, it was almost creepy.

After more research than I cared to admit, I was no closer to slapping a label on myself. I was kinda demisexual, a little bisexual, and a whole lot of not perfectly straight. If forced to label it, I felt most comfortable with sexually fluid.

And right now, it's Alec making the juices flow. I gave up trying to figure out why and accepted that maybe life and love aren't always the way you see in movies and read in books. Maybe you should just love the person and not care about the package they come in.

And I'm pretty sure I've loved him for a while.

"Why are you looking at me like that?"

He glances my way and I grin. I love the way his lip does this little tilt thing when he's teasing me.

"Like what?"

"Like you're shopping for groceries and just found something good."

I laugh. "Well, you're not wrong. I found something good. Real good."

Alec keeps his focus on the road ahead, but I notice the flex of his fingers on the wheel and the deep breath he takes. The sudden shift in the comfortable quiet.

"Uh, so we never talked about if you want this thing public yet or anything. I know it's new for you, but coming out can be...hard. It can be really fucking hard and I don't want you to rush into something that maybe makes life difficult for you."

I know he's right. To be fair, I hadn't really thought about it. I just know I want to be with him and see if we're compatible as more than friends. The rest seems like it's so far in the future I'd never need to think about it.

"I'm aware of the challenge it might bring, but I feel Bloomburg is an accepting town. Is this a huge concern for you? Like, do we have to tell people right away?"

We pass under the arch to The Broken Horn Ranch and Alec parks his truck in front of his adorable tiny farmhouse set off in the property's corner. He kills the engine, and the expressive blue eyes I am one hundred percent in love with are stormy.

"I will follow your lead for now, Zane. I just want you to feel safe and supported with whatever you do. If you need more time for us to work this out, I'm okay with that. But only temporarily. I will not be kept a secret. No matter how much I love you, I can't do that."

His voice hitches, but his gaze on me never wavers. My cowboy is a tough cookie, but not always with matters of the heart. That part is very clear now that I get to peek behind the curtain and have access to all of him.

"Thank you. I appreciate you telling me, and I don't *want* to keep you a secret. I want to take time to see if we work, though. If this doesn't go as we hope, I guess I'd like to not be public with a broken heart. So, yeah, following my lead for now would be great."

He nods, confirming his understanding, but I see the flash of doubt behind his eyes.

And I feel the pull to reassure him I won't hurt him, but a strange man knocks on the driver's side window, interrupting us.

"Hunter?"

Alec unbuckles and steps out. "You're not supposed to be here for a few more days."

Hunter pulls Alec into an awkward bro hug and Alec extracts himself quickly.

"Yeah, sorry. I didn't make the cut for finals. I figured I'd come up here early and maybe catch up. Blaze said I could board my horse here, so I just got her settled and was about to head to my hotel."

"Oh, I'm sorry you didn't make it. That must have been a rough round for you to be on the outside. How far off were you?"

Hunter smiles at Alec. An inside smile, like he knows Alec understands, but he also likes that Alec is sympathetic.

"I was out by one one-thousandth of a second. Totally sucks." His body relaxes, and he takes a half step towards Alec. "I was wondering if you might like to have dinner with me tonight. We could talk and catch up like old times."

Alec's eyes dart my way now that I've exited the truck and joined them.

I offer my hand to the guy and introduce myself.

"Hey, I'm Zane."

"Hunter."

He takes my offered hand with a nod, and then continues talking to Alec like I'm not even there. I'm trying to rack my brain for the name of the rodeo guy Alec told me about. He mentioned an old rodeo connection before who was closeted, and I wonder if this is the guy.

"Remember when we won that rodeo in Taber? We set the rodeo record. One of the best competitions I've ever been a part of. There's no faster heeler than you."

Ah, I was right. If there's one thing I've noticed in the years I've known Alec, it's that he's a magnet for both men and women. He gets hit on a lot and mostly he's oblivious, but sometimes he's not. This guy is into him.

He nods his head and changes the subject.

"So, was the drive okay?"

The guy clearly wants to puff him up and fawn over his roping, but Alec doesn't want that and Hunter doesn't notice.

"And then you did that rodeo before we teamed up and you won every tie-down roping round by miles. You had great hands. Do you still practice?"

"He ropes every day while working here. But he needs to practice for the upcoming charity rodeo." I'm hoping the guy just leaves, and I know that's bad manners, but I don't like him. Whatever it is I'm feeling about Hunter, it's not friendly.

"We could practice together. Just like old times."

Yep. I don't like this guy. He's not talking about roping.

"Hey fellas! I see you found Alec okay. Hi, Zane."

Blaze appears and shakes Hunter's hand.

"Nice to meet ya in person. You got your horse all squared away, I see. She's beautiful."

Without taking his eyes off Alec, Hunter says, "Yeah, she is."

Blaze pings his gaze to me and back to Alec.

"So, you all gonna do some ropin' then?"

"It's a great way to pass the afternoon." Hunter laughs, and Blaze motions for him to follow.

"C'mon. Grab your gear and we'll set up in the field behind Alec's house."

Hunter jogs off to his truck and Blaze heads to the gate off the meadow, leaving Alec and me together.

"He seems nice." I lie.

"He's the guy I told you about. I don't want to be with him."

"He's good at what he does, and you're supposed to practice. So practice."

"I said I'd follow your lead, Zane. Don't penalize me for that."

"I'm not. I was...I guess this was unexpected and you have a history with him."

Turning, I yank open the door of his truck and gather as many of the stuffed animals in my arms as I can. I'm jealous. Of course I am. Because accepting my newfound attraction to my best friend–my best *guy* friend–isn't enough to deal with. Now I need to sort this shit out, too.

Alec's hand on my hip and his lips near my ear as I bend into the truck help send some of the green away at least.

"History is the past, Z. I only look ahead now. I've already been waiting for you for three years. I can wait longer."

He steps away with a quick squeeze on my hip. "I'm going to get some ropes. I hope you still come and watch."

Alec walks away towards the meadow, a giant pink teddy bear tucked under his arm, before turning back to face me.

"There are Froot Loops in the pantry if you want that first."

"Since when do you buy Froot Loops? You hate that stuff."

He rubs his jaw and smiles.

"Since the first night I spent at your house and you ate them the next morning. You said you had to start the day with Froot Loops or you'd be in a bad mood. I wanted to be sure you wouldn't be in a bad mood if you ever spent the night."

He turns and walks off, leaving me with my arms full of stuffed unicorn while I watch a real one walk away.

Is there a prerequisite amount of time needed to pass before I return to Alec and Hunter in the field? I've never felt insecure before. By nature, I'm a confident person in most things I do. Whether it's changing a diaper on a friend's child, or jumping into a business venture I know little about, I've done it with the mindset that I'll master it. There's never been doubt.

I've most definitely never been jealous. How could I be when I've never been attached to someone enough to even know what love is? It's all new and weird and I'm so out of sorts, I need time to settle all these emotions jumping around my head like a damn kangaroo on caffeine.

After dumping the stuffed animals in the field with the guys, I promised that I'd be right back.

Instead, I watered and spritzed all of Alec's spider plants. I sang them all lullabies and told them how pretty they all were.

I turned his African violet a quarter turn on the windowsill and whispered my jealousy to it while praising how well it flowered. I repotted the violet that needed a bigger home and poured out my turmoil while gently feeding its regular dose of fertilizer.

I shouldn't be surprised that tending to the plants didn't ease any of these new emotions. But I'd had a few revelations. If I want to be with Alec and treat him well, I need to do two things. One was to not keep us a secret. This Hunter clown did that once, and I know how it hurt Alec. Two was to make sure I didn't push Alec away because I couldn't get a handle on my jealousy.

This whole '*grow wise with age*' bullshit is seriously annoying.

Fully prepared to declare my love and claim Alec in front of this guy, I marched out the door, turned down the side of the barn to the field and then… stopped. When I turned the corner and saw everyone laughing and enjoying themselves, I couldn't do it. I had heavy news to share and an announcement to make. Maybe this wasn't a good time, judging by the smiles and laughter.

"Hey, Zane. I thought you might have gone home or something," Hunter says with a smirk. My fists clench at my sides and I smile sweetly.

"Sorry to disappoint you. I watered the plants for Alec and got carried away."

"Oh thanks, Z." Alec smiles, and his forehead shines with perspiration.

"What did I miss?" I lean up against the fence with Blaze and survey the line of stuffed animals about ten feet away.

"Well," Blaze starts, "these two have been ropin' dinosaurs and bears at a long distance. They're about to change to the smaller ones and see who's more accurate."

"It's gonna be me," Hunter boasts. "Alec isn't as accurate as he used to be."

"Only when he's standing. On a horse, he'd beat you hands down."

Hunter's face drops, and Blaze laughs under his breath. Alec throws a shy smile my way.

"It's true." I shrug and look at Alec. "You know why."

"Why?" Hunter furrows his brow. His fake concern doesn't fly with me. I'm everyone's friend, but this guy can get lost in traffic. I don't like him.

"My hip. Remember when that steer kicked me when we helped that rodeo owner? We thought it was a deep bruise?"

Hunter's face remains blank, and there's a shift as Alec rushes on. "It wasn't. It was a hairline fracture and now it's a bone spur. It's also my plant leg, so I can't be as effective is what Zane was getting at. But it's not an issue on horseback."

"So what you're saying is I have an advantage right now."

Hunter laughs and Alec simply shrugs. "I guess so."

"He's a bit of a jerk, isn't he?" Blaze whispers as they set up the smaller bears for roping.

"I'd have chosen a more colourful name, but sure, let's go with jerk."

Alec and Hunter lay out the rules while Blaze and I listen, prepared to be judges if needed.

They trash talk each other mostly good-naturedly, but I can tell Hunter is far more invested in this than Alec. Even with Alec's hip as sore as it is, his accuracy is amazing, and he's roping the small bears with ease. He limped a little when he walked back from positioning the bears last time, too.

Alec is beautiful when in his element. And that's anything rodeo or on horseback. He makes swinging the lasso look easy. And hella sexy, because the corded muscle pops out as his arm flexes, and when his t-shirt lifts, I notice the muscle definition that's still there. He'll tell you he's too soft from beer and good food, but that's not true.

His lasso lands clean over the last tiny bear and he pumps his fist with a hoot.

"I win, Hunter!"

"Fine. I'll buy you dinner tonight then. We can practice more tomorrow."

"Oh, we already have plans for dinner tonight. Sorry."

All three men look at me, and while I might sound confident, inside I feel like a fish swimming next to a shark.

"He's right, we do. Maybe another night while you're here?"

Thank god Alec went along with that. We have zero plans, but I don't want him out alone with this guy.

"You're welcome to join me and my fiancé, if you'd like, Hunter."

"Oh, that's kind of you, but I think I'll get an early night tonight. Maybe we can set something up while I'm here."

Together we gather the stuffed animals and part ways with everyone outside of Alec's place. Blaze ends up giving his address to Hunter in case he changes his mind, and Alec and I go inside.

He hangs his Stetson on the hook beside the door and shoves his hands in his pants pockets.

"Do we really have plans for dinner?"

"We do now."

Chapter 11

Alec

Before I could question Zane, he was in my fridge again, gathering ingredients and creating something almost as mouthwatering as he is.

He's doing his best to ignore the tension with Hunter showing up, but I don't like ignoring things. Especially with Zane.

"He's not someone I'm interested in. In case you didn't hear me the first time."

He smashes a knife through the red pepper.

"I heard you. I just don't like him."

Zane likes everybody. He would never say that unless he had a specific reason to. The muscle in his jaw ticks as he keeps chopping random vegetables.

"How did you two meet?"

"You really want to know?"

Zane sets the knife down and hangs his head.

"Yes. I think I want to know."

He waits for my words and I step closer, pushing the knife away from his hand.

"We were drunk on the rodeo circuit and met at a bar. He went down on me in the bathroom. We exchanged numbers." Zane's chest rises and he keeps his eyes on the pile of vegetables.

"Who called who first?" he whispers, and I'm not sure why the details are so important to him.

"I called him."

He still doesn't look at me, and I reach out to lift his chin with a finger. When he finally turns his pretty green eyes my way, they aren't the bright lights I'm used to. This is not the Zane I know and love, and I rub at my chest with my other hand.

"Z, tell me what's wrong."

He shakes his head and reaches for the knife again. He keeps chopping vegetables for a dish unknown to me as I stand beside him like some forgotten scarecrow.

"Just give me a minute, please."

As he wishes, I back away from him at the counter and take a chair at the kitchen table. I don't know if that's enough space for him, but it's all I'm willing to give right now. He continues chopping and cooking, and the silence in the kitchen weighs so heavy I might suffocate from the weight of it. I need air, and it needs to come from Zane.

He finally turns from the stove and sits at the kitchen table next to me.

With a huff, he raises his eyes up to the ceiling.

"Okay. We've always been honest with each other. You mentioned a former partner and when I realized it was Hunter,

I…" his hands rub on his thighs. "And then he was all…like hitting on you and I, I…I got jealous."

I knew something was bothering him, but I didn't think it was that.

"Why are you jealous?"

Zane bites his lip and turns his gaze to me. I'm trying really hard to work out what he's jealous of. Hunter isn't a recent relationship. He's ancient history and we don't even keep in touch.

"Because he obviously wants to give you what I can't yet. He…he's touched you. He knows what you like. You've had sex with him." He inhales again. "I'm afraid you'll take him up on his offer instead of being with me."

He pushes out of his chair quickly, returning to the stove before I have time to react. He's losing himself in cooking, and I set the table in silence. Zane isn't the only one new at this. I'm at a loss for what to say because the only thing I want to say is, *'how can you even think that?'* But that's not right.

I watch quietly as he removes a dish from the oven. Baked chicken and potatoes.

I didn't even know I had chicken. I swear he's magic everywhere he goes.

It's not until he's plated our dinner that I take his hand before he sits and pull him to me.

"Zane, I know you're processing a lot, but I need you to know, just the promise of you is a million times better than any offer Hunter might make." I gesture to the table with the dinner he made. "This right here? I dream about this every night. Sharing supper with you and having you on my couch every evening. Yes, I want you in my bed. I have since I've known you. But the promise of all of you is far more appealing than the promise of one night with him."

He sags against me.

"I'm sorry. I've never felt like this and it's so weird. I'm so damn rage-y when he's talking to you and that's not who I am."

I smile and drop a kiss to his forehead.

"I love that you want to fight for me, but you don't need to. You've already won."

He looks away again, and I draw him in for a hug, needing his body against mine. He's still stiff, and he'll have to work through all this somehow to be comfortable with it in his own head. I just hope I can help.

"Let's eat before it's cold."

He kisses my cheek before stepping out of my arms and takes his seat.

"Tell me how it went. How did you feel roping the bears?"

"Fantastic, actually. I mean, rarely have I ever done it on foot, but it was a challenge." I puff out my chest. "And I still won. The washed-up, ex-rodeo star still has it."

Zane laughs at my very unusual bragging. It's not like me to speak of my accomplishments, but there was a part of me that shouted on the inside when my accuracy was far better than Hunter's.

"Do you ever wish you never left rodeo? Do you ever miss it?"

With a sigh, I finish the simple dinner Zane threw together for us. His question is something I try not to think about often.

"There're a lot of things I miss and a lot I don't." We stand together and work to clean up the kitchen. Zane fills the sink full of soapy water while I try to gather my thoughts.

"I miss the thrill of competing. There's nothing better than the rush of adrenaline when you've won. Hearing your name announced, doing the ride around the ring while you wave your hat to the fans. That's an incredible feeling."

He hands me a dish to dry. "I bet it is. All those adoring fans. Cowboys are next to rock stars in the adoration department. You probably felt like the world was at your feet. Ladies throwing their panties at you." He laughs and dabs a pile of dish suds on my cheek. I wipe it off with a grin and blow the suds back at him.

"It felt surreal, but the bad stuff was nobody told you that you'd spend most of your life living in a trailer with your horse. That was your home. Sometimes the places you would park didn't have proper water, so you couldn't have a real shower. Or that you'd spend three days in mud because it didn't stop raining and there was nowhere else to go. Or that a few of the event sponsors aren't always on the straight and narrow. Money won sometimes took months to get released because they were in financial trouble. Or that you'd just be constantly tired." I place the last pan in the cupboard as the dish water gurgles down the drain. Zane wipes the counter down and hangs the cloth over the tap and my chest grows tight.

This is the part you don't think you'll miss. The simple acts of domestic life. The ability to move around a stationary building and put dishes away without bumping into something. The stability of a relationship. A welcome home kiss.

Zane stands next to me, head cocked, waiting for me to continue.

"Where did you go there? You were talking and then you just drifted off."

"I remembered what I hated most about always being on the road."

Leaning my hip against the counter, I study Zane. His warm eyes wait for me, just like I'll wait for him, and I'm taken aback when wetness forms in my eyes.

"Alec? What's wrong?"

Zane reaches for me and I grab his hand, holding it against my cheek.

"For me, I was...still am, a romantic. I never had role model parents. They fought all the time and there was never any love there. I left home for the rodeo and they didn't even notice. I hoped rodeo would be my family. The bonds you build there, I wanted badly. And I had some, but only as friends."

Swallowing, I shake my head at my foolish confessions. "I was hoping to find someone to be my everything. The person who would keep me home and off the road. Someone who would care for me just as much as I do them. I wanted to find the dream, Zane. That all-consuming love where I'd lay down my life for someone

I loved. On the road…that wasn't a possibility. So the longer I competed, the farther that dream drifted from me."

Zane wipes at the wetness that somehow didn't spill down my cheek.

"You didn't like how lonely you felt?"

Nodding, I reach for him and bury my face in his neck. He gives me everything I've ever wanted. Dozens of friends who love you and care about you can surround you, but I longed for someone to hold and talk with. Someone to chase the loneliness away and share my day with. I want the boring, normal stuff nobody talks about. The one person who always has my back and will watch mindless TV shows with me with their head in my lap.

"I hated it. Still do."

"Can I ask you something?"

"Of course."

"Can you take me for a horseback ride?"

"Now?"

"Yeah. Can we?"

"It will be short because darkness is coming, but sure. Let's go. I can never say no to a ride."

And I can never say no to Zane.

It doesn't take long to saddle up Domino, and I choose one of the slower trail riding horses Dan rescued for Zane. Her name is Carmen, and she's the sweetest thing. She's perfect for a beginner rider.

"Have you ever been on a horse?"

"Never." He answers, but he's smiling that mischievous grin. "But I want you to take me. Teach me what it is you love about this."

I explain how to put his foot in the stirrup and mount the horse and, with a little help from me, he makes it on the second try.

"Nice work with the hand on my ass, cowboy."

I laugh out loud.

"You needed a boost. It was the easiest thing to help you along. Besides, I didn't hear you complaining."

I mount Domino with ease and find Zane biting his lip with a fire in his eyes.

"I'm definitely not complaining."

"Well, you might be in about twenty minutes, when your thighs burn."

"Good thing I know a guy with a hot tub, then."

Carmen is a trail horse through and through and really doesn't need to be told what to do. After showing Zane how to hold on to the saddle horn and the reins, Domino leads us out of the barn to the meadow. We won't go far tonight. I'm not a fan of riding in the dark, and Zane will be sore sooner rather than later.

But he's never asked me to ride before. Why now?

"It's soothing out here, isn't it? I see why you like it so much."

"It is. Riding for pleasure is a lot different from riding for work. But either way is an experience."

"So, with rodeo, you never got to enjoy this kind of thing? Just a ride for fun?"

"Rarely, no. There wasn't a lot of time. You had a competition, or you practiced. If you weren't doing that, you were grooming your horse or taking care of equipment. Or driving to the next stop. There wasn't a lot of downtime for moments like this."

Which is the truth. And while I enjoyed the competition, I longed for quiet moments like this. Even on days when my hip was extra painful, I'd never say no to this.

Zane leans forward to pet Carmen's neck, cooing to her about how wonderful she is for taking a newbie on his first ride. He's soaking up the whole experience. Looking up and down, wiggling his feet out of the stirrups and back in, even looking behind him to watch Carmen flick her tail.

Fuck, my heart squeezes so tight just watching him enjoy himself. Doing something I love with me, and when he smiles my way, bouncing back and forth with the steps of the horse, it's perfect. More perfect than the championship run for a belt buckle.

When we get back to the barn, he helps me unsaddle the horses while I talk him through it. He carries his saddle to the tack room, putting it away with great care as instructed. He brushes out

Carmen like I show him, marvelling at the way her hide twitches when he passes the brush over her flank. The entire time, he's smiling and just being his usual Zane self.

Happy. Shiny. A fucking dream that lives in my head 24/7.

And I want him more than I ever have before. I crave him in a visceral way that swamps all other rational thought.

Now that this door is open for us to be more, my fear of being hurt by him disappears. Right now, I'd bleed out just to have him for one night. Fear can take a back seat and just let me have this as my final memory.

He must have sensed my mood, because his light flirting and sunshine smiles come to a dead stop.

"Alec..."

My name breathless from his lips alone has me half hard.

I crowd him up against the wall in the barn and shove my thigh between his legs.

"Zane...how much can I touch you?" Trailing my lips down his neck, I groan with the sound of his gasps. He shifts against my leg, rubbing himself against my thigh, and my heart races. He's turned on. By me.

"Um, I don't know? This is ah, *fuck*, that feels good." I suck a spot on his neck and he thrusts his groin harder into me.

I can't and never will get enough of him panting like this for me. God, I want to drop to my knees right here and now and worship him for the rest of my days.

Instead, I give him space and force his glassy eyes to focus on me.

"Tell me if this is too much, sweetheart. I know I'm moving fast, but tell me if you want me to stop. I'll stop."

Zane never stops riding my leg while his eyes come back into focus. His cheeks are stained a strawberry-pink, lips parted in gentle wonder. If this is what he looks like during some heavy groping and kissing, I might likely die when he's finally naked with me.

"I want," he swallows, but never breaks our eye contact. "I want you to stroke me through my pants. And kiss me. You're an amazing kisser."

I haven't rubbed a guy's fully clothed dick since I was sixteen, but if it's what he wants, then it's what I'll do. It's awkward and more than a little weird, but he's into it.

His fingers curl into my shoulders as he rocks his denim-clad crotch against my hand. My lips alternate from his mouth to his neck and his jaw before taking his mouth again with a deep kiss. I love how he tastes of promises and sunshine.

Zane's entire body quivers like a newly strung wire fence in the pasture. Every thrum of his pleasure amplifies my own.

He presses harder into my hand with a breathy gasp.

"I'm gonna come, oh my god."

His body shakes, and he moans into my mouth as his orgasm pulses through his body. The warm wetness under my hand through his pants sends a shiver through me. I made him feel like this. It was *me* who gave him this experience, this euphoria, when nobody else could. The possibilities ahead for us make me ache to move his journey along faster.

When I step away, he reaches for me and pulls me back to him, resting his head on my shoulder.

"Thank you." He's still panting to catch his breath, and each warm puff against my neck sends a flash of heat to my dick. "Don't worry. It's okay. I'm okay."

"I'm sorry. I never want to force you. Never. But tonight was something different. You and me with the horses set something off and I...I wanted you. Like I always have, and yet like I never have before. Did you feel it, too?"

His sweet smile eases my guilt, and his hand on my cheek is an extra assurance.

"That's what I wanted. I wanted to share the things you love with you. I want to make the loneliness that sits at the edge of your heart go away. I want to be that for you, cowboy." He kisses me softly on the lips, lingering there. "I know I test your patience, but I'll get there. I liked this. A lot. So what's coming can only be better."

God, I hope he's right.

"Do you want me to take you home now?"

"Can I spend the night instead?"

A bigger man would likely say no, considering the change in our relationship and what we just did. I should let him process and chug forward instead of rocketing into another sleepover. But he's not wrong about the loneliness.

"You can always spend the night. Having you in my bed is something I'll never turn down."

Walking back to my tiny farmhouse from the barn, he reaches out and grabs my hand, locking our fingers together.

And all the padding I put around my heart dissolves.

It's all his now and I trust him to take care of it.

CHAPTER 12

ZANE

The aroma of freshly brewed coffee hits my nose and I stretch awake with a grin. Alec's bed is way more comfortable than mine. I should stay here more often. Comfortable bed, Froot Loops in the cupboard, and no raccoon break-ins. It's a definite step up from my place.

The room is still dark, but when I check my phone for the time, it's after 8 AM and I bolt up, scrambling for something to throw on. Then I remember Alec put my pants in the wash before bed and my skin burns lava hot remembering what put them there.

I can't believe I came in my pants rubbing up on Alec. But... shit, that was hot, and it wasn't just his hands and mouth on me that caused a shift. Our horse ride, the way he showed me what to do and how happy he was on our short outing. Alec's whole demeanour shifts when he's on his horse. From the way his body relaxes in the saddle to the peaceful expression on his handsome face, it's breathtaking.

Me riding with him gave him something he longed for. I wanted it as well. I just didn't know what to call it.

He's holding himself back and afraid to rush me, which is heart melting on its own, but I don't like him waiting for me. Especially now that I know he's been waiting so long. My head needs to catch up to what my heart and body clearly want.

Sooner rather than later.

Being with Alec will change my entire life. And I want that.

If the ridiculous flutter that settles in my chest every time I think of him is anything to go by, I'm in for a crazy ride. And now that I finally understand this attraction and have a hint at what it's like to be with Alec, I want it all.

This is the feeling that makes my friends get all mushy and heart-eyed over their partners. I could never understand it before. But I sure do now.

After yanking on a pair of discarded shorts from the floor, I wander out to the kitchen. Alec is nowhere to be seen, but his coffee maker beeps the signal to end the cycle. It's then I notice the sticky note on the counter and pad over to read it.

> *Zane,*
>
> *You were sleeping so deeply I didn't want to wake you. I hope the smell of coffee gets you out of bed and to work on time. Take my truck if you need to; the keys are by the door. Sorry I couldn't kiss you good morning. I really wanted to. By the time you wake, I'll be out of cell range, but I'll catch up with you tonight.*
>
> *Love, Alec*

Well then, insert lovestruck eyes now. Crushing the note to my chest, I sigh.

I've never wanted to kiss someone good morning. Ever. And here I am already scheming how to spend the night again and not miss a good morning kiss tomorrow.

Who knew I was such a sap?

After pouring a cup of coffee–Alec makes the best coffee–I peek out the front window to check if Martin's car is in the yard. If he hasn't left for work yet, I'll ask him to drive me in. I could use the commute to talk to him about all this.

But I don't get far because there's a loud squawk followed by a thump against the side of the house.

"Jeff! Get back here and into the box!"

One of the ranch hands, Heath, jogs across the yard, missing a shoe, and pulling some kind of cage on wheels behind him. I want to offer help, but this is one of those situations where I'm sure I don't want to be involved.

A large peacock skids around the corner of the house with another loud squawk and runs up Alec's front porch steps.

"Ah!" I jump back, clutching my chest.

Heath notices me in the window and waves. I'm not sure if it's a *'can you help?'* wave or a *'don't mind me'* kind of wave. I know I'm not opening the door, though. This bird looks unhinged and very unpredictable.

It squawks, hops over the porch railing, and takes off around the back of the house again. Heath leaves the cage behind and pursues the bird, still missing a shoe, and I back away after double checking the door is still locked. I don't know if peacocks are as crafty as raccoons, but I might as well be safe.

Instead of walking over and knocking on Dan's door, which I intended to do until the creepy bird showed up, I text Martin instead.

Zane: Are you going to the office today? I need a ride.

It doesn't take him long to respond.

Martin: I am. Still dragging my ass after the other night, but I can pick you up on the way. I'll leave in about 15, if that's ok?

Zane: I'm actually still at Alec's. Let me shower, and as long as there's no rogue peacock in the yard, I'll come over when I'm done.

Martin: Rogue peacock?

Zane: Heath was chasing it. It seems a little unstable, but I'll come over when I'm done.

Draining my coffee, I rush to the shower so I don't keep Martin waiting too long. I'll leave Alec a note before I leave and then I'll sprint across the yard to avoid any bird mishaps.

The laundry machines are in the bathroom, and while I towel myself dry, I notice my clean jeans and boxers folded nicely and sitting on top of the dryer. With a soft smile at his thoughtfulness, I yank them both on before searching for my shirt.

"Zane? Let me in."

Shit. Martin is ultra fast this morning. I jog down the hall to let him in while I towel off my hair.

"Get in quick. Did you see the peacock?"

"No. But I'll lock the door again."

I laugh to myself. Martin still isn't comfortable with animals of any kind, and the two of us locking a door for a bird makes me wonder how we've made it this far in life.

"Let me get my shirt and we can get going."

It's still on the bench in Alec's room, and after pulling it on, I find my wallet and keys and stuff them in my pockets.

Back in the kitchen, Martin peers through a crack in the blinds like he's a sniper on the lookout.

"I think Heath has the bird. He's dragging a cage on wheels behind him."

"Thank god. That was unnerving seeing a bird at the door so early. Or ever really, but I am curious as to why he was missing a shoe."

Martin lets the blinds drop before turning to me.

"I'm more curious about the hickey on your neck."

"What?!"

I rush back to the bathroom and stare in the mirror. This is what happens when you're distracted in the morning. There it is. Right at the base of my neck on my collarbone. Alec's mouth on me last night is something I'll not forget anytime soon, if ever. Now it seems like I'll have a visible reminder for a few days. Which, I admit, I'm not mad about.

When I return to the kitchen, Martin leans against the door, waiting.

"Now I'm not going to ask for all the details but...I'm asking for all the details because you were here all day yesterday and spent the night. Unless you had a mystery woman here... How do you have a hickey?"

This is a conversation I can't have on an empty stomach. And I need comfort food. I motion for him to take a chair and open the cupboard. My smile hurts my cheeks when I see the box of Froot Loops. After opening it to inhale the fruity goodness, I wrangle a large mixing bowl from the cupboard and pour half the box in. After adding milk, I sit at the kitchen table.

"How do you eat that shit? It's all sugar and food dye."

Shrugging, I spoon more into my mouth. "Sugar is delicious, and it's not shit. It's happy fuel."

His gaze is unrelenting, and I feel like a bug under a microscope. But I'm not answering his questions until I finish my cereal. When I lean back and let the spoon clink in the empty bowl, it's Martin who speaks first.

"Sorry."

"For calling my cereal shit? You should be."

He huffs a breath. "Be serious for a minute. I'm sorry for railroading you like that. You don't need to tell me anything until you want to, Zane. I was an ass demanding you tell me something so personal, and that's not fair."

Placing my bowl in the sink, I lean back against the counter and study Martin.

"No, it wasn't fair. Apology accepted, but I know it comes from a good place. You aren't forcing me to tell you anything. In fact, I'd love it if I could talk to someone about it."

Martin sags with relief and I'm grateful to have such a good friend.

"My door is always open, Zane. You know that."

"Well, yeah, I do know, but you were also drunk when I needed you the first time, so I couldn't really tell you anything then."

"Wow, I'm failing at friendship big time. First, I'm drunk, now I'm a bit of an asshole."

Sliding back down into the chair at the table, I drum my fingers before meeting Martin's gaze.

"You're a great friend, so stop that. But...I'm in love with Alec. The hickey is from him. We only made out in the barn for a few minutes. I'm...not sure what to call myself other than not straight. There's been a lot of self-discovery the last few months, and uh, I'm taking the next step."

Martin blinks and opens his mouth. Closes it. I know how he feels.

"Holy shit. I was not expecting you to tell me anything close to that."

"Well, neither was I to be honest. But I don't really know how to tell people and since you asked, I figured I'd just put it out there."

Martin sits quietly, and I bounce my knee. Then I roll the salt shaker between my palms.

"Stop squirming. I'm just processing this. I'm...sort of shocked, but...also not."

"Yeah, well, you didn't finally put the pieces together and realize what you were doing wrong your whole life."

Martin's hand shoots out to grab mine.

"There's nothing wrong, Zane. It was your path, that's all. But I hope whatever's changed has made things more clear for you." He chuckles the way only Martin can when he's in a particularly snarky mood. "And I want you to confirm if I'm right about the good head."

He waggles his eyebrows and my neck burns.

"I'm not going to kiss and tell when we get to that part, but...until yesterday we'd only just kissed and cuddled because..." I don't really know how to say it. What do I tell people when I come out? The truth? A whitewashed truth?

"Because you realized you're closer than most friends and that closeness is real love, but you didn't know if it was platonic love or a romantic love and now that you've explored it you have an answer?"

"Uh, yeah. That's, ah, really accurate actually."

"I think you're Alec's worst kept secret, to be honest. If there's anyone on this ranch who hasn't picked up on his, what do you want to call it, unrequited love? Then I'd be shocked. So for you to finally recognize your attachment to him, I'm thrilled."

"I am too. And what set me off yesterday was that Hunter guy. Have you met him yet?"

"No. What's the problem, and who is he?"

"Alec's ex and he's here for the rodeo thing. He showed up early yesterday and he was hitting on Alec so bad I wanted to punch him in the shoulder."

Martin chuckles. "Just the shoulder?"

"Well yeah, I'm not a fan of blood, so I'll avoid the face, but...he wants Alec, and I was so fucking green with jealousy, Martin. It was insane. I sulked in here and watered his plants while they roped out in the meadow."

"Jealous!? You? Oh boy. That's a new one for you, too." His expression softens as he studies me. "Are you sure you're okay? Jealousy can bring down the strongest of bonds sometimes."

My hand goes to the bite on my neck and I remember how alive I felt with Alec's hands and mouth on me. How it all felt so perfect. So natural and right. From the horseback ride to the time in the barn, and how he made sure I was okay after. Not a single moment did I ever feel uncomfortable or unsure. It was like figuring out the missing ingredient to a recipe that turned it from good to fucking amazing.

"It's all new, and we talked about it. He assured me he's not interested in Hunter. He told me he'd wait forever if he had to."

"Aww, Zane. I'm happy for you. So fucking happy. It's the missing piece, isn't it?"

Suddenly feeling very raw, very seen, by Martin, I swallow and nod.

"Yeah. I think it is."

"You wanna hug on it or just get to work like usual and pretend nothing happened?"

Laughing, I push out of the chair as Martin does and we hug.

"I'll need to talk to Dylan today, but we don't have to pretend we never had this conversation. Thanks for this, Marty."

"Don't thank me. I feel really fucking special that you told me what you did."

I rush around the house and run my fingers through my hair before I decide to borrow a ball cap of Alec's I find on a hook in the bathroom. I didn't think he owned a ball cap. He's never without his Stetson. Must be a rodeo thing, although Blaze always wears his, too. Maybe it's a rancher thing?

When I meet Martin at the door, I hold up a finger for him to wait and I write a note for Alec.

Alec,

I didn't know I'd miss kissing someone good morning until today. I hope we can remedy that soon.

Zane xoxo

I leave the note on the kitchen table where he should be sure to see it and add a smiling heart face.

"Okay, let's go."

As we walk to Martin's car, Heath appears carrying a shoe and shaking his head. Martin and I exchange a silent glance.

Waving, I greet Heath with a hello, and he waves back.

"Did you know peacocks have a mating season and will attack things when they can't find a lady peacock?"

"Uh, no."

"No man can ever match the frustration of a peacock with no lady friends. They are vicious." He holds up his shoe.

"Are you okay, Heath?"

He smiles back. "I am now! Jeff is on his way to meet Morticia and then I'll have a happy peacock."

As if he remembers the shoe he's holding should belong on his foot, he drops it and shoves his foot into the shoe. He waves again and whistles as he walks back to the barn.

"He's an odd one, isn't he?"

"I don't like to think about what he is, but he's something all right."

CHAPTER 13

ZANE

The whole drive in Martin babbles on about how he's still recovering from our dinner out, and I should never let him drink that much wine again. He's officially mourning the loss of his alcohol tolerance.

When Martin and I arrive late, Dylan is busy directing a delivery in the brewery, and Matts is on the phone with a seed supplier.

Once behind my desk and staring at the orders I have to deal with for the restaurant, the low-key anxiety brewing over telling my friends about Alec and me melts away. Because these guys are my family. Just like my sister, they've always been here for me and me for them.

There's no point in waiting to tell anyone about this. Even if things don't work out with Alec, it's a part of me that won't ever change.

"Morning, Zane." Dylan does a double take and narrows his eyes at me before leaning against his desk across from mine. "What's wrong?"

"Who said anything was wrong?"

He lifts an eyebrow. "You don't need to. I know. I can tell you how I know if you want me to."

The problem with being close friends with someone for so long is they know you better than yourself sometimes. Dylan is the most observant person I know. He likely has a list of eighteen things he's noticed about me since he walked in the room and he'll rhyme them off if I ask him.

"No. I don't need you to be any more smug than what you're likely to be after we talk."

"Well, that's rude. You're gonna penalize me for knowing you so well?"

There's a smile to his voice and I know he's just teasing me, but he's right. Next to Alec, Dylan is the one who knows me the best.

"Of course not. But I need you to be serious."

Martin stands and leans next to Dylan while Matts finishes his phone call and asks if it's required to stand for my news.

"You can stay sitting. Maybe you should all stay sitting. Well, except Martin, he already knows."

Three sets of eyes stay glued to me and wait patiently for me to speak. I have no speech prepared. No well-thought-out explanations and words. Just like most things in my life, I go into them headfirst and hope for the best. A Boy Scout I am not.

"I don't know how to say it other than to just say it. I'm in love with Alec and have been for a while. We're dating? Involved? I don't know what to call that, but we're together. I'm not straight and I'm not sure what to call that part either yet. So...ta-da!"

Martin sits back down with a smile since it's not new to him, while Matts and Dylan say nothing at first, but it's Matts that speaks first.

"You know, when you made him that special soup while he was sick, I suspected. But when you insisted on taking him a birthday cake in the field at the ranch—one you baked—and you fussed over it so much...I was certain then you had feelings for him. But I wasn't going to ask outright. I'm glad you figured it out. I'm happy for you."

"Hold on. What do you mean you suspected, and you knew?"

I've only just put all the pieces together myself. How could he possibly know before me?

Matts shrugs as he picks up his coffee mug and frowns at the bottom. "You had this way about you. It reminded me of when I was desperate to find a way to be with Jacob. You were so determined to make it work out. All of it. I'd never seen you so invested in the outcome of something before. Not even one of your kitchen experiments. It was just a birthday cake delivered and while it's a thoughtful gesture on its own, you made it out to be the single most important thing in your life that day. It just hit me and I was almost positive you were into him as more than friends."

"How come you never said anything?"

"I can answer that." Dylan finally chimes in. "We never said anything because it's not our place to question your feelings. Especially when it's new to you. Or in your case, not yet realized. We all knew if you wanted to talk to us about it, you would. Just like you're doing now."

"Wow. Martin said he knew Alec was into me and you two say you knew I was into Alec. I feel like I'm the slowest guy on the planet here. But you're also right." Dylan's face breaks into a grin and I wag my finger at him. "Don't say it."

He laughs. "I won't. This is far too big of a deal to gloat about it. So...how did you know?"

Running a hand through my hair, my lips tilt into a smile as I remember how it felt to have Alec hold me the first night. Every little touch and glance that we've shared has built this mountain of feelings. Feelings that I never took the time to explore because I thought it wasn't anything different from feelings I had for Dylan or any other of my friends. When I finally gave myself time to climb that mountain and actually explore it, a shift happened. There was a whole lot more on the mountain than just friendship.

"Remember the girl I last dated? Marla?"

He nods. "Yeah, you were pretty excited about her."

"I was, and she's such a nice girl, but...I never thought about sex with her. It just wasn't an interest, and she always wanted it. I liked her, but the few times we did have sex, I didn't enjoy it. Well, I mean, I liked it some. It's hard to explain, but it didn't make fireworks go off or cause me to profess my love. It was just something to do. Which made me rethink most of my girlfriends, and I never had that whole caveman attitude thing. They were never the single most important person to me. Like, I should have wanted them to be, but...I didn't care if I did."

Wow. That sounds harsh out loud, but it took me a long time to realize the lack of excitement over sex was connected to something much deeper that I hadn't learned about myself yet.

"Then I was at the shelter waiting for Matts and I heard some of the kids talking about how they couldn't just sleep with people for the sake of sex. They didn't have a connection or it just felt wrong. They said they had to almost be in love before anything physical happened and that really made me think." Swallowing, I shake my head as I replay several years of failed relationships. "I think I've always been this way, but I never let myself acknowledge it. I just thought it was like that with everyone. Over the last couple of years, hearing you all talk about being with your partners, it was a change. I heard it in your voices, and saw it in your eyes, and sometimes I saw it in action without my consent."

I cough for Matts' attention, and he looks up from his laptop.

"I told you I was sorry. Jacob has a thing when the lavender blooms and I wasn't going to say no to him. I didn't think you were still here."

"Eye bleach, Matts. I didn't need to see your...assets right before bed."

He shrugs and turns back to the monitor.

"Now you know to make noise around here in the spring."

Mental note to buy a damn cowbell.

"Anyway, I noticed how you all seemed to just be more glow-y and happy and I'd never had that. I also assumed when I did, it would be with a woman."

Dylan, always the father figure of our crew, motions me over for a hug and we hug with a laugh. But his gesture means so much.

"You know that anyone who's spent time around you and Alec can tell he's head over heels for you, Zane. He's carried a torch for a long time. How is he handling all this?"

We return to sitting at our desks while we talk and I shake my head when I look at the coaster on my desk. Alec gave it to me for my birthday last year.

In a garden of friends, I'd pick you every time.

It had a photo of his African violets on it. The one with a blue pot I bought special for him one Christmas was in the front. When I hugged him after, he held me a little longer than usual. I remember I teased him about being extra sentimental and he went really quiet. God, I've been so blind.

"He...he's very patient and I'm pretty sure he's happy about it. But I get the feeling he's more nervous than he shares with me."

"You can't blame him, Zane." Martin says. "He's only known you as the straight playboy he could never have. He's likely afraid of having his heart broken. I think he hides more than most of us know."

Dylan nods. "I agree. After what I went through with Travis, I think that's likely not far from the truth. He may be going slow for you because it's new for you, but maybe you should go slow for him to show him he's not just a passing fancy." He pauses. "He's not right? Like you think he's '*The One*'?"

The One.

Shit.

Life without Alec is one I don't ever want to know. He's my missing link. The other half of my wandering soul.

"If he made me come in my pants, it's probably a good sign I'll like that bit, right?"

Matts chokes on his water, and Martin laughs while Dylan's eyes bulge from their sockets.

"Oh yes," Matts wheezes. "That's a very, very good sign."

I smile, feeling the most sure I ever have.

"Then yes. He could be 'The One', but..."

The claws of anxiety, and the way Hunter looked at Alec, creep back in. I want Alec in every way, but I don't know how to deal with this new thing. This ick-filled emotion that makes me want to punch Hunter in his stupid, smiley, cowboy face.

"What is it? You know we'll help as much as we can." Dylan pauses from work, giving me his full attention.

"It's so dumb. But his ex is one of the cowboys here for the auction and rodeo. He showed up at the ranch yesterday."

"Okay? So what's the problem?"

"It's a 'me problem.' I don't like him and I don't want him near Alec."

"So you're jealous?"

Squirming in my seat, heat warms my neck, and I shrug.

"Yeah, weird right?"

Dylan chews the end of the arm on his reading glasses and leans back.

"It's not weird."

"When Dan and I went to the strippers one night, one of them was totally angling for him and it made me see red. You don't want anyone getting what's yours. Is it more like that or something else?" Martin returns to typing as I try to decode all the emotions that bubbled up yesterday.

Maybe that's all it is? I just want others to know he's now mine and nothing more. I spent a lot of time watering plants yesterday thinking about it. But my fear is I have no experience and he'll compare me to Hunter, ultimately finding me lacking in what he needs. Which is ridiculous. I know this. But it's not easy to just shake off.

It's like trying to tie a bow when the string is too short, and no matter how hard you try, you can't make the ends meet and work together.

Logic and my broken thought process don't see eye to eye.

"I think you need to talk to Alec about this. He won't know or understand this version of Zane. He's likely thinking of how this changes everything with you being together. He has his own worries and I think you need to talk it out before it's a problem." Dylan returns his glasses to his face and focuses on his computer screen.

With a sigh, I run my hand over my face. It feels like I've been here for a week when it's barely been an hour.

My phone buzzes and the instant smile and warmth that fills me when I see it's Alec can't be hidden. I might have sighed.

"Oh god. It's him, isn't it? You look like a teenager with their first crush." Martin teases and I can't help but laugh.

He's not far from the truth.

Except I'm thirty-eight and in love for the first time.

Even emo teenagers aren't as scary as that.

Chapter 14

Alec

The tires of the ranch's three-quarter-ton truck hit the rumble strip along the highway's edge. I snap my head up and wipe the drool from my chin.

"What's got you so sleepy today? You never fall asleep when I'm drivin'."

Blaze laughs when I turn my sleepy stare his way.

"True. You know it's because you sing and drive and I literally can't fall asleep with all that screeching you call singing. So maybe I should ask why you aren't singing first?"

He smirks, and I wish I hadn't woken up.

"I have been singin'. I needed to drown out your snorin'"

Great. He'll never let this drop now. I may have dozed off for thirty minutes last night, but that's it. I held a naked Zane in my arms after I made him come in his pants. How was I supposed to sleep after that? It was a miracle I could remember how to get dressed this morning.

"Since you'll find out anyway...Zane spent the night. I didn't sleep a wink."

Blaze snorts in surprise.

"No shit. River owes me twenty bucks."

"You bet on me? What the fuck?"

Blaze nods with a grimace. "Sorry buddy. But I only did because I felt certain there would be a happy endin'. So, is it out there now? You two are a thing? He was mighty uncomfortable with Hunter around. If I knew gettin' an ex to come over would get Zane riled up, I'd have done it sooner."

"What did Zane say to you?"

"Nothin'. I just watched him once he came down to watch you two ropin'." Blaze flicks the turn signal on as we pass a slower vehicle. We dropped a few rescue horses off at their new homes this morning and the drive back is taking forever. "I've watched a lot of people over my time in business and he was all kinds of uncomfortable and, if I'm not mistaken, jealous."

Scrubbing my hand over my face, I reach for the mug of sweet tea I bought at the last rest stop. It's not as good as the stuff Zane makes.

"He was jealous, he admitted it. But, and this is in confidence, being attracted to me was something he didn't understand at first. He's been really open with his feelings and what's going on in his head. I think Hunter confused him even more because he'd never felt that way before. He's never felt our relationship was threatened."

Blaze nods. "That's a huge shift to process for anyone. Now here's a question for you. If he didn't like Hunter around, how is he gonna feel with you in the cowboy auction with people oglin' your ass in those jeans?"

I hadn't even thought about it. Why would I? Jealousy was something I didn't do or understand. You're with me or you aren't, there's no need to overthink all the possible scenarios. And we hadn't even figured out how we worked together yet, so it was definitely not on my radar. I only told Zane I'd follow his lead.

"I guess I'll have to ask him. I'm still doing it since it's for charity, but if our conversation last night is anything to go by, he won't like it."

Blaze stops the truck and trailer as we get stuck in a construction zone and I groan at the size of the backup.

"Do you have a plan at least? Like how you're goin' to approach this?"

"Shit, Blaze. It's not every day the guy you've been in love with for years realizes he's loved you too and wants to take things further. Even if I had a plan for this, I'd likely go off the rails. I want to go full speed ahead, but I'll be truthful and tell you I'm as nervous as a cat near a rocking chair." Swallowing, I stare out the window. "What if it all goes sideways and we're making a mistake?"

The truck inches ahead half a car's length and we stop again.

"Ah...the old what-if questions. I understand, I do. And I could say somethin' poetic or deep and meanin'ful, but that's not my style either."

I laugh to myself because he's right. Blaze never sugar coats anything.

"But I will say this—the regret of never knowing is worse than the regret of tryin' and failin'. It will haunt you forever if you don't take this, Alec. I know I can't see the future, but I don't think you'll go up in flames. I really don't."

"You're probably right. Even though Hunter is ancient history, I remember how I felt when he chose keeping us a secret over standing up for me. I was devastated, you know? It confirmed he didn't value me, and that was a really low point in my life. Even if I was still interested now, I can't forget how he threw me away."

It's hard to forget the day reality crashed in and I realized my lover would never be the person I wanted him to be. Or put me somewhere in his hierarchy of importance that was higher than second. Hunter had good qualities, but thinking of how his actions hurt others was not one of them.

"I think Zane struggles because he's just tryin' to piece it all together, Alec. He's hung up on being attracted to not just his best friend, but a man. It's like your first time all over again. My thoughts are that he's afraid of lettin' you down in the bedroom since he's now met Hunter. That guy is the total opposite of Zane. He's all rough-and-tough, manly cowboy. Zane is —"

"A fucking angel on earth and the most beautiful man I've ever met. Hunter doesn't hold a candle to him."

Blaze smiles again with a chuckle.

"I love how much you love him. It's statements like that that carry a lot of weight for people who don't know either of you. The mind is a funny thing, though. He likely knows how you feel, but those doubts are still there." He takes a drink from his mug. The same tea I got at our last rest stop and he filled his pink, sparkly

Like a Boss mug with pride. "He's just in a weird place and he'll work it out. I have faith."

"You should be in social work or something. You're good to talk to." I point a finger at him. "Don't let that go to your head."

Blaze laughs and beams a smile at me.

"I told you before. I watch and I learn things. People interest me."

Finally, the line up moves us along and we almost reach the flagger before we're stopped again.

"This trip took longer than I thought it would. There's a meeting with Jacob tonight about the auction. Could you drop me off at the brewery? I'll see if I can borrow Zane's car to make the meeting on time."

"Of course. We'll be in cell range soon, and you can let Jake know you're runnin' late."

The joys of rural living. Patchy cell phone service.

"Ah! I have a signal. I'll send him a message now."

Since we'll be passing the brewery before we hit town, it's easier for Blaze to drop me off and take the horse trailer back to the ranch. It can be dicey navigating this truck-and-trailer setup on the narrow streets downtown near the shelters. Besides, I already miss Zane, and the sooner I see him the better.

After texting Zane, it doesn't take long for him to get back to me and his message has me shifting in my seat.

Zane: Of course! If I drive you, that means I can also take you home and hopefully spend the night again.
I want a good morning kiss, cowboy.

"Everythin' okay?"

Blaze smirks at me. How the fuck does he just know everything? It's creepy.

"Perfectly okay. Zane will drive me."

I send a quick text to Jacob as well, letting him know I might be late.

"How come you aren't doing this auction? I seem to be the only one roped into it. No pun intended."

"Oh, I'd never do one of those! I'd feel like a side of beef bein' graded at the warehouse. No, thank you." He mock shudders. "I don't know how people can do that."

"So you offered your friend up instead. Gee, thanks."

"Well, you're the better man for the job. With those eyes and that smile, you'll bring in more cash than I would. It's for the greater good, trust me."

I shake my head as Blaze laughs. I'm sure part of Jacob's meeting is to walk us through how the auction itself and the date afterward will go. I hadn't even thought of that part. If someone bids on me, what is it they want exactly?

We've finally cleared the construction zone and Blaze pushes the truck a little faster. As usual, when we work together, we talk about everything from work to River's new business and everything in between.

It's always easy to talk to Blaze. I wasn't kidding when I said he picked the wrong profession. He's a man that's lived more than his forty years with all the experiences he's had. I trust him completely, and our talks have grown more personal over the last year as I struggled with my feelings for Zane. Blaze always knows what to say, and this time is no different.

As we finally turn down the road to the brewery, I let Zane know we're almost there, and the fluttery feeling I always get when I'm about to see him hits me with an extra punch this time. Before, it was soft and like putting on your favourite sweater on a chilly autumn day. When I see him exit the brewery and wave as we get closer, that flutter morphs into a full body shiver, and I swear I hold my breath.

It's not the same sweater-soft happiness to see him. It's 'sitting too close to the fire and feeling the flames almost lick your skin' in anticipation of seeing him.

"Man, you are so in love it almost makes me wanna vomit. But I know that look on your face and I can't do it."

"You can't make fun of me, Blaze. You're the sappiest fucker I've ever met. Just stop this truck so I can get out, would you?"

After thanking Blaze for finally stopping, I jump out and jog over to Zane.

"Is it okay if I go to the meeting with you?" He reaches out and takes my hand, tugging me a step closer. "I've missed you."

I hum under my breath and let his words settle over me.

"I think that's a good idea." His free hand slides up my chest as I step the rest of the way to him. "I've missed you, too."

Ducking my head, I press my lips to his, and he immediately opens for me. His tongue slides against mine, and he nips at my lip with a playful ease that makes my heart sing. Grabbing his ass, I press him against me and he tilts his head back, green eyes twinkling with mischief.

"We're gonna be even more late if we stay out here doing this."

With a sigh, I release him and step back.

"You're right. Jacob knows I'm running late, so let's get this over with."

I make sure to kick my boots off before slipping in the passenger side of Zane's BMW. He likes to keep it pristine, right down to the car mats.

"How was your day?" I ask as he drives us back to the highway.

"Interesting. And long."

"What was interesting? Did you create a new dish?"

He makes the turn onto the highway and quickly glances at me.

"I told the guys about us and they weren't at all surprised. In fact, it seems like the only one surprised is me."

"So they're okay with it? You didn't get any doubters or them telling you it's a mistake?"

They're all good guys, but would they council him away from his friend if they felt it was the wrong step? I don't think so, but you never know.

"No. The opposite, Alec. They like you and they support my decision, but Dylan mentioned something I think we should talk about later."

He turns onto the town's main street and heads toward the youth shelter where Jacob requested our meeting be.

"I don't want to talk about it now because you should focus on the meeting." Parking the car outside the building, he turns to me. "It's not a bad thing. I promise."

He leans over and kisses me. His lips linger and he kisses me more. Each one increasing in its intensity, and the fire in my belly burns hotter the longer his lips stay on mine.

"I love kissing you." He breathes against my lips before going in for more. "I don't know what it is, but I could do this all night."

"I'd be up for that."

He laughs softly before sitting back. "Alec...I..." he smiles and dips his head. "Let's go to the meeting and we'll continue this after."

Zane opens his door and waits for me before we buzz ourselves in at the youth shelter. Jacob wanted us all to meet here so we could see where the funds will go. Which makes complete sense. He's built the LGBTQ shelter to be such a pillar in this small town. The youth shelter and the animal shelter give so much more back to Bloomburg than they take. The people here know that and it shows in their support whenever he has to ask the community for help.

Once we enter the building, a teenage boy leads us to the giant common room where everyone else is already settled. I nod hello to Hunter, and shake hands with Jimmy and Mike, my other rodeo friends who arrived in town today.

The other people I don't know, and I wait for Jacob to make introductions.

"Hey Alec, thanks for coming. We ended up giving everyone a tour before you arrived, so you haven't missed anything." He gestures towards the three beautiful men seated across from my friends.

"My brother is a model and he couldn't be here for this event, but he sent three friends from his modelling agency to attend the auction. This is Sasha, Roman and Liam."

Each of them stands up and shakes my hand. I smile back and Sasha holds my hand a little longer than necessary.

"Nice to meet you." He purrs and bats his extra long eyelashes at me. "I love cowboys."

"That's very kind of you. Thank you."

Releasing his hand, I sit next to Hunter. Sasha still holds uncomfortable eye contact with me until a young woman with bright purple hair enters the room and hands Jacob a folder.

"You could've told me there'd be cowboys here tonight. I'd have worn something nicer that makes my tits stick out."

Jacob blushes and groans. "Katie, language please. These men are here to help with the auction."

"Oh? So you're for sale? How much for a night?"

She snort-laughs as Jacob narrows his eyes at her.

"First, you can't afford them. Second, it's a conflict of interest and third," he takes a deep breath. "I said no."

Her lips twitch. "I'm an adult now, Jake. I can do what I want."

"You're my sister and I won't allow it." He shoves her towards the hallway. "Thank you for bringing me this. Please go stay out of trouble."

She huffs and runs a hand through her hair. "Fine. But I'm telling Matts about the belt buckle thing then."

Jacob turns a lovely shade of scarlet as we all try not to react, but Jimmy can't help it and asks the question anyway.

"What's the *'belt buckle thing'*?"

"Oh my god I'm going to kill her. I think they're sexy, okay? I like the big ones with the championship stamp and stuff."

"I didn't know you had a sister." I offer as a change of topic. Jake takes the change in conversation with a smile.

"Well, technically she's not my sister, but I was her guardian while she was here for a while. We're very close and if I adopted her legally, I'd be her dad, and that was just weird. So I call her my sister, but Matts and I are her parents, if that makes sense."

"I understand why you like buckles, though." Sasha chimes in. "The bigger the buckle, the more interest I have." He sends a gaze my way again. "Because it probably comes with a great story."

He licks his lips, and I focus on the pattern in the hardwood floor.

"Of course. They all come with a story." Hunter adds. "I'd be happy to tell you about mine." He hooks his thumbs into this belt loops so the buckle he's wearing pops out.

Sasha flicks his gaze up and down Hunter's body before crossing his legs. His haughty model vibes fill the room. "I'll think about it."

But when Hunter winks, the satisfied smile on his face tells me Sasha won what he was after. A cowboy's attention.

"Okay, let's get the details out of the way. In two days, you're all on the auction block, and the goal is to bring in as much money as possible for this place. So I want you to be ready."

"I was born ready." Sasha quips and I wonder if he's talking about something else.

Jacob launches into some boring legal stuff and I zone out as I watch Zane give a little wave as he leaves with Katie.

As the conversation buzzes around me, I barely process a single word of it.

I'm still thinking about kissing Zane in his car and what he wants to talk about.

And how much longer this is going to take.

CHAPTER 15

ZANE

"**H**ow long are you home for?"

Katie hands me a cat while she places a clean blanket in its kennel. When Jake shoved her out of the meeting, she pulled me over to the animal shelter next door with her. I wasn't about to protest. Having been here before, I know what the volunteers do here and I love animals.

It's also a welcome distraction.

"Just a week. I start a new placement in Rosevale right after that. Jake told me about the auction and I've been helping out here while he's been busy planning it." She takes the cat from me and returns it to its kennel before handing me another one.

"He always gets so swamped right before these events with all the final prep. He lets other things slide, so I'm just picking up the slack." Katie smiles over her shoulder while she cleans up the kennel. "I miss coming home. School and work take up a lot of my time."

The cat I'm holding is an adult. The kennel card says her name is Layla, and she gazes at me with giant green eyes. Too bad Alec has so many plants; a cat would love all his windows.

"I can see why you miss coming here. Jake and Matts are great people. They've always made me feel welcome."

Tilting her head, she studies me. A small smile flirting on her lips.

"What about you? How come you're here tonight?"

"Oh, Alec needed a ride, and I figured I'd hang out so I could take him home."

Katie's eyebrows shoot up. "Huh. I didn't think you were like that."

"Like what?"

She takes Layla from me and I give her an extra scratch and a kiss before she's back in her kennel.

"Into guys. How long have you two been together?" she grimaces. "Sorry, subtlety is not my strong point. I promise I'm professional with clients, but away from the office I tend to just remove filter and speak. Especially when I'm here."

Blinking, I stare at her. She's not wrong about that. The purple hair was a giveaway for me that she's not someone who likes to be under the radar. But her line of questioning doesn't make me uncomfortable at all. In fact, like I seem to do more and more these days, I welcome someone to talk to about my new situation.

"Uh, that depends. He's been one of my best friends for three years, but I've only figured out recently I felt more than that. It's still new since I told him, and we, ah, did some stuff."

Okay, I haven't shared that kind of information with anyone yet. But Katie has an air about her that puts me at ease.

"Ooh, I like stuff. A lot. Good for you. Too many people get so hung up on these things. Like, I met Jake and came to the shelter when I told my parents I was bisexual. That, of course, was all wrong for them. There was only one box I could be in, one path to follow." A cloud passes over her face and leaves just as fast as it came. "Imagine their faces now if they knew that not only am I bi, but I'm in a poly relationship. They'd likely shit a brick." She pushes another cat into my hands and I cuddle it close. "Sexuality is just as individual as the clothes you wear in my opinion. It's not a one-size-fits-all, and some things just don't fit no matter how hard you try to squeeze into it."

"That's...a great comparison. I was definitely trying to squeeze into something that didn't fit."

The cat I'm holding meows in agreement and licks my ear. Katie motions for me to take it over to the visiting area and sit with it. She joins me with another older cat that sticks firmly to her lap.

"Zane, I'm not someone who blends into the background, as you can probably tell. I'm loud. I have brightly coloured hair and I stand up for things I support. It's why I went into the same line of work as Jacob. Teenagers and adults alike who struggle with the boxes society puts out for them speak freely with me. And I make a difference." She smiles down at the cat on her lap. "I might not come off as someone who has a motherly instinct, and I certainly don't sugarcoat things, but I'll be your biggest supporter—and I give great hugs."

I laugh as she grins at me and I can see why Jacob took to her and loves her like his own.

"I have great friends who support me, and I'll add you to the list. You made the right career choice and I bet Jacob is proud as heck about that."

She snort laughs and the cat on her lap startles. The giant orange cat grumbles and spins around on her lap before settling back down. Katie shushes them with a chin scratch and she's instantly forgiven.

"Jacob is crazy proud of me. He and Matts are amazing and I'm so fortunate to have met them. I wouldn't be where I am today without their support." She leans forward and whispers, "If you ever want to tease Jake, show up with something lavender-scented."

"Oh god, no. You forget I work with Matts. I've seen things that can't be unseen already."

Her booming laugh has me bark out one of my own at the shared insider information. But this whole interaction with Katie has felt like one giant hug. I'm lighter and excited about what's to come. Yesterday's time in the barn is all I've been thinking about and like Katie said, it's not a one-size-fits-all situation.

"I should probably get back to the meeting. I don't think it should be much longer."

"Of course. Let's put these two back and get over there. You can volunteer here, you know. Anytime. You like the cats and they seem to like you. You're the first one who has held that one without her complaining."

"This cat complains?" She's been purring and snuggling on my lap the entire time. How strange.

"All the time. She hates being held. You have the touch, I guess."

I'd never even considered volunteering here at the animal shelter. Maybe I should. I can't have one of my own. I'm barely home for that. But I could do this.

"I may look into that then. This would be nice."

She leads us out of the animal shelter and back over next door.

"I'll leave a note for Micha. He'll fill you in on what's needed and you can decide then."

When we enter the kitchen of the youth shelter, Jacob's voice still carries, but it's obvious that things are winding down. Katie wishes me a good night, leaving me alone while I watch the group of auction attendees in the open concept room they use as a living room.

"Use the models' advice, fellas. Or not. But they're the ones who know how to walk a runway. Maybe they have tips to escalate bidding."

"What kind of tips are we talking?" Jimmy says.

"Well, how about the way you walk?" Sasha jumps up to demonstrate. I wouldn't call it a walk. It's more like sashaying, and I don't think a cowboy would ever walk that way. Definitely not Alec.

"I don't think I can walk like that with my hip." Alec stands and winces. "What else can I do to be more appealing?"

Not a damn thing, cowboy. You're perfect just like that.

But of course I don't say that out loud.

Sasha smiles and moves into his personal space.

"Sugar, you're mighty appealing already. But you can always play to the crowd if it feels natural."

"Um, like how?"

One of the other models, Liam, joins in.

"If you notice an interested bidder, blow them a kiss or give them an extra look at your ass. Are *Wranglers* the dress code for these guys, Jacob? They should be."

"Oh good idea, Liam! Blow them a kiss is always a good one. Like this."

Sasha puckers his pouty lips and makes a show of kissing his hand and blowing the kiss towards Alec. He winks and his sultry smile is the cherry on top for flirting.

Alec rubs his neck and steps away with a smile.

"I don't think I'd like doing that, but thank you. I'll think of something if I need to, I guess."

"It's not a prerequisite," Jacob says. "Just go with the moment. Whatever you do, I know it will be great, but be comfortable with it. I don't want you doing anything you don't like. However..." His cheeks pink, and he clears his throat. "If you could all wear your best belt buckle and jeans for the casual portion of the show, I'd appreciate that. I mean, for the bidders. Not me personally or anything."

"I support that." Sasha purrs and his sex eyes on Alec aren't helping my little issue with jealousy. And anger. Alec is clearly not comfortable with Sasha so close. Of course, he's too damn nice to say anything about it, too.

Stepping out of the kitchen, I join the group and lean against the wall in the common room.

Hunter chews on his lip as Sasha prances around, suggesting other enticing moves. The other two models join in and before you know it, it's our own private runway show. Hunter isn't trying to hide how much he likes what he sees, and Jimmy seems more amused than anything.

All three models are attractive. Perfect smiles, good skin, bodies tight and toned. Even Hunter and Jimmy are good-looking guys with their classic rugged '*I just stepped out of a western movie*' good looks, but it's only Alec who stirs something more in me than just an appreciation of high cheekbones and tight asses.

He's the full package, and he lights up every damn nerve in my body like a dang Christmas tree. With a million little extra sparkly lights. And glitter. Buckets of glitter.

Alec turns his head, like he feels me thinking about him, and the smallest smile flirts on his lips. Yep, twinkle lights activated. Those ocean-blue eyes focused on me with a half smile on his plush lips that I know feel amazing on my neck, make my knees weak.

Pushing off the wall, I walk up to him and place my hand on his chest. His eyes widen as I place a soft kiss on his lips.

"Let's go home." I whisper against his lips before stepping away.

Alec spins to find everyone watching us like we're the main feature at the theatre on a Sunday afternoon.

"Thanks, Jacob. I'll see you at the auction. It was nice to meet you all."

I take his hand as we walk out, the voices of the others fading behind us, and once we're at the car, I follow him to the passenger side. Placing my hand on the door so he can't open it I wait for him to turn and face me.

"I thought you said you wanted to go home."

"I do. But I need to do this first."

Grasping his face between my hands, I smash my mouth to his and press my body against him, pinning him to the car. His hands grip my hips and I gasp into his mouth. His ever-present cowboy hat falls to the ground when I card my fingers into his hair. He pulls away, panting and staring at me. Eyes wide with hope.

"Zane?"

"I don't like that guy undressing you with his eyes. I want to take you home and undress you myself. I want you to be mine. All of it, Alec. I'm tired of wearing a shirt that doesn't fit."

His brow wrinkles.

"What?"

I shake my head, and kiss down his neck. "I can't think right, but trust me, it means I want to be me. And I want to be with you, and I want this whole thing with us."

There's a hitch in his breath and his hands push me away with a gentleness that makes my heart ache.

"Then you should probably stop kissing me and take us home."

With a deep breath and all the fortitude I can muster, I step back and pick up his hat from the ground. After dusting it off, I hand it to him with a smirk.

"Would you ever wear the hat during sex?"

"Jesus, Zane. What's gotten into you?"

I don't answer at first because there's so much bubbling up. So many emotions and words wanting to break free. So much I don't even know how to describe yet.

"I just want to show the man I love how much he means to me."

"Sweetheart..."

Alec swallows and dusts his fingers down my neck. "I've been waiting years to hear you say that."

CHAPTER 16

ALEC

Our drive home is quiet. The inside of the car crackles not with tension, but a static of anticipation. The thrill of what we're about to step into thrums through my veins. I know I've wanted this from Zane for years. For him to tell me he feels the same is like I'm in an alternate reality. The sky is still blue and we're still in his car, but none of this feels like it's real.

"I need to stop at my place for a change of clothes and stuff first. Is that okay?"

"Of course it is. We could stay there, too, if you prefer."

He shakes his head, lips pressed together in a tight line. "No. You need the hot tub and pain meds tonight. I don't want you to sacrifice your comfort. I'll only be a minute."

"Okay."

I mean, what else do I say? Zane always puts me first. Even when he barely knew me. At first, I thought it was just him being a good host and tending to his guests. The more time we spent together, the more I noticed he rarely does anything for himself first. It's a wonder his heart stays in his body. I couldn't be luckier to have a part of his heart to call my own, though. Maybe I'm selfish to admit that, but it's the truth.

I don't know what changed with him since last night, but I'm ready to take the chance. Blaze was right about regretting it if I didn't take the risk. I might be terrified of a broken heart, but I can't keep him at arm's length, even if I wanted to.

He kissed me. I've kissed him. I know what he sounds like when he comes. What good would it do to try to slow things down when he's on board with it?

Zane pulls into his driveway and we both groan. There's garbage everywhere.

"Didn't you get special cans?"

"Yes! And the stupid things are hard to use! Ugh. That damn thing better not have broken in again." He turns to me. "Just ignore it. I'll be quick."

"I'm not gonna ignore it, Zane. Give me some gloves and I'll clean up while you get what you need."

He concedes to letting me help, and once we get to the back deck, it's not that bad. I pick up the trash, right the cans and secure the clips. The clips really are hard to use. He's not lying.

Entering the back door, I toss the gloves into the garbage under the sink and wash my hands. Zane always has lemon scented soap in the kitchen. For years I've always thought of him when I used anything lemon scented. I don't think that will ever change.

"I think I'm ready."

Spinning around, I find Zane with a small duffel bag in his hand. He bites his lip and his free hand twists the edge of his t-shirt.

"You don't seem ready."

He shakes his head and stalks towards me. My breath hitches as he slides his nose along my jaw and his lips stop next to my ear. The whisper of his warm breath as he speaks sends a shiver through me.

"I'm ready, Alec. I'm tired of being scared and nervous." His tongue flicks my earlobe and I bite back a moan.

He steps back and his cheeks have a rosy glow, giving him an innocent vibe, but his eyes are anything but innocent. They sparkle with mischief and, if I'm not mistaken, desire.

"Let's go then. Make sure the door is locked. I don't want you to come back to another raccoon invasion."

"Maybe I don't plan on coming back."

He stares me down and the pull I've felt towards Zane since the moment I met him is at its maximum. If he wanted to move in tomorrow, I'd let him without a single question asked.

"Take me home, Z."

"I've been trying to, but you won't stop talking." He chirps as he walks to the door, with me right behind him.

"Maybe I'm only talking because my mouth isn't occupied with something else."

His feet actually stutter and he trips. I chuckle.

Zane shakes his head with a smile. "Get in the car, cowboy."

I don't know what Zane is cooking, but my mouth waters with the scents drifting outside through the kitchen exhaust fan.

When we arrived at my place, Zane fell into his default setting—taking care of me. He immediately started making dinner even though it was well past the time for a full supper. He knew I didn't have time for a proper meal today, and there's no arguing with Zane. If he thinks you need food, you shut up and eat what he makes you.

After he dropped his bag in my bedroom like it was the most natural thing to do, he ordered me to hit the hot tub.

The only thing different about tonight is he packed a bag to stay over. And he helped me take my jeans off when he noticed how swollen my knee was. Clearly, I can't avoid a doctor visit any longer.

At least I have a nurse to help me with recovery. I wonder if he'd wear a cute little costume if I asked?

The timer on the hot tub jets reaches its time limit, cloaking me with silence. The soothing bubbles stop and I'm left in the calm warm water of the tub. I linger a little longer with my eyes closed and imagine Zane in full nurse mode with a cute little skirt that shows his ass every time he bends over to adjust my leg. Yeah, that would be awesome.

Without a second thought, I take myself in hand and let the naughty little scene unfold in my mind. Oh, think of the sponge bath fun we could have. He'd do it, too. I know he would.

Lost in my own fantasy, I don't hear Zane come out.

"You starting without me, cowboy?"

His voice is ragged and rough, like he needs a tall glass of water. Opening my eyes, I find him watching me with an intensity I've not seen before. Like he's noticing me for the first time and I suppose he kind of is.

"I was just thinking about you being my nurse if I need one. Wearing a little skirt to show off your perky, perfect ass. Would you?"

He licks his lips and steps closer for a better look. I'm fully hard now and slowly stroking myself under the clear water.

"Role play stuff, you mean? Do you like that?"

"I love it." I growl and his pupils dilate.

"Yeah, I'd do that. What else do you like?"

He adjusts the front of his pants and sits on the edge of the tub, getting as close to me as he can without hopping in. His breath comes faster and I turn my head to watch his reaction. Shamelessly, I spread my legs wider so he can enjoy a better view.

"A lot of things. Toys, being in charge...ropes."

His eyes fly to mine, and he swallows.

"I'd try those, uh, that. Or..." he huffs a shaky breath, "I'd do all that with you."

It's been a long time since I've held someone's attention like this. His eagerness and innocent curiosity are so very Zane. And I'm dying to experience every level of it.

"Supper's ready."

He swallows again, and it's an effort for him to tear his eyes away from what I'm doing under the water.

"Should I eat now, sweetheart?"

"Yeah, yes. I mean, you need to eat and I should maybe dry you off."

He moves to grab one of my towels, but I grab his arm. "Kiss me first?"

Without hesitation, he bends to meet my mouth. His lips slide across mine with a tenderness I wasn't expecting. His tongue licks against my lips with an ease that feels like coming home, and my whole soul aches. When he pulls away, he snags a towel, but doesn't hand it to me. Instead, he holds it open and out of reach.

Rising from the tub, I run my hand through my damp hair and face him. His lips part as he drinks in my nakedness and steps forward to pat me dry. The air crackles between us and when he kneels at my feet, I damn near combust. But he's only drying me off. With the same care he takes in everything he does, but his hands shake and his breaths are short and ragged. As he stands in front of me again, he wraps the towel around my waist and dusts his fingertips across my stomach.

"Are you hungry?"

"Why do you ask? You said I needed to eat."

He hesitates before reaching his hand under my towel to grip my cock.

"I can't concentrate enough to eat right now." His hand moves to cup my balls and I drop my head back with a groan. "But I don't want to keep you standing when you hurt. Can we...can we just continue this in the bedroom?"

Lifting my head, I find his green eyes shining back at me and I take his mouth harder than before. He returns the kiss with equal intensity, moving his hands to my ass with a squeeze.

"You worried I'm going to hurt myself making you feel good?"

"I always worry about you, so yes."

The honesty in his voice squeezes my heart. Even though I want him naked and pressed up against me right now, I'll do what he asks.

"Okay. I'll lie down for you and we'll eat later."

Taking his hand, I pull him along behind me into the house. When we reach my bedroom, Zane huffs a breath and stops at the end of the bed.

"So ah, earlier when you said you like to be in charge, can you...can you tell me what to do?"

"Because you like the idea or because you're nervous?"

He licks his lips and meets my gaze.

"Both. I think it's hot for you to tell me what to do, and I'm not nervous about being with you. It's more like I don't want to disappoint you. You've been waiting for me all this time. Maybe you have it built up in your mind. What if I...what if it's not as good as you hoped?"

Fuck me. Zane speaks so freely with me it steals the breath from my lungs.

Stepping closer, I slip my hand under his shirt and smooth my palm across his skin where it meets his jeans. Zane shivers with my touch but never drops his gaze.

"You will never disappoint me. I've been dreaming of this for almost as long as I've known you. No matter what you do, I guarantee I'll love it because it's you."

His eyes close, and he whispers my name. There's a touch of sadness in his voice, but he could never have known how much I wished I could make him mine in every way. Not then. "I told you I'd follow your lead, and that still goes, okay? Don't do anything you don't want to and tell me if you don't like it."

Zane nods and places a soft kiss in the centre of my chest.

"I didn't know I could feel like this before we even get to the good stuff." He sighs and rests his forehead on my shoulder. "You have me all twisted up inside, cowboy. Is this too much too soon?"

"Sweetheart, look at me."

He lifts his head and clutches at the towel still hanging around my waist like it's the only thing tethering him to reality.

"I won't lie and tell you I'm not nervous as fuck that this could be a mistake and we'll never be able to go back to how it was. But I'm also so in love with you Zane, I don't want to not try. There's no time limit on these things. I've known you and wanted this for years. So it doesn't feel like it's too soon for me. It feels like it's been forever and this is finally our time."

He nods and locks his gaze on me.

"What I said we needed to talk about earlier, it's...it's my issue. I don't want you to think this a game or something I don't take seriously. But when Hunter was here I just..." he sighs and my heart breaks a little, watching him struggle to find the right words. "I think I'm just feeling exposed now that my heart knows what it wants and I'm afraid of...I don't fucking know what I'm afraid of, but I don't want this jealousy issue of mine to come between us. I'm asking you to understand and be patient with me."

He buries his face into my neck, and I hold him tight. He fits like he's meant to be there, and there's no way someone could be more perfect for me.

"I think you know I'm patient, and there's only so many times I can tell you I won't run off with an ex, or the next pretty thing to flirt with me. But maybe tonight might help you see it's only you I want, Z. It always has been."

Kissing the side of his head, I whisper in his ear, "When you're ready, take my towel off. This is what you get. Nobody else."

He steps back, sliding his hands under the towel and tugs where he tucked it in. It falls to the floor, and he raises his gaze to mine again.

"I'm going to lie down and be comfortable, just like you wanted. When I'm ready, I want to watch you undress."

Zane waits, but it's not with patience. His hands flutter from the zipper on his pants to his shirt hem and he's already hard, if the multiple adjustments he's made to himself are any indication. That makes me preen like a damn peacock in full strut.

"Take it off, sweetheart. All of it."

He whips off his shirt and drops it on the floor before wiggling out of his jeans and almost falling over.

"It's not a race, Z. Take your time."

"Don't want to," he grunts as he flicks his pants off his foot with a triumphant grin. When he moves to take off his boxers, I tell him to stop.

"Turn around and bend over when you take them off. I want to see your gorgeous ass."

He gulps, but spins so fast around he makes me dizzy. He does as I ask and stays bent over for an extra beat, which I appreciate. I've never seen an ass I want to bury my face in more than his. It's perfection. Maybe I only think that because it's Zane, but either way, I like what I see.

"Did I do good, cowboy?" he asks as he turns around, and I get the full frontal of my best friend.

He's always had fair skin, and it extends for miles. I want to cover every inch of it with my mouth and mark him up a bit. Make him remember he's mine. My cock twitches at the thought.

This moment seems even more surreal than the makeout session in the barn.

"You did great, sweetheart. You're gorgeous, you know. My living wet dream."

He ducks his head with a bashful grin and there's a pink flush around his neck. I don't think I've ever seen Zane so shy. His uncertainty isn't about the two of us. I think he's just a guy who prefers to not have the pressure on him in the bedroom. He wants to be led, and he's never been with anyone who gave him that. Perhaps another self-discovery.

"Come here."

He crawls up the bed next to me on my non-sore leg side and places a kiss on my chest. His eyes dart to me when I suck in a breath and he moves closer to my nipple. When his tongue darts out and swirls around the hardened nub, I close my eyes with a sigh.

"Kiss wherever you want to. I like it everywhere, Z."

"Do you have a favourite spot?"

He hovers over me on all fours and begins kissing me on the neck, the collarbone, and then drifts further down.

"I do, but it's more fun if you find it yourself."

Tucking my hands behind my pillow, I watch the top of his head as he moves down my body. He mostly kisses, but he also licks or nips in places, hoping to find my favourite spot.

I hold my breath as he draws closer to my cock, but he doesn't even touch me there. Instead, he veers off and trails down the inside of my thigh and nips a spot near the crease of my groin and I groan.

"Did I find it?" he smiles against my skin before doing it again, and I squirm.

"You did. But that's only one spot."

"I bet I know another one."

He moves his lips over my leaking cock and slowly laps across it with the tip of his tongue. His heated green eyes are locked onto mine the whole time, and even if I wanted to lie and tell him that's not another favourite spot, I couldn't, because my hand shoots forward to grip his hair and hold him in place.

"And I found another one." he grins, like he already knows my body like the back of his hand. "Should I go for lucky number three?"

"Are you feeling lucky?" I rasp.

He smirks at me. "Yes."

He scoots down and with zero hesitation, and even less finesse, he kisses my balls before sucking one into his mouth.

My hands fist the sheets and I will my hips to stay put and not break his face as my whole body quakes with pleasure.

"Bingo." He laughs as he crawls back up my body and settles overtop of me.

"I don't think you get to say that until we come."

He laughs again as he adjusts to line up our dicks.

"No, I think that would be '*jackpot*', wouldn't it?"

"Make me come and find out, then." I sit up to take his lips and he kisses me so deeply my toes curl. How could he possibly think he'd disappoint me? He's barely done anything and, hands down, it's the best night of my life.

He follows my mouth down as I lay back and I clutch at his shoulders. We pant and paw at each other as he swivels his hips and keeps just the right amount of friction between us to bring us both close, but not over the edge.

It's both heaven and hell and I tear my mouth away from his, pushing him to sit up.

"Jerk us both off. I want to watch you come."

He fumbles, and his hands shake, but after a few tries he finds a grip that has our eyes rolling back.

"Holy shit!" Zane gasps as his orgasm hits, bathing my abs and his hand. The reality of Zane coating me in his come after all the times I've thought about it is too much, and I come with a shout.

His slippery hand continues to stroke me until I have to ask him to stop.

"I didn't think watching you come would be so hot." He brings his hand to his lips and tastes it.

"Jesus, Zane. Don't do that."

He cocks his head, a cloud of doubt shadowing his previous post sex-glow.

"Do you not like that? Sorry, I should have asked or —"

"Stop." I wrap a hand around his neck and pull him down to me. "It's incredibly intimate and erotic for me to watch you taste me like that. I'm already aching for you again, but I need food and rest. You did nothing wrong, sweetheart. It's all too damn right. "

Our tongues slide together again and I can't get enough of feeling him everywhere. His touch. His smell. His everything.

"Can you take a sick day?"

I laugh and release him as he stands gingerly.

"I probably could. What about you?"

"Me too. Can we make some calls and spend tomorrow together?"

I've never ditched any responsibility before for anyone, but there's a first time for everything.

"We have to meet at the fairgrounds in the evening to go over the events, but I'll call Dan now if that's what you want to do."

"I do. I really do."

With a smirk, he throws the towel on the floor to me and I stare after him as I wipe myself off.

Good idea on the sick day. There's no way either of us are getting much sleep tonight.

Chapter 17

ZANE

Rolling over, I find Alec's side of the bed empty.

Again.

I don't like not waking up with him.

The sun filters through the curtains, signalling it's much later than either of our usual wake up times. But it doesn't matter. We planned a day off for a reason. A smile fills my face and I close my eyes again, replaying all the things we did last night.

The soft caresses. The exploring. The kisses. God, he's the best kisser. The epic orgasms unlike anything I've ever experienced.

I've robbed myself of almost twenty years of amazing sex. Twenty missed years of sexual satisfaction because I didn't know any better. I've never craved another person sexually like I do Alec. He makes me feel so different and it's hard to put a finger on exactly what it is. Sure, it's new being with someone who isn't soft and curvy with different parts, but it's so much more than us being two men.

Alec knows what I need, and it's uncanny how he reads my mind. Maybe it's because we were so close before we became lovers. Or maybe he's just that skilled in the bedroom. Whatever it is, it doesn't overshadow the soul-deep contentment of sharing this level of intimacy with someone I love. It's all fluttery hearts and I love yous, but this time I know it's real and I can easily return the sentiment. And that's what I've been missing.

This isn't an experiment. This is where I'm supposed to be.

"Sleeping Beauty finally awakes."

Turning my head, Alec leans against the doorway. All sleep mussed and mouthwatering in his low-hanging sleep pants.

"How long have you been awake?"

Pushing off the doorframe, he walks over to settle next to me and props his head in his hand as he stretches out beside me.

"My internal clock went off at 5 AM. I watched the sun rise and fell asleep around six on the couch. It's 9:30 now."

"You should have come back to bed. Or woke me up."

With a newfound confidence, I graze my palm over his covered cock and he leans in to kiss me.

"You needed sleep. You were up late."

"So were you."

I chase after his lips again, and our kiss is slow, dreamy, and intoxicating. I lose myself in it completely. In him.

"Good morning," he whispers against my lips before rolling me over and blanketing his body over mine.

"It *is* good." I sigh and his body shakes with a quiet laugh.

"I can make it better." Alec trails his lips down my neck and I tilt to give him access. His morning scruff rubs across my skin and a trail of goose bumps races down my neck.

"Yeah?"

"Oh, yeah."

He shifts and pulls the sheet out from between us, and just like that, I'm naked underneath him. His lips burn a path down my chest and in my eagerness, I spear my fingers through his hair and guide him where I want his mouth.

"Hands to yourself, Z. I'll get there."

"Can't you get there faster?" I groan, and he lifts his head. His blue eyes are stern and I swallow hard. Holy cracker jacks. That look just made my toes curl.

"Hands over your head, sweetheart, and leave them there. I don't want to find rope right now to make you stay."

"*Ohmotherofgod.*" I whoosh. "What if I want you to?" He told me he enjoyed using rope, but I didn't think I would so easily. Turns out I'm wrong.

"I'll take it under advisement."

How did I not know I liked this kind of power trip in the bedroom? Doing as he asked, I keep my hands above my head and grip the metal of his headboard. The cool metal in my sweaty hands grounds me while I allow Alec to do what he wants to me.

Much like we did last night, he uses his mouth to cover my body with kisses and bites and when I glance down my body, there're more than a few marks showing. He lingers on the spot he discovered I really, really like on the inside of my knee, and I clutch the headboard harder.

"Goddamn, cowboy. You can make me come just by doing that."

I roll my hips with a whine. Taking my dick in his hand, Alec jerks me off. I can't look away from his fingers wrapped around my dick, working me over like he has the most magic of hands. My hands tingle on the headboard. I'm not gonna make it.

His gaze meets mine as he nibbles at my odd erogenous zone and strokes me faster.

"I want you to come. That's the point."

"I can't feel my hands."

His gaze sweeps to my trembling arms before settling on me.

"Let go, baby. Don't hurt yourself. Look at me."

Letting my hands unclench, I let my arms lie limp above my head as he dips his head to lick along my dick before closing his lips over me with a satisfied hum. Those ocean-blue eyes watch me from under his dark lashes as he moves his talented mouth.

The lightning races up my spine. "Gonna blow."

He moves faster, and I come down the throat of my best friend. I watch him swallow as my body quivers. Aside from closing my eyes once when it felt like I took a short trip to some sort of spiritual plane, we never break eye contact. It's the hottest thing I've ever done.

It's also the most intimate.

Alec wasn't and isn't looking for a returned favour. He did it for me because he wanted to and knew I'd appreciate it. Who wouldn't mind having a hot cowboy blow them in the morning? But his touches were all ministered with a reverence I felt right to my bones, hell to my embryonic state.

He loves me, and nothing has ever felt so right in my life.

Licking his lips, he prowls back up my body. My chest still heaves and my limbs feel like limp noodles.

"You broke me."

Alec chuckles and kisses me so sweetly it's hard to pair this kiss with the bossy man who ordered me to keep my hands to myself.

"I hope not. I like you whole." He stands up and I notice his wince again.

"Are you okay? I know you just blew my world, but you haven't been this sore before."

"I likely did too much last night. It will be fine."

"Cowboy, don't be tough for me. Let me make it easier."

With a sigh, he runs a hand down his face and I sense my plans of lazing around in bed together are about to be changed.

"You make it easier being here. But…it's good we took the day off because I could get a cancellation spot at an orthopedist this afternoon."

Standing to join him, I search his face.

"That's a specialist. Should I be worried?"

He draws me to him, and I wrap my arms around his waist.

"I'm not worried, so you shouldn't be. It's more like I'm afraid of what they might say if that makes sense. But I wouldn't mind you being there with me."

"Of course I will. When do we have to leave?"

"An hour. The doctor is in Arpinville, which is an hour's drive. But I'll buy you lunch and let you choose the radio station."

He's about to drag me into the shower with him when there's a squawk and a yell outside his door.

"What the hell?" He mutters as he stalks to the door to peer outside.

I grab my discarded boxers from last night and tug them on before running out to join him.

"Oh god, it's that damn peacock again, Jeff. I thought Heath had that handled?"

We stand at the window watching as Jeff shows his feathers and squawks at Heath.

"Huh. I thought when he brought it to the lady's farm to meet the female, this behaviour was supposed to stop."

"My expertise is with four-legged, furry animals. I know nothing about ones with feathers. But...Jeff isn't being aggressive. I think he's showing off."

The peacock keeps strutting close to Heath, and it's whenever Heath tries to put distance between them that it squawks. If Heath stays, the bird seems happy.

"Do you think the bird has a crush on Heath?"

Alec snort laughs and keeps watching the scene in the ranch yard.

"Who the hell knows?" He turns away from the window and grabs my hand again. "Whatever the situation is, he can handle it. I'm off the clock. We have a shower to take and an appointment to make. So let's get to it."

When we get to the shower and he shucks his pants, he wags a finger at me.

"And hands to yourself. For real. We're on a time crunch."

Alec bounces his good leg in a sporadic pattern. Each time he does, it vibrates my thin plastic chair.

Placing my hand on his knee, I squeeze.

"I thought you weren't nervous?"

He shrugs, but takes my hand in his and laces our fingers together.

"I half lied. Sorry."

"Half lied? What the hell is that?"

"Promise you won't laugh."

I slide to the edge of the uncomfortable chair and angle towards him.

"We're in a doctor's office waiting for results and a consult on your hip. I don't see myself laughing at anything soon."

His eyes dart to the side, and he bites his lip before exhaling.

"I'm not worried about whatever the diagnosis is. I'm just...I'm afraid of needles. And that's why I never went for the cortisone shots suggested years ago. I *will* pass out. It's not a good look for a cowboy."

His lips tilt in an embarrassed smile, and I squeeze his hand again.

"Uh, okay. I wasn't expecting that, but it's not unheard of. Lots of people are afraid of needles and we'll figure it out. I'm here to help you remember."

"Is it bad to wish for complete anaesthetic and be sick while recovering from it instead of a less invasive day surgery and needles that are definitely the easier route?"

The nurse at that moment calls us back into the consult room.

"Breathe, we'll figure it out. I've got you."

The comfortable chairs of the doctor's consult office are a relief. Why don't they spend money to have a more comfortable waiting room? Alec rubs at his sore side absently and I reach over to fiddle with a skeleton model on the desk.

"Hey, look. I've got a boner in my hand."

Alec at least shakes his head with a smile at my foolishness. When the door opens, I do my best to reassemble the model, but it clatters on the desk in a pile of plastic pieces.

The doctor glances at me, then at Alec before taking her seat behind the desk.

"What is it with grown men and toys?" She says it with a smile, thankfully, and logs in to her computer. Turning the screen towards us, she just launches into Alec's diagnosis with zero preamble.

"Mr. Blackwell, you have a bone spur that has broken off and lodged itself near the joint of your hip." She uses a pen to point to the area on the screen, then enlarges the image. "It's irritating the lining of the joint and that's causing you hip pain. It's also what's causing your knee and leg to swell. What are you taking for pain now?"

Alec sits forward. "Usually I alternate between acetaminophen and ibuprofen. I also have a topical CBD cream I use when it gets hot to touch. And I have a hot tub that helps too."

"The good thing is that your hip joint is still in good shape. It doesn't need replacing, but we do need to take the spur out before it does real damage to the joint."

I watch the blood drain from Alec's face in slow motion.

"And how...uh, how do you do that?" His voice squeaks at the end, and I squeeze his hand.

"It's a day surgery. Your spur is in an accessible area, you're lucky. You would get a local anaesthetic. Then we make a small incision and remove it arthroscopically. Because of the spur's position, it should be straight-forward and easy to remove. You can go home in a few hours."

"So with needles. Okay, ah, is there...?"

Kneeling in front of Alec, I draw his head down to rest on his knees.

"Take a deep breath, cowboy. Great, take another one. It's all good. I got you."

Rubbing my hand on his back, I turn to find the doctor watching closely.

"It's the needles. He has a phobia. Are there other options?"

Alec slowly sits up and there's a bit of pink back in his face.

"General anaesthesia could be arranged, but getting an OR booked for that may take longer. I could offer him a sedative to take the day of the procedure. Many people respond well to that when they're anxious."

"And if I take a sedative would I forget what's happening?"

"Sometimes. Everyone reacts differently. But you'd definitely be less stressed with the procedure."

"What if I don't do the procedure? What will happen?"

The doctor points to the hip joint on the screen. "This area here will erode and irritate the bone so much you'll likely never want to walk. It would become that painful. You'll need a hip replacement and a minimum of six months to recover. Intense physical therapy and no horseback riding."

That gets his attention. Do not take horseback riding away from Alec. It's his life.

"And if I do the first option?"

"Four-to-six weeks while the incision heals and your body adjusts. Physical therapy as needed and you'll be back on a horse much quicker."

As he processes the new info, I decide to ask my own questions.

"If he goes with option one, what kind of help will he need at home? I'm assuming he shouldn't be allowed to drive."

She nods. "He can't drive the day of the procedure, obviously, and especially if he takes the sedative. He'll be sore for a few days, but he should try to walk every day to encourage healing. No horseback riding until the incision heals, so seven-to-ten days. He'd likely be okay on his own, but someone to help out and make sure he follows directions wouldn't be a bad thing."

I lean in closer to her. "What about sex? How long is that off the table for?"

"Really, Zane? You had to ask about that?"

The doctor tries to hide her smile and fails.

"I'd say only a few days. As long as there's nothing vigorous or rough where he may injure the joint, I think you're in the clear."

I beam back at Alec, who's now pink with embarrassment. But at least he's not hyperventilating or stuck in doom mode.

"Can I think about it and let you know?"

She passes Alec her card. "Of course. I'll have the options we discussed in the notes, and you can book through reception. I strongly suggest the inpatient procedure soon."

Alec nods and pockets the card. As we return to his vehicle in the parking lot, my phone chimes with a message.

> **Martin:** I know you played hooky today to do all the things with the new boyfriend, but I'm gonna need you to stop in tonight if you can. I think I screwed up your kitchen delivery.

With a laugh, I return his message. Never let the marketing guy take over the organization, I guess.

"Hey, I need to stop at the brewery on the way home. Martin thinks he screwed up my kitchen. Could you drop me off there on the way back and I'll just get him to take me to the ranch when we're done?"

"You want to spend the night again?"

Following him to his side of the truck, I tug on his belt loop, so he turns around.

"I want to spend every minute I can with you. Just like I always have. Only now I get to kiss you."

Looping my arms around his waist, I tug him closer. "Cowboy, you are my sun, my moon, and the force that keeps me standing. Don't forget, I've known you long enough to know you're freaking out about this inside. I'll always be here."

And as long as I'm breathing, I will be.

Chapter 18

Alec

After dropping off Zane, I head to the new fairgrounds. It's local knowledge that the town sold the old grounds to the guys for the brewery, that's why they named it Tilt-A-Whirl brewery. It was a nod to the fair that, in its heyday, meant a lot to this small town. After a lot of consideration, Bloomburg decided to bring back their annual fair, but in a new location. One that didn't have a tragic memory attached to it.

A town resident sold one of his farm fields for the grand price of one dollar to the town of Bloomburg and for the last two years, they've been clearing the land and turning it into a useable location. It's not that far from the old grounds, but sometimes a fresh start is all that's needed, even when it's still close to home.

Jimmy, Mike, and Hunter are already at the show ring with Jacob and Blaze when I arrive, and I hurry over to join them.

"Sorry I'm late."

Blaze grins and winks, and I smile back. We exchange an entire conversation without a word and he approves with a tip of his hat. He, more than anyone, knows where my thoughts have been for months. I'll have to thank him for the nudge and the support with actual words later.

"Oh, hi, Alec!"

Jacob bounces over, clipboard in hand, with the other cowboys trailing behind.

"We're all trying to work out the best way to do this roping thing. Did you have any thoughts?"

Dang, he's so excited about this. I love how he's found a cowboy hat to wear, too. It may be made of straw, and likely won't make it through a season, but he's embracing his inner cowboy with gusto.

"Simple was my thought. You're selling tickets and will have multiple winners, right?"

"That's my plan, yes. Blaze already donated the prizes, and I have them printed out on certificates for the winners to claim."

"Since we all rope to some degree, I know Mike and Jimmy are more riders than anything, but what if each winner picks one of us and a stuffy then we rope it for them? They find their prize pinned to it or some shit like that?"

Jimmy agrees. "I'm a bronc rider, but I still work on my farm and know how to rope. I'm cool with that. Each of us will do something differently."

"That's a good idea. I'm fine with making a show out of how I rope a teddy bear." Mike chuckles. "Did you at least get a stuffed bull?"

"I didn't pick them out, Zane did. But we could look for one if you really want."

"Where is Zane, anyway?" Hunter smirks. "At home, watering your plants again?"

Narrowing my eyes, I glare at him. "There's nothing wrong with watering plants."

"Do you still have all those stupid violets with all their dumb names?"

Jacob's eyes bounce between me and Hunter.

"Boys," Blaze steps up. "There's no need for shit talkin' about someone who isn't here or the names of plants. This is a friendly event, remember."

Hunter nods, backing down from whatever it was he was trying to start.

"My apologies. I'm okay with the rope idea. I think it's cool. But if you want to give them an extra show, perhaps Alec and I could do a roping demonstration."

Jacob bounces from foot to foot. "I want as much cowboy stuff here as possible. It's not too late for me to get you a steer if needed, and you already have horses here. Could you do that team thing you used to do? I mean, I called it a rodeo and made the mistake of not looking into what I really needed to make it a rodeo, so this is all I've got. And the mutton busting for the kids."

He bites his lip and blinks those giant brown eyes at me. He's usually so thorough and such a planner, so I'm shocked he didn't look into what a rodeo set up entails before announcing it. And I can't let his event be a complete flop. It wouldn't look good for anyone.

"Yeah." I find myself saying. "Get us three to five steers and Hunter and I will do a team roping demo." Pausing, I know I might regret this, but I add, "And I'll do a tie-down, too. So two events you can arrange easy enough with the steers and a calf or two."

His shout of joy is all I need to know that I made the right choice.

"Thank you so much, Alec! Oh wow, okay. I'm going to call my friend right now. Excuse me."

He pulls out his phone and dials while he walks away, leaving us all together in the rodeo ring.

"Is it weird for you to be back in a ring?" Mike asks.

"A little bit? It brings back memories, though." I glance over at Hunter. "Not all of them were good."

Is it a low blow? Absolutely. But he took a shot at Zane earlier, and I think it's only fair.

"I did what I had to." He bites and takes a step closer. "It couldn't be all rainbows and unicorns like you wanted, Alec. Some of us didn't have the freedom to live in the open like you."

His words make me bristle and I push forward, crowding into his space.

"You let your family's money and position cloud your judgement and you never did the right thing. You could have stepped away!" My lip curls as I remember what he said to me that last day and how he turned his back on what I thought was something meaningful. "You were a coward, Hunter. And you left me to deal with it on my own. I wouldn't call having a target on my back after that freedom."

He presses his lips together and I'm not sure what shade of red his face turns, but he balls his hands into fists at his side. He can throw a punch at me if he wants, but he better make it a good one. One is all he gets.

Blaze steps between us with a menacing growl and shoves us apart.

"May I remind you both, Jacob is right over there excited for the two of you to work together and bring a bit of rodeo to this event? Whatever fuckin' issues are still between the two of you, leave it alone right now. If you want to go beat the shit out of each other behind the barn away from pryin' eyes, be my guest. But none of this shit goes down right now. None. You hear me? Drop it."

"Sorry, you're right."

I offer my hand to Hunter, and he hesitates before shaking it quickly.

"Sorry."

Jacob, unaware of the tension, scurries back up. "It's all set. He said he has something to work as a chute for you both and it won't be a bother. He's gonna come by and set it up tonight so we're ready."

I smile, genuinely happy he's thrilled with the idea.

"That's great Jacob. What else do we need to do here?"

There's a commotion in the parking lot as Sasha appears on the fairgrounds with the other two models. After abandoning the rental car in the middle of the parking lot, they link their arms together and march towards us. Each of them carries a large manilla envelope, and if I'm not mistaken, Sasha is wearing high-heeled cowboy boots. Which is impressive. The ground here is soft and even I know how hard it is to walk in heels and soft dirt. He makes it look effortless.

Along with the sparkles, painted-on jeans, and full make-up, he stands out.

A lot.

"Hi Jacob. I'm so glad we found you here."

"I told you I'd be here?" Jacob scrunches his brow and Sasha waves his hand with a giggle.

"Listen, my friend worked his magic and look at these photos! You boys are F-I-N-E, fine."

He passes an envelope to Jacob, who squeals with delight when he opens it.

"These are gorgeous!"

He holds up 8x10 photos, one for each of us. Mike and Jimmy's look recent and they're action shots at rodeos. An inset of their face is on the bottom. Hunter's is also an action shot, but it's while he's in the chute and you can read the concentration etched on his face. Mine is...

"Where did you get the poses to make these?" I ask.

"Oh, my friend went online and purchased photos from event photographers that were unique. I'm not sure where yours came from."

My gaze drifts to Blaze.

He shrugs. "It's a nice photo, and I didn't pick it out."

I know when this photo was taken. After one of the first conversations I had with Blaze about my feelings for Zane, Blaze snapped the pic when I was on Domino, heading out to deal with the sheep. He'd smiled and said, *'that's some real cowboy GQ shit right there.'* He pocketed his phone after that and I forgot all about it.

"What are these for, anyway?" Hunter hands his photo back to Jacob.

"These are your photos to autograph. After the event here you have a time to sign autographs. People make donations for the photos and, of course, you might pose for some. You'll also sign autographs briefly after the cowboy auction. Some people won't go to both events."

Sasha hands us a photo of his own and we all fall into an uncomfortable silence.

"This one is mine. I had it done exclusively for this event. Do you like it?"

It's likely not what I consider a family-friendly photo. He's wearing short-cut jean shorts and one of those loose fitting, flowy tank tops that show more skin than it covers. He also has pink cowboy boots on with a sequined pink-and-white cowboy hat. He's a very pretty man and this photo would have gone well on my wall when I was a teenager.

Jimmy clears his throat and passes it back to him. "That's, ah, nice."

"Oh, keep it. I signed them all for each of you. You know, to remember all this together? A memento, as my gram would say."

"Oh, thanks, that's kind of you." Mike smiles and the rest of us murmur our thanks.

Sasha takes over the conversation, organizing a night out with everyone and asking Jacob if any of the kids at the shelter would like to hang out with them. I'm touched he offered to include them. Jacob will appreciate that.

Blaze motions for me to step away and I join him a few feet away at the fence of the show ring.

"What was that all about with Hunter? I thought you two were okay?"

"We are mostly, but he's just being a dick and trying to rattle me. Maybe he's jealous of Zane." I laugh at the thought of two men fighting for me. "It's nothing."

Blaze nods and flicks a toothpick around with his tongue.

"You happy with that photo?"

"Yeah, it's a good one. Why?"

He shifts against the rail and turns to me.

"Zane picked it a few months ago. I wasn't asking him to choose a photo of you. I was showin' the markins' of your horse. You hadn't got to the bar yet for your usual dinner." He chuckles. "I know your routine, too, you know."

"I had no idea I was that predictable."

I do, but I didn't think it was that big of a deal.

"Anyway, we just started talkin' like we always do and horse markins' came up and he mentioned a black-and-white one. So I showed him that photo and let me tell you, Alec, that man stopped breathin' and didn't even notice. He studied that picture for a good minute and I'm no expert, but he wasn't lookin' at the horse."

"So, what are you saying, Blaze? You already know we're moving this thing forward and I've had him in my bed. I should hope he finds a picture of me on my horse attractive."

"I'm just sayin' Zane is the type of guy who focuses on one thing. Right now it's you. I know he's not fond of Hunter."

"He hates him." I correct.

"I don't want him gettin' himself into any trouble goin' after Hunter. I think Zane has a possessive streak a mile wide, and if you want to do this with him, you need to get that under control."

Sighing, I lean on the rails and watch Sasha flirt with Hunter and the others. Hunter laps up the attention like a thirsty dog. He always liked being the centre of attention.

"We've already talked about it. I know where he's coming from and, for what it's worth, Blaze, I don't hate it. He's not interfering with my life and causing havoc. He's...in a place where he wants me to himself, I think."

Blaze nods and flicks his toothpick again.

"So he's not gonna go trash your place or anythin' when he sees that photo of Sasha?"

"The opposite for me, actually." I grin at Blaze, and he shakes his head.

"Ah, no, don't tell me about some kind of hot, claimin' sex you two have. That's not healthy. Or likely safe." He laughs and I join him.

"It's okay, Blaze. Really. He's working on it and I think once people know we're a thing, he'll ease off."

"I like him. I always have, and I want you to find your happiness, Alec. I know that lonely feelin' eats away at you when you don't even know it's there. I'll do everythin' I can to make this work for you."

"I appreciate that. And I think we'll be okay."

"Hey, you two want to join us at The Burgatory tonight?" Mike calls over and Blaze and I rejoin the group. "Jacob said there's a mechanical bull there this week. I want to try it."

"It's not as good as the real thing. You know that." Jimmy laughs.

Hunter slaps his hand on my shoulder. "What do you say? We can watch Jimmy get bucked off a kid's toy. Shoot some pool. Eat some burgers."

While Jimmy and Mike laugh and joke around some more, I realize how much I've missed these outings with old friends. Not so much Hunter, but the rodeo talk and camaraderie. The want to join them is strong.

"Yeah, I'll join you for a while. What about you Blaze?"

"I can't tonight. River needs a hand with some deliveries and I promised I'd help."

Sasha and his gang leave, promising to meet us all there by 8 PM. Mike and Jimmy linger a little longer to survey the show ring that will be transformed for the events overnight by Jacob's friend.

Hunter calls out. "I'll meet you all there, too. Here's to old times with new friends."

After a short chat, making sure Jimmy and Mike know where they need to go, I call Zane.

"Miss me already, cowboy?"

A zing shoots up my spine with his low laugh.

"I always miss you. But that's not why I'm calling. Do you know how long you'll be there tonight?"

His dramatic sigh pulls another laugh from me.

"A while, actually. My head chef had to leave because his daughter is sick, and the sitter thinks it should be a hospital visit. So I'm in the kitchen for the next few hours at least. And I need to organize the stock Martin misplaced."

"Oh." My bubble of excitement for a night with the guys deflates. I wanted to have Zane there, too. "Well, are you still coming over tonight?"

"I told you. I want all the nights in your bed I can get. Is everything okay?"

"Yeah. I just wanted to ask if you'd like to join us at The Burgatory tonight. There's a mechanical bull there and Mike wants to try it. I was hoping you'd be done soon."

"If I could, I would. It sounds fun. But I'll just let myself in tonight. You go have fun with them and tell me all about it over coffee tomorrow."

"I won't be out late. And yes, I'll tell you all about it in the morning."

There's a crash of metal in the background and Zane groans.

"I gotta go. Have fun, cowboy."

"Hey, Zane?"

"Yeah?"

"I love you."

All I can hear on the line is the ruckus in the kitchen and Zane's soft breath over the phone.

"I love you, too. I'll keep your side warm until you get there."

CHAPTER 19

ALEC

The Burgatory is a burger joint and arcade until 9 PM. After that time, it's a bar only, and no minors are allowed. It transforms from a family-friendly restaurant into a party bar where adult games appear and the music is cranked to encourage dancing and drinking.

A giant wall slides out, cutting off the entire side of the restaurant where the more tame pinball and Skee-Ball games are found. The bar side contains the pool tables, dart boards, and this week, a mechanical bull. The wall dividing the establishment has been up all week due to the novelty hunk of metal and fake fur. Wheeling it into a corner during the day isn't easy. To prevent children from climbing on it during family hours, it was easier to just keep the wall up.

The latest pop and rock music pulses in the smaller space, vibrating the floor through my boots as soon as I step inside. The scent of beer and young men wearing far too much cologne wraps around me. There were days in my youth I'd often go home smelling the same. While it was fun and most memories still make me smile, I wouldn't want to make this my usual Friday night anymore. Occasionally a night like this with the guys is great, though.

I shake my head with a smile when I spot the group I'm meeting. It's not hard to find Sasha and his crew. His hair and make-up are still the same, but the boots he's wearing have me do a double take. I'm sure I'm not the only one to do so either.

As my well-worn cowboy boots pull me closer to their laughter, Sasha spots me.

"Alec! You made it. Come sit with me!"

They've pulled two tables together with extra chairs squished around it. Once I'm close enough, I confirm Sasha has thigh-high boots on and the tiniest pair of booty shorts. My handkerchief is probably bigger. He might as well be wearing nothing at all. Which, if I had to guess, he'd likely prefer as well.

"I saved you a seat and Mike told us to drink this stuff, but it's rather hideous."

He holds up a glass while pointing to the jug of amber liquid on the table and I laugh.

"You're drinking draft beer? I hope it's a good kind."

Mike pipes up. "It's decent. It's *Budweiser*. Hard pass on the *Molson Canadian* for this guy. They don't call it Skunky Canuck for nothing."

Sasha wrinkles his nose. "*Eww.* Maybe I should say thank you for not making me drink skunk juice, then? That's nasty."

Laughing, I take the seat next to Sasha and Mike fills a glass, sliding it my way.

"Alec, listen, I already asked Mike, and he said no."

Sasha smiles my way, batting his pretty eyelashes with an aura of hope.

"I didn't say no. I said I didn't think it was a good idea."

Mike shakes his head with a raised eyebrow. Sasha dismisses his comment and runs his manicured finger down my arm.

"I want someone to ride the bull with me."

Snorting, I shake my head and his pout could rival any toddler's. "No way am I getting on a bull, mechanical or otherwise. Sorry." I sip my beer and glance at Mike again. He's clearly amused by Sasha and his friends.

Liam and Roman play pool with Hunter and Jimmy in the corner. Mike's constant laughter at the antics around the pool table brings back memories of the days we used to do this almost every night. All the guys would look for bed partners and I went just to be close to Hunter. The night always started well enough with beers and laughter, but more often than not, it ended with me lonely in my trailer because Hunter was afraid of being caught with me. A drink at a table with twelve other people is the closest we ever came to a public date.

Hunter's laughter draws my gaze, and he looks over, catching me watching. He holds the eye contact, and it's me who breaks it when I turn to smile at Sasha again.

"How come you're not playing pool with the others?"

"Silly bar games aren't really my thing." He shrugs and peers into his glass of draft beer. A fog of melancholy settles briefly over his smiling face before he shakes his head, as if clearing an unwanted memory away. "Besides, if I was playing pool, I wouldn't get to sit here with two handsome cowboys all to myself."

His devilish grin returns just as fast as it disappeared and Mike chuckles into his beer. Sasha is the biggest flirt I've ever met, and judging by the stares he's getting from other men in here, he could have his pick. I'm certain Hunter would take him to bed, if he hasn't already.

"Okay, I give up. Your friends are pool sharks." Hunter takes the seat on the other side of Sasha with a laugh. "Liam just cleared the table and took my twenty bucks."

"And mine, too." Jimmy says as he joins us and pours himself a glass of beer. "You should have warned us."

Sasha laughs, throwing his head back. "If I warned you, then I'd also lose out. Those two are my wingmen. They usually ask for more than twenty dollars, though. They're getting soft."

"So you all work together to con men? That doesn't sound like a good idea." I frown at Liam and Roman still at the pool table discussing the rules with the next pair of challengers.

"Don't worry about us. If there's trouble, they give the money back. It's just a thing they started to prove they could do something other than look good in nice clothes."

"I'm sure there are better ways to do that. It could be dangerous with the wrong guys, Sasha."

He smiles at me and I know he's trying to dust away my concern like the crumbs off the table, but it falls flat. "I'll take your concern as a sign that you care. It's not every day a fine specimen like yourself says something sweet to me."

The music fades and the DJ's voice booms out, sending everyone into excited chatter and my further questions for Sasha die on my lips.

"It's a fantastic evening here tonight! Who's ready to try their hand at the mechanical bull?"

The crowd all roars and Sasha's hand grips my leg. "Oh my god, I want to try this so bad. Do you think I could do it?"

"They have speed settings. Ask for the slow one and you should be fine."

The DJ runs through the rules and asks everyone to sign up at the table and fill in their waivers in order to try. There's a beginner and an advanced section and Sasha squeezes my leg again. "Okay. I'm gonna do it."

He races off to the table to sign up without any more doubt. On the way there, Sasha draws whistles and catcalls and the hair on my neck stands up when I watch a man hand Sasha a pen and clipboard. I've always followed gut feelings, and it's rarely steered me wrong.

"I don't like the guy at the controls. You getting weird vibes?" Jimmy leans over, speaking in my ear, and I nod.

"Keep an eye on him, Jimmy. I'll watch out for Sasha."

Leaving the table, I walk along the perimeter of the crowd lined up for their turn on the bull. Usually at these things, they have all the slower riders first, then move on to the daredevil-type riders. The ones who can hang on for close to eight seconds or longer at the jerks and speeds of something closer to a real bull. Those are the guys, and sometimes girls too, who are strong enough to stand the blow when they fall. Tonight they're alternating and after a few of the slower riders, the DJ's voice booms again, calling out Mike.

"You're in for a treat tonight folks! Mike McCoy is here for the big event this weekend and since there are no real bulls around, he's in the house tonight for a ride on this old hunk of metal. Mike is a multiple championship winner in bull riding. He's won the Morris Stampede twice, was runner-up at the Calgary Stampede this past year, and is on his way to the PBR finals in Vegas for the third time!"

The crowd stands and cheers so loud my ears ring. Mike waves his hat around at the crowd, waving and thanking everyone for their cheers. Mike has always been a humble man and keeps to himself, except for a few close friends. He's a genuinely good guy and appreciates all the fans. I can't say that about every man in rodeo.

After taking a few moments to get himself on the bull just like any real ride he'd take, he nods to the guy at the controls as if he was actually in the bucking shoots to signal for the gate to open.

Immediately, the bull spins to the right and jerks hard, throwing Mike forward before it changes, bucking and spinning in erratic patterns. Mike holds firm, working his legs like he would on a real bull, and when the buzzer sounds he jumps off with a whoop. Just a walk in the park for Mike.

Sasha's wide eyes focus on Mike and a flush spreads over his cheeks. Mike gives Sasha his hat with a smile and exchanges words that only make Sasha's grin grow larger.

Mike notices me against the wall and heads my way instead of back to the table. Breathless, he smiles and bumps me with his shoulder.

"Nothing beats a real bull and the smell of the ring, but that was pretty good."

A woman presses herself against him with a sharpie in hand and bares the top of her breast. "Can I have your autograph?"

Mike nods and takes the marker, gingerly signing her skin as she fixes her dark eyes on him. "You can add your phone number, too." She purrs.

"Thank you, but that's not my style."

He hands her the marker back with a nod and she leaves with a shrug, rejoining her girlfriends in the corner.

"Do you think Sasha will be okay? Even the slow speed seems fast. I saw his hands and they're not working hands. Know what I mean?"

"Yeah, I know. But he seemed genuinely excited. You don't think it's another hustle, do you?"

"I don't think so. I mean, I barely know him, but what would he be trying to prove if it was?"

"I don't know, but I'm keeping my eye on that group of guys over there." I nod my head towards three men huddled around a table near the sign-up table. I'm not sure if they're locals or not. I don't go out enough to know, but they don't exactly give me queer-friendly vibes. I saw how they looked at Sasha when he signed up.

A few more slow riders take their turn. One rider is a woman who's so drunk they shouldn't have allowed her on. Her turn lasts less than a second as she slips off the side in hysterical laughter, plopping onto the mat in a giggling heap.

Sasha's name is called next, and he waves Mike's hat to the crowd, just like Mike did. In his thigh-high boots and short-shorts, I know he'll be sore no matter how long he stays on. You never ride a horse like that and you certainly don't ride a bull showing skin either. But this isn't real life, so there's some leeway given. Not much, but some.

The woman who had Mike sign her cleavage hoots and cheers and blows Sasha a kiss. He pulls Mike's hat down so tight his ears pop out, and then throws himself over the top of the bull to the amusement of the crowd. He wiggles his ass in the air and laughs at the whistles. From where I stand, he seems to be having fun.

"Do you think he knows how to hold on and keep his balance?"

Mike shakes his head. "I doubt it. He's full of surprises though, so who knows?"

The bull moves at a pedestrian pace and Sasha's face beams with pride. This is a much bigger deal than just riding a bull. Maybe he'll tell me about what it is after tonight. I'm happy Mike or I didn't agree to help him because he's doing just fine on his own. If we were with him, it wouldn't mean so much. This is all him, and that giant smile has a story to it.

But his smile vanishes and all hell breaks loose.

The bull speeds up, taking Sasha by surprise, and he's flung off the back of the bull like a rag doll. Mike and I both launch through the crowd to get to where he lays in a heap at the edge of the foam mat.

"Sasha! Are you okay?" Mike kneels next to him, and I can tell Sasha's right arm is bent in a way that's not natural. His tear-filled eyes beg for comfort and Mike slides closer.

"N-no. My arm. And probably something else. Why did it go so fast? You said it only goes slow, Alec." He sniffs and struggles to push up with his good hand.

"It's supposed to." I growl and turn towards the control operator. The man who was operating the bull is already in the grips of Hunter, and out of nowhere, Heath sinks next to me.

"Jimmy and I saw the whole thing. Some clown in a backwards ball cap with an offensive slogan on it distracted the controller. His buddy made the speed switch, and they hightailed it out of here once Sasha was airborne."

"Maybe go let Hunter know that before he smashes an innocent guy's nose."

Heath follows my gaze and curses. "I'm on it."

Mike holds Sasha in a protective embrace. He's so small next to Mike. Almost childlike in my large friend's arms. "He needs to get to the hospital. Can you drive?"

"Let me tell Hunter and the others. I can take you."

Liam and Roman hover next to Sasha.

"Don't let this get you down, Sash. We're coming with you."

"I'm in so much trouble." Sasha wails as he holds his injured arm.

His friends exchange a worried glance, and Mike effortlessly carries Sasha out of the building. After a quick word with Jimmy, I toss some money toward our tab on the table and push my way outside to find my friend with three hysterical models.

"He's not going to fire you."

"You'll still be in the fashion show. We'll ask for a pink cast. We can bedazzle it!"

"I just wanted to prove I was capable of...of anything! I'm not just a pretty face," Sasha sobs into Mike's shirt.

Jogging to the parking lot, I start my truck and pull up to the curb. They all pile into the cab, with Sasha refusing to let go of Mike. Thankfully, the hospital isn't too far away, so I ignore their lack of seatbelts. I just hope we didn't do any damage to his arm by not calling an ambulance. Sasha whimpers and his sniffling is enough to break my heart. The concern Liam and Roman have for their flamboyant friend is strong, and I wish this wasn't the ending of what could have been a great night.

Mike gently extracts himself from the truck with Sasha near the emergency entrance and takes him inside while I find a parking space and get a quick background of why Sasha is more upset about his job than his injury.

"It's in our contracts to not partake in activities that might damage our physical state. Nothing dangerous." Roman worries at the hem of his shirt. "Sasha has been butting heads with our agent for a while now and I don't know how this will go over."

"But if he only broke his arm, that's not cause for dismissal, is it? He can still walk and function. His face isn't damaged."

"Alec, with all due respect, we make a living by looking perfect on magazine pages. Any blemish that can't be airbrushed out is serious. It's pretty hard to hide a cast. And while bruises can be edited out too, it's...more complicated than just what a good photographer with editing software can do."

I can't wrap my head around living my life dictated by a contract that doesn't allow me to hurt myself. If Sasha fell outside and broke his arm, would they be this distressed about it? Or is it just because he made the decision to do something *he* wanted for once and it ended in injury?

"Does he have any family we should call? I know it's not serious, but is there anyone we should try contacting? Do you all even have insurance?"

Liam laughs softly. "We do, and Sasha is Canadian with a US work visa. He has the same coverage you have here because he returns for long enough every year to keep it valid. So he's okay that way. If he wasn't, we'd just pay out of pocket and get reimbursed later."

Once inside, we're led to a bank of exam rooms where Mike already has Sasha on a bed. It's clearly a very quiet evening in the emergency department for that to happen.

"Oh, good, you're here. He needs his health card. He said you guys have it."

Nodding, Liam removes a small wallet from his pocket and pulls out a green piece of plastic and hands it to Mike as he fills in admittance forms for Sasha.

He snorts when he reads it.

"Your real name isn't Sasha?"

"No, and if you repeat it to anyone I'll fill your coffee with laxative before the rodeo."

Mike gasps as the others laugh.

"Damn. You're vicious...Solomon."

Liam grins, not at all afraid of what his friend might threaten him with, as Sasha drops his mouth open.

"Traitor! Ugh. I thought you were my friend."

"It's just a name. And I am your friend. I'll be here all night if you need me."

The nurse enters the room with a wheelchair and a questioning gaze on all of us jammed into the tiny room.

"Okay, radiology is ready for you." She takes the card and clipboard from Mike. "Are you okay to continue, Solomon?"

"Please call me Sasha." he groans.

"I can do that Sasha. The sooner we get some x-rays, the sooner you can go home."

With Sasha gone, I speak to the others about how to handle this. Liam and Roman refuse to leave without him and Mike says he'll stick around to make sure they all get back to their hotel okay. I trust Mike to keep them all safe.

Since Sasha has enough support with him, there's no sense in me staying, too. It's after midnight when I leave the hospital and I never did get to have that burger like I wanted.

And more than ever, I just want to be with Zane.

Chapter 20

ZANE

I haven't been truly asleep since I arrived at Alec's. I'm in his bed, drifting in and out of that space that's not quite awake, but not fully asleep either. My brain refuses to decide until I hear the door open and know Alec is home safe.

When he told me he wouldn't be out late, I assumed he'd be home by 11 PM, but it's close to 1 AM before the door opens and clicks softly behind him. The deadbolt slides into place with a thunk, and I know that even in the dark, Alec is sneaking down the hall to not wake me.

A rustle of clothing and a heavy clunk of his belt buckle hitting the floor, followed by a soft curse, make my lips curve in a ridiculous grin. I've never been in this position. Waiting for someone I love to come home and witnessing how much effort he's taking to not wake me up.

It may not seem like much, but it's a direct arrow to my heart.

"I'm awake, cowboy."

"I'm sorry to wake you. I was trying to be quiet."

His voice is still a hushed whisper, even though he knows I'm awake.

Sliding under the blankets, his strong arm immediately pulls me back towards him. Snuggling into his body, I grip his hand in mine, kissing his palm and pulling it against my chest.

"You didn't wake me. I've been half asleep waiting for you. I guess I couldn't fall asleep not knowing when you'd be home."

His warm lips press against my neck.

"I should've called you. I'm sorry. There was…an incident at the bar. I had to take Sasha to the hospital."

Releasing his arm, I roll over to face him. Alec's face, so close to mine in the dark, is now visible, and the sadness I find there pains my heart.

"What happened? Is he okay?"

With a sigh, he strokes my cheek with his rough palm.

"He broke his arm. There were some queer haters and Sasha wanted to ride the bull. You should've seen how proud of himself he was, Zane. He reminded me of a kid who rides their bike without training wheels for the first time."

"Oh my god. Did you catch them and punch them in the face? I sure would have."

He laughs softly. "No, I didn't, but there were witnesses. Heath saw it and likely, some others did, too. Mike and I focused on Sasha and getting him help. His friends gave me the impression this could jeopardize his job."

"I'm so sorry. God, what a mess. He's here out of the goodness of his heart to help a friend's charity, and this bullshit happens." I may not have liked how flirty the guy was with Alec, but he doesn't deserve that. Nobody does. "Are you okay?"

Running my hand down his side, I linger on his hip. He always sleeps with the sore side up. Which I've known for years. Funny how I adjusted the side of the bed I sleep on without even thinking about it.

"I'm better now that I'm here with you." His lips find mine when I tilt my head back and my body trembles with the sweet emotion. The pure gratitude he passes through his kiss for me being here. Instead of my heart breaking at the magnitude of what happened to Sasha, it soars. Because I can be this for him. His comfort after a stressful evening and perhaps a safety he never felt before. I've always been there for him as a friend, but as a lover, it feels exponentially more. Like I get to see a part of his heart nobody else ever will.

"Alec..." I whisper in the darkness as our hands roam with not just a sexual urge, but a want to comfort and promise that whatever happens, we know we're here together. "It's okay if you're not okay. I'm not going anywhere."

He rests his head on my shoulder and his hand slides between my legs.

"I'll be okay. I just want to...I want..." He swallows, the click in his throat extra loud in the quiet room. "I want you to know I love you. All of you. Just as you are."

"I know, cowboy. And I'm really fucking lucky."

He rolls us back, pulling me on top of him, and I gasp with the strength he exudes. We're almost the same size and he can lift me with so little effort, I barely noticed. His hand pulls my head down for a kiss as he rocks his hips up.

I'm consumed with need for him. With showing him I'm serious about this and there's no way in hell I want to go back to the monotony of life before love with this man.

My hands and hips do the work. We're in tune with each of our wants, like we've been lovers forever. Alec's hands cup my face, but he won't let me sit up and I really can't complain. His kisses are like a drug of the sweetest kind. Kisses that lift me so high I should attach a weight to my leg so I don't fly away.

"I'm so close." I squeak out against his lips when I finally draw a breath.

Alec's harsh breaths fill the room and he pushes me to sit up. His hand finds mine and together we jerk each other off. It's rough and tender and somehow more intimate than anything else we've done. In the room's darkness, I moan when the tingle runs down my spine and over my balls. I spill over Alec's hand with a gasp.

"Zane..."

My name on his lips in a quiet moan as he coats my hand with his orgasm is overwhelming. This man gives me every bit of himself. He always has. This moment isn't just him getting off for the sake of it. This isn't just sex to him.

Collapsing against him, not caring about the mess between us, I swallow the lump in my throat. Alec has flipped everything I once believed about myself on its head.

Intimate moments. Passionate moments. Waiting for him in the dark to come home. I've never had someone carry my heart outside my body like this before.

It's scary as hell, but my word it's so worth it.

"Cowboy? Where have you been all my life?"

"Right in front of you, sweetheart."

"Well, you best get used to being in front of me forever now."

His body shakes with a quiet laugh.

"That's a really long time. You sure?"

"More sure than when I found that sale on Froot Loops and knew I'd go home with as many boxes that fit in my car."

He whistles long and low. "That's pretty sure."

"I know. So we should probably go to sleep now, in case this is all a dream."

"Some dreams do come true, you know." He whispers with a brush of his lips over my cheek.

I agree with another kiss in the dark.

After the late night at work and then the even later night in bed with Alec, I'm grateful today is a scheduled day off.

Alec barely made it out of bed when his alarm went off, but he kissed me before he left and it made me all gooey inside. He has to talk to Dan about the peacock that keeps escaping before greeting some new horse boarding clients. If I stay here, he said we could have lunch together before getting ready for the cowboy auction tonight.

With a stretch and a groan, I roll out of bed, pull on a pair of nearby sleep pants, and snag my phone from the dresser on my way to the kitchen. My heart just about explodes when I see the giant sticky note on the coffeemaker.

> *Good Morning again,*
> *Press start and call me once you're awake.*
> *Love, Alec*

After pressing start, I flop on the couch and call Alec.

"Good morning, Cowboy. I'm checking in as requested."

"It's almost afternoon, Z. But I'm happy to hear you follow orders."

His low, rumbly voice sends goosebumps down my arms.

"And if I didn't?"

"I might have to bring this piece of rope home with me. Maybe teach you a lesson about following simple requests."

I think the noise in my ears is all my conscious thought leaving while I imagine Alec naked with rope and all kinds of wicked things. Too many, probably.

His low chuckle snaps me back to the present.

"Huh?"

"I was asking you if you liked that idea, and all I heard was some kind of gurgled form of words I couldn't understand."

"Oh, well, that makes sense since I think all my blood drained from my brain and you've left me with a raging hard on just by mentioning rope and leaving it to my imagination."

"Well," he drawls in that deep, smooth voice, I feel all the way to the soles of my feet, "I only have one more boarding client to check in, then I'm free for two days. I'll be back there in an hour. I could take care of that for you."

I don't want to sound too eager. A man has to make him work for it a little, right? Pretty sure he knows I'd run through a wall of spider webs for him without a second thought, but it's the principle.

"Could you, now?"

"I could."

"I haven't had my coffee yet. I really need to wake up and think about this a little more. Make sure I weigh all my options and such."

"I don't mean to sound bossy, but it's only on the table for this phone call, sweetheart. So before I hang up, you're gonna have to tell me if you want to...come."

His seductive chuckle does nothing to quell the situation below and I press a hand to my crotch as the coffee maker beeps.

"I want you to come." God, is that even my voice? Since when do I sound so desperate?

"I'll see you in an hour."

He ends the call without me even saying goodbye and I don't need coffee anymore because I'm more awake than a pack of squirrels who found a stash of espresso beans.

What the hell do I do until he gets here? Should I google it? Jesus Christ, what do I even google?

What should I do while I wait for my hot cowboy boyfriend to tie me up for sex?

To be fair, it is *Google* and I bet someone has searched it before. But I have something better than Google.

Choosing his contact and pressing call, I pour a coffee with a shaky hand and wonder when my life took such a sudden swing to the better. I've gone from lacklustre dates and feeding a stray raccoon (yes, I fed it!) to someone waiting for their boyfriend to come home and tie them up to do kinky things. I'm so hot thinking about it, I might just melt into the floor before he gets here.

And that's another thing. Boyfriend. Or is partner better? Do people our age even say boyfriend? Something else I should ask, I guess. As long as I call him 'mine', that's all that matters.

"Hey, Zane. What's up?"

Martin's voice is his usual get-right-to-business self and for a moment, I think maybe I shouldn't bother him.

"Zane? Is everything okay?"

"Yeah, it's good. Great. Fantastic even."

A crazed laugh bubbles from my lips.

"Sorry, I just. I need to ask you something. Personal."

"Okay. You know you can ask me anything. It's not a big deal. We're friends."

"Right. I know. It's why I called you and not Google."

"Google? I don't follow."

Glancing at the clock on the microwave, panic simmers in my chest. I've lost fifteen minutes already.

"What should I do before Alec gets here to tie me up?"

There's a sputter and cough, and I sip my coffee while I wait.

"Warn me next time you're about to drop something like that! I just spit coffee on my desk. Give me a second."

There are muffled movements and other voices until silence again with only Martin's voice.

"I had to move to the supply room. I know we're all friends, but this isn't exactly a water cooler conversation, I don't think. So, what do you need to know?"

"Uh, everything? Are you into that kind of thing? I guess I don't know what I'm supposed to do. He said he'll come home and tie me up to take care of possibly the biggest hard on I've ever had. It's like my dick just grew three sizes too big. Like the *Grinch's* heart kinda thing when he said he'd tie me up. I didn't think I liked that stuff, but obviously I do." I laugh again, but keep my nervous ramble running like an out-of-control freight train. "Marty, I'm at Alec's waiting for him and what do I do? Is there some kind of protocol? Should I be naked in bed with my ass in the air? This just feels like I should be, I don't know, in character or something. I really don't want to let him down."

"Take a breath, Zane. This is a lot to process for me, too. I was only kidding by the way when I said I wanted to know if he gave great BJs, so keep that to yourself."

Gulping the rest of my coffee, I pace to the living room and fidget with some of Alec's violets.

"Every couple will do different things in the bedroom. It's not much different from one of your previous girlfriends showing up in sexy lingerie. It's just something you choose to do to heighten the experience."

"I asked him before we got to all the naked stuff to tell me what to do and he said he would. And he has. But...I guess I want to be prepared instead of being some new kid, you know? Maybe step up my sex game?"

"Well, I'm flattered you asked me," Martin laughs. "But I mean, other than have a shower and shave your bits, I have little else to offer you."

My mouth drops open.

"You *shave*? Like, all of it?"

Martin laughs more heartily now. "Not that you need to know this, but Dan likes me smooth, so I manscape all the time. Maybe Alec likes that too. I'm just throwing it out there."

I glance at the clock. I only have thirty minutes.

"Okay, I'll take it into consideration. But he'll be here soon, so thanks Marty. Sorry to dump that on you and if the coffee ruined anything."

"Nah. It's an excuse for me to go shopping, so it's fine. I wouldn't panic, though. Alec won't make you uncomfortable, so just enjoy it."

"He's bossy as hell, you know. Total turn on."

"Okay, TMI my friend. It's barely 11 AM, and I'd need wine to keep on with this conversation. Just...be yourself."

Ending the call, I toss the phone on the kitchen table and sprint to the bathroom.

After sifting through my shave kit, I shuck my pants and head to the shower.

Here goes nothing.

CHAPTER 21

ALEC

"Polly will fit right in with the other horses boarding here. Babe's stall is next to hers and she's the sweetest thing. She makes friends with everyone when they first get here."

The young girl nods, but I know she's struggling with leaving her horse somewhere new and I'm running out of comforting things to say.

"And the stalls get mucked out daily? Always fresh water, even in the winter?"

"By me personally. This is my responsibility, and I'll take care of your horse like it's my own." Pointing to Domino in the pasture, I add. "That's my pretty lady there. I could never go a day without bringing her a carrot and an ear scratch. I'll do the same for Polly. You have my word."

That seems to ease the tension, and she smiles.

"Thank you, Alec." She spins my card in her fingers. "Can I...would it be weird if I asked you to text me pictures this week? I'll be gone on a work trip for a week and I'll miss her."

"Not at all. Send me a text and I'll send a few along."

She doesn't want to leave her horse and I know how it is, but I'm growing impatient. Ever since I threw out the rope idea to Zane almost an hour ago, it's all I can think about. In fact, I'm impressed I can still carry a conversation with this woman.

"Okay. I've taken enough of your time. You come highly recommended, so I know there's nothing for me to worry about."

"You do *not* have to worry one bit." I step towards her truck and she finally follows along. "Drive safe and we'll be in touch during the week."

With a wave, she slides behind the wheel and closes the door. I try not to walk away from the boarding stable too quickly. I don't want her to think I'm running away from her, but I *do* want to run to my house that seems like it's in another country right now and not just across the yard of the ranch.

My hand fingers the length of tie-down rope in the pocket of my jeans, and my feet move faster. Zane breathless in my ear when I gave him the option to be tied up has been on repeat and I've never been more focused on something in my life.

I'm almost to my front porch when Jeff, the troublemaking peacock, charges across the yard in front of me. Heath follows behind him in hot pursuit.

"Hey, Alec! It's under control. Don't worry!"

It better be. I spent two hours working on a more secure pen for that damn bird today. I give Heath a thumbs up and run up the few steps to my door before anything else can side track me.

Once inside, I lock the door and pull the window shades down while struggling out of my coat and boots. If anyone needs either of us, it better be because the house is on fire. Anything less than that is unacceptable.

Walking down the hall to the bedroom, the bathroom door clicks open and Zane steps out with a towel around his waist followed by a billow of steam. Zane is attractive anytime of the day, but I've always appreciated how carefree and boyishly cute he looks fresh out of a shower. His tussled blonde hair and a few stray drops of water trickle down his chest. When he notices me, he brings his hand to his chest.

"Shit. Am I late? Has it been an hour?"

His green eyes search for a clock and my heart squeezes with how hard he's trying to please me and follow my instructions to a tee.

"You're not late. It looks like I'm right on time."

"Yeah?"

"Oh, yeah." I skim a fingertip over the top of the towel across his stomach. "There's something about you in a towel that just works for me."

God, the pupils in his eyes swallow the beautiful green and the pulse on his neck draws me in like a siren's call. Bending down, I kiss the space on his neck, licking up a few stray drops of water while I'm there. He clutches my shirt with a breathy sigh.

"You work for me." He gasps as I lay more kisses up his neck.

He works his hands under my shirt and I back away, gently taking his wrists in my hands.

"Keep your towel on and lay down on the bed for me."

Dazed, he nods and scrambles onto the bed. The tent under the towel should be comical, but to me it assures me Zane is just as turned on as I am, and that's the biggest rush ever. I didn't mean to bring rope to the bedroom this soon. It just sort of happened and once it did, well, I'm not about to backtrack on something that rendered him speechless just thinking about it.

Placing my hat on the dresser, I peel off my t-shirt and he inhales sharply.

Zane presses a hand against his erection, and I shake my head.

"Hands above your head, sweetheart. You don't get to touch a thing. Not even yourself." Pulling the piece of rope from my pocket, I let it dangle from my fingertips and Zane licks his lips.

"Okay. Please."

"You can watch me tie it first." I murmur and bring his wrists in front of him again. Kneeling over him I rest his hands on my thighs, and loop his wrists just like I'd do a calf, but slower. I end it with a quick-release knot and show him how easy it is to remove if he needs to.

He understands and lifts his trussed-up wrists back over his head. I'd love to tie him down to the bed completely, but I think I should let him get used to this first. And I only brought one rope with me. Next time I'll do it properly. Maybe I should get more intricate if he really likes it. There's a class that teaches shibari in the city and I've never had a reason to learn more about the art. Simple ties to bed posts were all I ever needed. Perhaps this is a sign I have a reason to explore the more sensual side of the kink and my simple rodeo tie-downs need an upgrade.

My lips wander down his body, enjoying every exposed inch. Zane's skin marks so easily; all it takes is a tiny bit of suction to leave a mark behind. Every time I do, his body hitches, and his tied-up hands twitch. He's dying to touch me and I love that

I'm the source of his passion. That it's me leading him on this self-discovery and there's no better person out there for the job.

After covering every exposed piece of skin I can reach with my mouth, I sit back to admire Zane. Sometimes I think it's a cruel trick of fate and he's not really here with me. Maybe it's just one of those weird breaks in reality and I'm dreaming in real time. Falling in love with Zane was something I couldn't help. Loving him from afar was what I was prepared to do.

But I also know this is very real. Dream Zane has never looked at me like he is right now. And it squeezes the air from my lungs.

"Are your wrists okay?"

He flexes his fingers and nods. "I'm okay. Next time you can, uh, tie me down. But I like this. A lot."

Swallowing, I lean down to place a kiss on his lips. "How are you so perfect?"

"I could say the same about you."

We're not perfect, of course. But we sure as hell go great together.

Zane's breath puffs in shallow pants as I slide back down his body and dip my finger under the towel knot.

"I'm impressed the towel stayed on with all the squirming you've done."

"You're not the only one good with knots, I guess."

Chuckling, I yank gently, and his knot gives way for me to peel back the towel.

And it's my turn to be speechless.

"You...you shaved. Everything." Gone is the golden bush of curls at the base of his cock and, on closer inspection, his balls are naked too. I have no preference. Or, at least, I thought I didn't. But I have to loosen my belt buckle and zipper now because there's been a change of plans.

"Do you like it? Is it okay?"

The waver in his voice has me rushing to assure him.

"Sweetheart, I love it. And I'll show you."

Dipping my head, I run my tongue up his leaking cock, and he bucks his hips. I want to hold him down and make him wait, but all my self-control has evaporated.

"Be careful when you reach my right nut. I nicked my ball sack, and that bleeds like crazy. It was touch and go for a few minutes. I thought I might need to call for help."

Resting my cheek on his thigh, I shake with laughter.

"Zane?"

"Yeah?"

"I love you. Don't ever change. And I'll be careful."

"Okay. I trust you."

Once I catch my breath from laughing, I glance up to find Zane peering down at me. His eyes still burn with desire and since he took the time to do this for me, you better believe I'm going to reward him.

My tongue maps its own course. Licking, swirling, and sucking on all his newly shaved areas. His groans and pleas to make him come only drive my want higher and my hips move on their own, seeking friction against the bed. I don't want to take my hands or mouth off Zane.

"I want to see you. If I can't touch you, let me see you. Please."

Zane's plea is thick and raspy and the only thing that makes me change from my intended course.

Pushing off the bed, I stand at the foot and shove my jeans and boxers down enough for me to free my cock.

"Is this what you want to see? How hard and aching I am for you? You want to watch me come apart for you, sweetheart?"

"*Fuuuckk*. Yes. Please, cowboy."

I scramble out of my pants the rest of the way before kneeling over him again. His gaze locks on my hand as I stroke myself off over him and he licks his lips.

My whole body tingles, alight with a flame that's about to consume me from the inside.

"Fuck!" I knew I was close, but the force of my orgasm takes me by surprise and I come over my fist onto Zane's stomach. His needy whine doesn't go ignored, and I wrap my lips around his straining dick and swallow.

He cries out, and hot spunk fills my mouth. I swallow it all, not wanting to waste a drop until Zane begs me to stop and I release his softening dick.

With my chest still heaving like I ran a marathon, I shimmy up to his head and pull his hands to me. The knot releases with ease and, even though he wasn't tied tightly, I still massage his wrists and place a kiss to each one.

"Are you okay? That wasn't what I planned, but you surprised me with landscaping."

"I'm more than okay. I'm just glad you liked it."

Swiping a shirt off the floor, I mop up the mess off him and toss it near my hamper before laying next to him, pulling him close. He twines his legs in mine and spears his fingers through my hair.

"I don't think there's anything about being with you I won't like."

I place a kiss on his forehead and pull him closer as my eyes grow heavy. "I'm your safe place, Zane. I always will be. If you ever want to try something with me, just ask."

"Thank you for being patient and understanding. I was worried I'd be too new for you. Like, innocent, I suppose. I thought you might want to be...I don't know...whatever you want. I just thought I'd not be it. It doesn't make sense, I know, but that's what's in my head. That you'd want a man who knows his way around, you know?"

"Zane, I love you. It's you I want. We'll learn about all this stuff together. You know your way around just fine."

He traces his fingers down my chest and he's quiet, but there's a gentle thrum in his body.

"What are you thinking? I can feel you vibrating." I murmur with a kiss to his lips.

"I was thinking maybe you should show me the toys you like next?"

My eyes fly open and the fuzzy sleep that was creeping in vanishes.

"You will never stop surprising me. But yeah, we can absolutely do that next. But first I need a nap. I have an auction to attend tonight."

He smiles and snuggles in next to me.

"Good idea. Nap. Auction. Sex toys."

His soft snores drift into the room, but I can't sleep.

How can I when all I can think about is what we'll discover together next?

CHAPTER 22

ZANE

"This is where you're supposed to get changed?"

I try to sound like it's not a big deal...but it's a big deal. There's zero privacy here.

"Um, yeah. Sasha said the set up was just like one of his modelling gigs and not to worry."

He expects me not to worry?

"There are no doors. Everyone is just..." My words die on my tongue as Roman, one of the models, strips in front of us. He's bare-assed right there for anyone to see and, oh dear god, is that a jockstrap?

"Hey, Z, open your eyes."

Alec's voice is soft with laughter, and I turn to him before opening my eyes.

"Everyone will see you back here." I whisper.

A make-up artist bumps into us with a withering look. I yank us closer to one of the walls, away from the main path. And by wall I mean curtain. Anyone can just walk back here and get an eyeful!

"Eh, let them look. They can't touch. That's only for you."

"Yeah, well, I don't like it."

Not sure when I got so territorial, but I know for a fact that I don't want anyone back here to see any naked part of Alec.

He laughs and drops a kiss on my nose. "You don't have to like it. It's just one auction."

"I know," I grumble. I hate that I'm so green about this, but god dammit, he's my cowboy to look at and nobody else's.

"Oh yay! You're here! I can give you the tour." Sasha greats Alec with a flirty smile. He may be sporting a cast on his arm, but his flirt game isn't broken. "I'll show you where your stall is and what to expect." He loops his good arm through Alec's and bats his eyes at him. "We can take it from here, Zane. Thank you."

"I'm sorry about your arm. Are you feeling well enough to do this still?"

His smile slips a little, but not enough for me to be okay with him hanging off Alec's arm.

"Thank you. I may be small, but I'm tough. I've been through worse than a broken arm." He smirks at Alec. "Besides, I wouldn't miss seeing these glorious men in their full attire." He fans himself, and I clench my teeth.

"Oh, for sure. Alec will be a little tied up later with plans. It's best to get all your fill of looking now."

Yeah, I said it and I don't regret it.

Alec shakes his head with a small laugh, and Sasha watches as Alec kisses me on the cheek. Someone else motions for them to follow further into the maze of curtains and Sasha glances back at me as they leave, arm in arm. His expression catches me off guard. The flirty Sasha knows I'm struggling. With a soft smile and a nod, he acknowledges my feelings and creates distance between him and Alec. Behind his back he attempts a thumbs up with his casted hand. While the push and pull of jealousy still wars within me, Sasha's gesture puts me somewhat at ease.

With Sasha, at least.

Still won't change the fact this will be the longest night of my life.

People mingle in the ballroom, enjoying appetizers and desserts while they register to bid on four cowboys and three famous male models. All the 'dates' are set to happen tomorrow before the rodeo event while everyone is still in town. A large whiteboard is on display, with the dates listed beside each man. Roman is 'Dinner at the steakhouse with up to four people and personalized make-up lessons.' Mike has 'Two hours of manual labour followed by a privately catered dinner in your home for up to four people.'

Alec's date is listed as to-be-announced. Great. More of the unknown.

Flipping through the program, I pause at Alec's bio. His photo would make you think he's one of the models here. It's the same photo I told Blaze to send in for his autograph sheet for after the rodeo. It might even be one of the triggers that made me re-examine my feelings for Alec, so it holds a very special place in my heart.

I have my auction paddle tucked into the pocket of my blazer and ready to go. There's no way in hell I'm not bidding on Alec. Even if I drain my savings account to do it. It's a good cause for the shelters and for my heart. If I have to endure him on a date with someone else, even when I know it's not a romantic date, I might lose my mind.

Dan waves from a table in the middle of the room, and I push through the people toward him. He purchased a table for the event and invited all of us from the brewery to sit with the ranch staff. Blaze sprung for the bar tab, so the whole night should be one of fun and laughter with my friends, but I'll be tied up in knots the entire time.

"Hey, Zane!"

Heath plunks down next to me with a plate of cookies and other sweets.

"Hey, Heath. Starting with dessert tonight?"

He nods, biting the head off a horse shaped cookie, and I cringe.

"Get it before it's gone. It's from that bakery downtown–Crumb and Cake, I think it's called? Anyhow, dude is a fantastic baker. You should go get some before the table is empty."

"Oh, yeah. That's Parker's business. We hired him to do the cupcake thing at our grand opening. I'll be right back."

Needing something to do other than obsess over men seeing Alec naked backstage, I wander over to the table and I'm greeted by... a man in a horse costume. He must be sweating buckets in that thing.

When he turns to me, I smile, recognizing Parker's cheerful face.

"I should've known you'd be here. Don't you have staff for these events?"

"Zane! Hi! Nice to see you again." He puffs at the hair falling in his face, as his hands, covered in hoof mitts, hand me a plate. "I do, but I love doing the events myself. Especially for Jacob. It's just a little way to give back to him and the shelter."

"Where do you want all these shortbread cowboy hats? And honestly, Parker, I thought you were going to ditch the hoof mitts."

"Hey, Owen." I wave, and he gives me a chin tilt.

"Hey, man. I haven't seen you in for coffee for a while. Did you ditch me?"

"Hell no. You still have the best cappuccino in this town. I've just been going to work in a different direction these days."

And by different direction, I mean that I don't drive through town because Alec makes it for me... and usually wakes me up with more than caffeine.

"Well, come by again soon so we can catch up." He's still holding a huge tote of cookies, and Parker taps his arm before pointing where he wants it. He bends down and kisses Parker's sweaty cheek and I almost say, '*aw*' out loud. They're so cute. I wonder if people will think that about me and Alec?

Parker waves at me as he speaks to more people, and I wander around the ballroom munching on the sweet snacks. I should bring one of these shortbreads to Alec. He'd like it. I'm totally not trying to check up on things backstage. He legit loves shortbread. So I pop behind all the curtains where I left him not that long ago.

And I immediately wish I hadn't. The first person I bump into, literally, is Hunter.

"What are you doing back here?"

"Bringing Alec a cookie."

When I move to step around him, he grabs my arm.

"Are you actually with Alec? Be honest. This isn't some kind of act to make me jealous, is it?"

The fuck?

Pulling my arm away from him, I narrow my eyes.

"No, it's not fake, and it's really none of your business." I snap with maybe a bit more malice than I intended. "Good luck out there."

I'm barely two steps away before he calls out, "His ass is still great. It was nice to see it again, even if he was across the room. It's a shame I didn't get the full Monty."

Without dignifying that with a reply, I turn the corner to the open area and find Alec in his first outfit. I think I stop breathing.

Alec is dressed in a fitted blue suit that clings to his thighs like saran wrap. A crisp white shirt paired with a plain black tie and a matching blue jacket. It's the perfect shade of blue to complement his eyes. I've always loved his eyes. They're so expressive, and the more I think about it, they're usually on me.

His hair is styled in a cute bedhead kind of way and his quirky little smile lights up his face when he sees me.

"What are you doing back here?"

"Bringing you a cookie." I hold out the plate and frown when I see the horse's head broke off. I probably snapped it after Hunter's remark. "Oh, that's a bummer. Now it looks like I'm offering you some kind of cursed godfather cookie."

He adjusts the cuffs on this shirt with a smile and plucks the cookie from the plate.

"Thank you, Zane. Shortbread is my favourite."

"I know." I sound a little breathless and I think it's because Alec in a suit is another sight I've failed to appreciate all these years.

Titling his head, he steps closer and whispers in my ear. "You're staring, sweetheart."

"I like what I see, cowboy."

His lips feather next to my ear as he lowers his voice. "Thanks for the cookie. And while you're watching me up there, don't forget you're the only one who goes home with me."

"The formal part of the auction starts in ten minutes!"

Alec straightens up and smiles.

"I guess it's showtime. Go have fun with the guys and cheer for me."

Finally remembering I know how to speak, I wish him good luck.

He's herded off with the other guys, all dressed in various styles of formal wear, and I slip out back to our table that's now mostly full. Heath saved me a seat, and no sooner does my butt hit the chair than a drink is placed in front of me.

"Long Island Iced Tea. Figured you'd need a few of these tonight."

Blaze smiles at me as he settles in the chair beside me.

"Thanks. You know me well." I gulp half of it back to settle my nerves and River peers around Blaze. "You know it's easier when you just rip off the bandaid. Chug the whole thing and sit back."

"No, I don't want to do that. I need to pay attention for Alec's turn…" I wave my hand at the stage, "at this thing. Gotta make sure others know he's…unavailable."

River snorts and punches Blaze in the shoulder.

"Yeah, I know what you mean. Blaze told me about this Hunter guy. Is he chafing your ass? If so, the only way to shut him up is to *'stake your claim'* as they say. Make it known."

River sips his beer and winks at Blaze.

"He's rememberin' when he almost threw a punch at my ex. I don't always approve of that, but that was one time I would've been okay with it."

"Oh god. I'm not a fighter. I don't want to punch him." Although it would probably make me feel better since he's been intimate with Alec and knows him in ways I don't–yet. Jesus, I have to stop thinking like that. "I just want his stupid ass out of here."

The master of ceremonies, Dominic, greets the crowd and explains how the event will work. The men first model their formal wear. After a short break, they model their casual garb. Bidding won't start until the casual part. That means I have a lot of extra time to wind myself up and obsess over who might win a date with Alec. Which I know is dumb. It's completely dumb. But try talking to my brain.

I'm the one Alec kisses and says *'I love you'* to. He knows I drink coffee in the morning and tea at night. He knows I like to eat Froot Loops every morning and keeps some at his house for me. For god's sake, he's had my dick in his mouth, and just today tied me up and marked me as his own.

I know the names of his plants and that he keeps his underwear in the bottom drawer of his dresser because it makes sense to him for clothes that cover your bottom to be on the bottom.

Alec is mine. I know it. My closest friends know it. But maybe it's time for other people to know. Maybe I'll stop being so possessive if it's public knowledge. Because there are clearly doubts if Hunter's comments are anything to go by. I'm definitely not faking a single thing with Alec.

The crowd hoots and cheers for the first man to walk onto the stage. Roman struts out in a gorgeous, slim fit tuxedo and the table next to us goes wild. Hooting and throwing fake money in the air towards him. Dominic reads his bio, and it sounds like a dating profile. He likes to take long walks along the beach, lay in the sun, and sip wine around a fire.

The group drooling over him look young enough to be new college grads and Roman plays up to them. An extra wiggle in his step and blowing kisses, as he does what comes naturally to him.

"Do you want another drink?" Heath elbows me and points to my glass.

"Sure. Looks like I'll be here for a while. Why not?"

With Heath gone to the bar, Martin slides over to take his place.

"So? How did it go? But don't give me dirty details. Just an outline is good."

Martin's eyes dance and I bite my lip to keep from cracking up.

"It's hard to look you in the face now that I know you trim the hedges."

He raises his wineglass with a naughty smirk.

"You did it then?"

"You're drinking red wine. Is Dan okay with that?"

Leaning close, he whispers in my ear. "He's more than okay with it because I keep the hedges trimmed, as you so nicely put it. Be happy I didn't tell you to wax. Now stop changing the subject."

Heath sits a drink down in front of me.

"Stay there, Martin. I have to talk to someone about a vacation plan. I'll be back."

We both watch as he waves at the side of the stage and disappears behind the curtain.

"He better not see Alec's naked ass back there."

"Oh, would you stop?" He smacks my arm playfully. "He's a grown man and clearly crazy about you. Stop being so...possessive. It's weird." His sharp elbow nudges me. "So what happened?"

The crowd roars as Mike gets his chance to strut. His table of fans is near the back and very vocal. He plays it up, asking them to scream louder, and they do. Women can screech at ungodly decibels. A younger man I don't know runs up to the stage and tosses something at Mike. He catches it and blushes before showing the audience. It's a jockstrap with his name in sharpie across the front. Winking at the man, he stuffs it in his pocket.

I wonder if Jacob knew this event would involve undergarments being tossed around?

Martin won't be leaving anytime soon, so I turn back to face him.

"I took your advice. He loved it. Be happy I didn't ask for you a lesson, because doing that is hard. How do you not cut yourself all the time?"

Martin snorts and sets his wine down before he dumps it on himself while laughing.

"Practice, Zane." He wipes away tears of laughter and leans in closer. "But what about the rope stuff? Is that something I should try?"

A flame of desire ignites when I remember how the rope felt on my wrists and the heat in Alec's eyes as he tied them.

"Yep. A thousand percent, you should."

I gulp more of my drink because it's hot in here. No other reason.

"Damn. Good to know."

Damn right it's good to know. "Knowledge is power, as they say."

Martin laughs as Dan waves for him to come back to his side of the table.

"I know what I'm learning tonight, then."

"That's oversharing, Marty."

He leaves with his wine and a wink, and instead of sitting next to Dan, he perches on Dan's knee. Dan smiles as Martin leans in to kiss him. He whispers to Dan next, and I have a good idea what he's saying when Dan's eyes bug out of his head.

Martin wiggles his eyebrows with a grin, and I wonder if they'll stay until the end of the auction.

CHAPTER 23

ALEC

"You did great, Alec. The crowd loved you."

The make-up artist dabs something on my face as Sasha watches closely.

"What shirt did you bring for your casual wear?"

I currently don't have a shirt on since I was told it would be better to sit for make up without one on. Since I trust these guys, they're models after all, I kept my shirt off.

But the three of them hanging on to each other while fully dressed has me question their sincerity.

"I brought a blue one that Zane picked out."

Sasha manages to fish it out of the garment bag for me and holds it out.

"Excellent choice. He has good taste."

His gaze stays on mine and I nod.

"The best. I trust him completely."

Taking my shirt from him, I pull it over my head and the collective sighs of disappointment are a boost to my ego.

"Can I ask you something?" Sasha motions for the others to move out of our space and it's just the two of us. Dominic's voice is muffled, but he's introducing the next round of the auction and hyping the crowd for the bidding portion of the night.

"Sure. Is everything okay?"

He picks at a sticker on his casted arm. It's glittery and says *'Fabulous!'* I think one of the kids at the shelter placed it on his cast tonight.

"First, I want to apologize for being so over the top with you. I feel like I might have caused tension between you and Zane, and I'm sorry. I didn't know you were together."

"There was no tension, but apology accepted."

Sasha kicks the toe of his sparkling cowboy boot on the floor and clears his throat.

"And I, uh, I wanted to know if you'd have time to show me how to ride a horse before I leave? I know I only have one useful arm, and maybe I shouldn't have gotten on that mechanical bull, but I came here to taste the country. I wanted to see what it's like outside of the city."

"That bull wasn't your fault. And I was damn proud of you for even trying."

He snaps his head up. "You were?"

"Yeah. You may come across like a diva who doesn't want his nails chipped, but you wanted to prove something to yourself." Nodding, he looks away. "And it took guts to do it."

"Thank you for saying that. I might lose my contract because of it, but that means a lot, Alec. Thank you."

Heath pops his head behind the curtains.

"Hey, Sasha! I've been looking all over for you. Do you still want to talk about the vacation? I have a place you might like."

"Oh! Yeah! I'll be right there."

He turns back to me with a hopeful smile.

"Thanks again Alec. That shirt looks great on you. Zane's a lucky man." He pats my chest. "I bet you bring in the biggest amount tonight."

"I doubt that. But thank you. I'll make sure to get you on a horse before you leave."

"Hey Alec! You're up next!" Mike nods his head at Sasha as he leaves. "It's chaos out there."

"How much did you go for?"

"I don't mean to brag, but two grand!"

He dusts his knuckles across his chest with a laugh.

"Wow, good for you. Do you know the buyer or what you have to do yet?"

"We meet after the auction, but I think it's a group of older ladies who want me to do yard work." He laughs with a shake of his head. "Could be worse than being a thirst trap for a bunch of seventy-year-olds, I guess."

"Alec! You're on!" Roman yells out and I grab my hat off the nearby table before rushing out.

"Shit. I'll see you after, Mike!"

Jogging around the back of the stage I find Roman smiling beside the entrance.

"He's just introducing you and then you're up. Shake that ass and make some money."

"You make it sound like I'm stripping or something."

He hums. "Now that would've been a good idea."

"The pride of Bloomburg and our homegrown cowboy–please give Alec Blackwell a huge welcome back!" Dominic's voice fades to thunderous applause and Roman smacks my ass. Hard.

"What the hell, Roman?"

"It's for good luck. All the sports ball players do it." He shrugs with a grin and I step out onto the stage.

The parade around with my suit was a walk in the park compared to the absolute insanity now that bidding has begun. Searching the crowd, I find the ranch guys whistling and cheering. Zane sits while everyone stands, but his eyes find mine and he smiles before dipping his head back down.

Not exactly the support I was hoping for from him, but the show must go on, as they say.

Sasha's voice sounds across the loudspeaker and I swivel back to find Dominic has passed over his duties and I wonder what the hell is going on.

"Thank you, Dominic, for allowing me to take over for a few moments. You've all got your programs in front of you, and you had time to gaze upon Alec in his suit earlier. Wasn't he fine? Tell me what you thought of him in his formal wear. Make it loud!"

I freeze in the middle of the stage when the entire room erupts with everything from whistles and cheers to catcalls and a few inappropriate comments.

"That's what I thought, too!" Sasha agrees with the crowd and settles them down while I walk to the end of the stage and wave at a grandmotherly type woman. She wiggles her eyebrows and blows me a kiss.

"Now, Alec doesn't need me to hype him up anymore. But I want to tell you why I'm not bidding on him myself. You see, last night, this man and the one before him, Mike? They rescued me." The crowd murmurs and falls silent to listen to Sasha. "Alec swooped in last night when I had an unfortunate accident." He holds up his cast. "I don't need to bid on his time because he gave me an incredible gift last night for free. A friendship I'll cherish forever."

Sasha smiles my way, and I tip my hat. Of course we're friends. But where is he going with this?

"Which is why I'm donating to the date you get to have with him if you're the lucky bidder. But I'm not going to tell you what that is yet. Just know it's delicious." Paddles start going up immediately, and even Sasha is overwhelmed.

"Bidding starts at five hundred dollars!"

He makes a terrible auctioneer, but I do what I'm told and walk up and down the stage. In my boring, everyday clothes. My favourite jeans, cowboy boots, and the t-shirt Zane told me to wear. And I can't forget my ever-present black Stetson. Ball caps have nothing on cowboy hats and I'll die on that hill.

The bidding rises quickly, and we've already reached two thousand dollars. I'm going to top Mike's bids!

An attractive older man near the back stands up and bellows, "Two thousand five hundred!"

I don't know who he is, but he seems intent on winning as he stares Sasha down to end the bidding.

A few more bids trickle in and Sasha keeps selling me to the audience.

"Don't you all love how he fits those jeans? And those eyes! Look how blue they are with that shirt on. He's all country heart and so delish to look at. He's a cowboy, folks. Big, strong hands for any of the yard work you might need done or just to help you into your jacket after your date. Surely he's worth more?"

"Five thousand dollars!"

My jaw drops as Zane launches to his feet and shouts his bid. Everyone stares at him. Including me.

Sasha laughs softly. "Seems like this one is set on winning. Going once. Twice..." Sasha lets the last beat hang in the air for any last-minute bidders. The man in the back shakes his head. Zane drops his bidding paddle to his side, and I can't read his expression. I swallow as he stalks towards the stage before Sasha ends the bid, gaze laser-focused on me.

"Sold! For a whopping five thousand dollars to the lucky man who I think may have something he wants to say to Alec."

Zane hops up the stairs and hands his paddle to Sasha while he strides towards me. My heart beats an off-kilter rhythm and my throat runs dry. Zane reaches me and his green eyes flash. Possessive and kind. Soul searching. Love.

"I love you. I know you wouldn't do anything with anyone who might have won your time. But I couldn't let that happen. I'm too greedy to share you with someone else for even a minute. I'm yours and you're mine, and I want everyone to know that."

He fists his hands into my t-shirt and yanks me to him, kissing me with a fierceness so strong, it's hard to keep my wits about me. I kiss him back with my hands on his face and my hat goes tumbling off.

"Fucking hell, I couldn't handle people not knowing you're mine, cowboy." he mumbles against my lips before resting his head on my shoulder. "I'm sorry if I embarrassed you."

"I'm not embarrassed. Quite the opposite. I've always wanted to tell people you're mine, but you did it first." I can't help kissing him again, and I ignore the hoots and hollers behind us. "Do you even have that much money to honour your bid?"

He shakes his head. "Blaze. He told me he was more than happy to make whatever donation I bid. And he was even happier to *see us get our heads out of our asses and get on with it.*'"

I laugh and kiss his neck. "Sounds like Blaze."

"Uh, guys?"

Dominic taps Zane's shoulder. "You can take it offstage."

Zane's eyes burn into mine. "I like that idea."

With the cheers following us offstage, Zane drags me to the back into the curtain village.

"Why isn't there anything with a damn door back here?" He mutters as he keeps walking.

"Why do you need a door?"

He stops and spins and I crash into him.

"You're right. I don't need a door. I want everyone to see."

"Are we moving on to public sex now?"

He stares at me and shakes his head. "Shit. No. I saw jockstraps back here and who knows what else. I don't need that. Can we leave?"

"Uh, I think I'm supposed to stay and sign those autographs for a while. But I'd love it if you were with me."

He huffs an impatient breath.

"Damn it. Okay. The sex can wait then." He laughs. "Never thought I'd ever say that. But sometimes waiting is worth it." His eyes soften and I know he means more than just whatever he wants to do with my body tonight.

"It sure is, and I'd do it again for you."

"Let's go meet your fans."

He twines our fingers together and we find our way back out to the seating area where Jacob has a station set up for us to speak with people, pose for photos, and the like. Most of these people live here and know me, so it's weird to sign pics of myself, but I do as I'm told.

The entire time, Zane stays nearby. He brings me a drink or kisses my cheek. He mostly watches from a table over, but there's a lightness in his gaze now whenever I catch it.

Blaze appears and smacks his program down open to the page with my bio.

"Your autograph on a photo is priceless, and I need to have it."

I snort and look into the smiling face of my close friend.

"You didn't have to do that for Zane, but I appreciate it."

"I couldn't let him sit there and be so down. It was killin' me. Besides, I think he was likely goin' to make a public display even if he didn't win."

"Maybe. Only he knows. I'm just glad he did. Not that I doubted him or anything. I just wanted to...I don't know. Show him off?"

"Well, who wouldn't? I think he finally realized he wanted that, too. He's not jealous in the way he doesn't trust you. He's proprietary. He wants everyone to know you're off the market. Nothin' wrong with that and I'm happy he figured it out."

Glancing around Blaze, I watch Zane and Sasha talk and laugh together, and I wonder what they're talking about. Both of them look my way and burst out laughing before resuming their animated conversation.

"Was it like this when you and River got together? Did everything just feel like it was right in the world and you could just die happy now?"

"Well, aren't you a closet romantic?" He laughs at me and leans in close. "But yes, that's what it felt like. It didn't matter whatever happened in life. Once I was wakin' up to him every day, that was the only thing I wanted. And I will move heaven and earth to make him happy."

Blaze and I are the only ones left at the table for autographs, and with surprise, I notice most of the hall has emptied out. The first event seems to have been a hit.

"Hey, do you mind if we talk about this again later? I have someone I need to take home."

He laughs softly and claps me on the shoulder as I brush past him, focused on Zane. Zane turns his head my way and Sasha follows his gaze. Once I'm at their table, Sasha stands with a friendly smile.

"You two are what people dream of. Best of luck to you both." He pats my arm. "We'll talk tomorrow. Thank you for everything. Both of you."

Zane surprises me by jumping up, hugging Sasha, and speaking close to his ear before Sasha waves and disappears.

"You've made a new friend."

"I have. He's a nice guy. I think he's learned a lot the past few days."

We stare at each other for a moment before he smiles and places his hand behind my head to pull me to his lips.

"C'mere."

I meet his lips with the biggest smile on my face, and he laughs.

"It's hard to kiss you when you're smiling like that."

"You might have to get used to it. I don't see my smile going anywhere soon."

"Take me home, cowboy. I'll give you something to really smile about."

He twines our fingers together, pulling us to the exit.

"You've turned into a sex fiend. I can't say I'm disappointed."

Zane cocks his head. "Me neither. Just hope you can keep up with that bum hip of yours."

Laughing, I steal a quick kiss before we get into my truck.

"I assure you, it won't be a problem. I'm a man of many resources."

"Smart *and* sexy? I feel like I won the damn lottery."

He's not the only one.

CHAPTER 24

ZANE

The drive back to the ranch is quiet, but the air is thick and shimmery, like a haze on a summer's day. You can't see it, but you can feel the same anticipatory heat. The kind that takes your breath away once you step into it.

The small uptick of Alec's lips hasn't left his face since I kissed him on that stage in front of everybody. It's a Mona Lisa smile. One that's confident, happy, and satisfied, but also has a tiny bit of mystery still attached.

The truck rolls to a stop outside of his little farmhouse at the back of the ranch property. It's tucked away with one large maple tree in the front and one of the barns next to it. I've never noticed how much this house reflects who Alec really is.

Maybe it's because I see him in a different light now.

From the small covered porch with its wooden rocking chair to the path of patio stones to the back where you find his cherished gazebo and hot tub. It's understated, but packed with so much care and love. Nothing fancy. Not even the truck he drives.

"Are you going to get out or just stare at my house all night?"

Shaking my head, I open the door and step out into the cool evening air. Summer hasn't arrived entirely. The cool nip of spring is still present, but it's welcome on my warm skin.

"Is everything okay, Z? You've been really quiet."

"I'm fine. I'm just noticing how much your place really is like you."

"I hope you don't mean the paint I need to redo. I don't want you to think I'm flaky."

He elbows me with a smile, proud of his bad joke, and I reward him with a soft laugh.

"Definitely not. It's just…" God, the wave of emotion slams into me and I blink furiously.

"Hey, what's going on?"

Alec's gentle palm on my face draws a deep sigh from my lips.

"Is this too fast? Are you having second thoughts now? We can slow it down, Z. I know it's been a whirlwind of a week for you. I don't —"

"No second thoughts, cowboy. Not a single one." My voice catches and this time I let the wetness in my eyes flow. "It just kind of smacked me once we parked that this is you. Your warm, welcoming little house with a view of the meadow and a path to the gazebo." I swallow back the lump building. "Even how close your house is to the barn for the new rescues. You're never more than a few steps away. I've been coming here for three years and not really seeing you."

Turning, I stare into his blue eyes. The ones that really do show me his soul. If I'd have paid attention, I might have had all this sooner.

"I want to spend the rest of my life with you. I've never been more sure of anything–ever. I'm new at this whole 'being in love' thing, but I know you're the part I've been missing, Alec. Everything just keeps clicking into place and it's all because of you."

He stares back at me. His lips parted in shocked wonder.

"It's not because of me, sweetheart. It's because you took the time to pay attention to what your brain was telling you. And your heart. You put the pieces together. Not me." He dips his head and kicks a toe of his boot in the dirt. "I'm sure glad you did, though."

I launch myself at him, wrapping my arms around his neck, and smashing my lips to his.

He grunts and stumbles a step back, but presses into me, grabbing my hips and pushing me into the front of the truck. We're a wild mess of panting, pawing, and sweet whispers of affection. My desire burns from the inside out and I just know I need him. It's a visceral want. A primal need for him to be mine.

Every memory, every tear, every beat of his heart. Mine.

And every intimate experience.

"Can you...ah, fuck..."

"Can I what?" He holds my chin, forcing me to stare into the blue orbs I'm obsessed with.

"I want you to...go all the way with me." I huff a laugh with my awkward phrasing. "Like, have sex. The whole," I gesture between us and the flush rises on my body, heating my skin just thinking about it, "ball of wax. Not just hand job stuff."

He smiles and drops a kiss on my forehead.

"We can do that. I'd love to. But you'd be doing me."

Wrinkling my eyebrows, I don't quite follow. He kisses me again.

"I prefer to be the bottom, Z."

"Oh." My brain kind of goes offline as I process that before I snap back to attention. "Oh! Okay, that just ah, opened up a lot of scenarios I like. A lot. Can we do that?"

He groans and pushes his groin into mine.

"Good god yes, we can do that. I might last three seconds, but we can definitely do that."

Somehow we stumble up the stairs to the front door and I've ripped Alec's shirt off. But not too hard because it really is the prettiest blue and highlights his eyes.

"Fuck, I love it when you're like this," Alec gasps as I push him against the front door and kiss him again.

"Like what? Desperate to get your dick in my mouth?"

He groans, dropping his head to the door with a hard thud.

"Goddammit, Z. You'll kill me if you keep saying shit like that."

"I need you alive. Don't do that."

My fingers fumble with his giant belt buckle and I don't know what everybody sees in these things. It's harder to deal with them using one hand, and it's so big it might cause an earthquake when it hits the floor.

Alec shoves my hands aside and unlatches it with ease.

"Not that I want you to stop, but let's go inside."

Alec opens the door and pulls me in with him. We laugh and stumble as he kicks the door closed behind us. Neither of us can stop touching each other. My shirt comes off. Shoes and boots are somehow scattered down the hallway, and by the time we make it to the bedroom, I only have socks on. Alec still wears his pants.

"Seems you're better than me at getting clothes off." I joke as I slide my hands into the back of his jeans and push them until the sheer weight of his belt pulls them the rest of the way to the floor. It thunks against the hardwood and Alec pins me against the wall before sinking to his knees.

"Because I wanted to do this."

"Shiiitttt..." My gaze stays glued to Alec's mouth wrapped around my cock and my breath stutters as he works his magic.

His saliva flows down my dick, trickling onto my balls, and I have to tap him gently to stop.

"Cowboy, I'm too wound up."

He releases me and winces when he stands.

"Did you hurt yourself?"

"I'll be okay. But I should probably lay down." His cheeks pink. "And it kills me to admit that."

"I was only kidding about the bum hip thing. I'll do whatever you need."

He settles himself on his back and motions for me to join him on the bed.

"If you reach under the bed, there's a small shoe box. It has what we need."

I locate it easily and settle next to him.

"Is this your sex box?"

"You could say that. Open it."

Flipping open the top, I take one look at Alec and lick my lips.

"Have you used all this stuff?"

"Well, yeah. I'm a single man. Sometimes I want more than my hand." He shrugs and I'm still fixated on the items he keeps here.

"Just get the lube. We can use the other stuff later."

I hold up the piece of rope that I'm certain he used on me already... and there's another longer one in there.

"As long as you promise we can use this later."

His eyes darken, and he bites his lip.

"Yeah, we can. I'd love to do that, but right now, I need you to fuck me."

I wrinkle my nose and smooth my hand on his chest. "I don't like that phrase. It sounds so cold. Like the intimacy is gone, and I don't want that. Not now, maybe not ever. I realize burying myself in you is beyond intimate, but call me old-fashioned...I don't want to say that word. Like this."

Alec takes my hands to his lips and I melt in a giant puddle of goo. His eyes are so soft and I swallow hard.

"That's okay. It means a lot to know you feel that way. Call it what you want and I'll do the same."

"I don't know what to call it. Making love is so corny, fucking is so cold. I just want to show you I love you and it means everything to me to be with you like this. Everything." My voice cracks and that fluttery thing that always happens now around Alec sets in.

"I don't want to be a guy who cries with sex. I've had sex, but I've never had it be so...meaningful? Right? I don't want the significance of that to be lost. It's stupid, I know, but this is...this is me giving my best friend, the man I love, all of me."

Blinking hard, I shake my head. "I just ruined the mood. Sorry."

"No. Not one bit. I'm a little overwhelmed by how much this means to you. Maybe I didn't consider your feelings enough. But you know I've only ever dreamed of having you like this, right? Not once did I ever think I'd be here with you. I kept that tucked away, so I didn't break into pieces every time you went on a date with someone else. I didn't mean to cheapen this for you at all. This is literally a dream for me, Zane. You're a dream come true and I want you to be with me."

Forgetting the box and all the questions I have about what's inside, I drape myself over Alec and press my lips to his. No more awkward words or spilling my guts. I want to make him feel good and I want to show him I'm in this.

For the rest of my life.

Our kisses are slow and deep, the hurry gone, as we touch and slide our bodies together. I know what I need to do, and when my hand moves between his legs, he spreads them with a breathy sigh. Pausing, I fumble with the lube and squirt some on my hand and coat his cock.

His breath catches, and while I've done this with him before, I see it through different eyes. He relaxes into the pillow and lets me take control. God, the moans from his lips are so different from before. Even his deep blue eyes watch me with a look I don't have a name for. But I feel it.

Sliding down, I kneel between his legs and reach for a pillow to prop him up. My gaze stays glued to his face as my fingers do their work. Alec's chest rises in short puffs and there's a strawberry-pink flush to his skin. His lips are puffy and swollen from all our kissing and he's the most head turning handsome man I've ever seen.

"You're so gorgeous, cowboy. God, I wish you could see what I see."

He bites his lip, and tilts his hips slightly, urging me on.

"Please, sweetheart." His voice cracks. "Show me."

"Is your hip okay?" I murmur as I settle between his legs and spread him open more.

"Maybe don't push that leg so far." I adjust my grip, releasing the tension on his sore side, and notch my cock at his entrance, pressing forward.

He huffs out a breath as I slide deeper, and once I'm seated, he clutches at me to bend down. His mouth meets mine with a kiss that's overflowing with years of longing and love. It's heartbreak and new hope all in one. It's gratitude and a promise there's no love like this. I gasp with the intensity of the emotions coursing through me.

"I love you, cowboy." I pant as I pull away and move inside him. It's an exquisite pleasure. While, of course, the physical sensation is impossibly good, I'm overwhelmed.

Alec reaches for his cock while I experiment with the speed and depth of my thrusts. Watching his face, I catalogue his reactions for later. I'll remember what he likes, so he doesn't need to tell me.

I piston my hips faster when he increases the pace of his hand.

Slapping skin and our moans of pleasure float through the air as Alec jerks himself. Next time I want to do that for him.

"Alec, I'm so close."

"Come in me, sweetheart. Make me yours."

Words should not be that powerful. "Oh, fuck!" I couldn't stop this orgasm if I wanted to. Gasping for air, I try to keep moving through it for him, but it's only short jerks and spasms I can manage as I empty into Alec. Stars burst behind my eyes and I keep them screwed close. The enormity is too much.

Holy shit.

Alec explodes across his stomach with a shout and somehow I still have the frame of mind to be careful and not press against his sore side as I settle next to him.

His satisfied, but sleepy smile from his pillow squeezes at my heart.

"You okay?" He asks with his fingertips on my cheek.

"I couldn't be better. Overwhelmed, but in a good way. You?"

"Like I discovered a hidden treasure."

And with Alec, I know he means that. He treats me like a treasure, always has.

"Do you want to shower this off or just a wipe down?"

His rough palm slides over my cheek.

"I don't think I want to wash this away for a while. Just lay with me."

I roll over and toss him my shirt to wipe up with before settling back next to him. My head rests over the steady beat of his heart and I drift off to sleep with his lips on my head and a murmured promise of never letting me go.

CHAPTER 25

ALEC

"Did you ever think you'd be roping a pink unicorn in front of a crowd of people and calling it rodeo?"

Mike and Jimmy shake with laughter and their smiles tell me they're enjoying it maybe a little too much.

"I don't use the rope much with round-ups, but I can honestly say I'm happy the target wasn't moving." Mike adjusts his hat and glances at the young woman while she opens the envelope attached to the animal she chose. Jacob hovers nearby and when the woman breaks into tears of joy, he does too.

"If you're wondering why we're all crying here," Jacob speaks into the mic, "It's because Jocelyn's prize is airfare to anywhere in North America. Until she opened this, she wasn't able to attend her brother's wedding in Vancouver due to the cost. Now she can!"

She hugs Jacob and then Blaze, who holds her a little longer and leads her out of the ring. She cries fresh tears and they speak a little longer and if I know Blaze, he likely offered to throw in a hotel or whatever else she needed, too.

It seems all our winners of the 'Lasso Your Prize' event were deserving, and it makes it that much sweeter to be a part of it.

"So, are you and Hunter going to pull off this roping show without killing each other?" Jimmy tilts his chin towards the chutes where the steers wait. Hunter roped his teddy bear first, and he's been absent since disappearing after the winner claimed their prize.

"I hope so." I sigh. "I don't know why he's been so confrontational. It was all water under the bridge until he started giving Zane a hard time."

"I like Zane. He's good for you." Mike adds and I warm with my friend's approval.

"He is. I'm a lucky man."

My gaze floats to the stands in search of Zane, and I find him seated in between Sasha and Roman, smashing cotton candy into his face and laughing. Like he knows I'm watching him, his gaze lands on mine and he beams a smile my way.

"Hey! Alec! You want to talk strategy before we go live?" Hunter yells over to us, and I excuse myself before walking toward the cattle pen. Right now, the mutton busting is about to start, but Mike and Jimmy have it under control. Kids signed up earlier today for a chance to take part. Now they're fitted with a helmet before they try to ride a sheep for as long as possible. It's an event that always makes me smile because it's how I got hooked on rodeo. Maybe one of these kids will go on to do that too.

Hunter motions for me to step to the back of the pens, and he leans on the rails. A pang of nostalgia squeezes. Back when we were partners, he used to stand like that before every event. He'd scan the steers and make comments about which one he hoped we got based on if it looked sleepy or whatever else his brain told him was a good sign. It was his way of getting into the right headspace before an event.

He'd run his rope through his hands with one foot on the railing while he chewed on a cinnamon toothpick. He pulls the wrapped splinter of wood from a package and flips it into his mouth. When he runs the rope through his hands, I'm transported back to a time that was both joyful and heartbreaking. It's weird to be here like this, remembering it all as if nothing bad ever happened with us.

"Before we talk about the event, I want you to tell me why you've been such an asshole since you showed up."

He spins the toothpick around and stares out at the first kid bobbing along on the back of a sheep.

"When Blaze called me and said you'd given him my name, I guess I was hoping it meant more than that."

He glances at me, jaw set, before staring back at the action in the ring.

"I didn't think you'd take it that way. He wanted to know if I still knew any talent in rodeo that might be able to help out at an event. You have talent."

"So it's like that then."

His hands falter on the rope and squeeze into fists.

"It was never meant to imply anything other than you were a good roper, Hunter. I wasn't asking for you to come back. I didn't even know why Blaze was asking me all the questions."

The crowd roars with laughter as a little girl still hangs on to her sheep while sliding under its belly.

"My grandpa saw me with someone. He, ah, just was out and about, you know?" He swallows and casts a quick glance my way. "I'm not that golden boy anymore."

"Am I supposed to just forget how you treated me when I needed you on my side? I had nobody but you." I shake my head, not willing to believe we're having this conversation after all these years. "We had some good times, Hunter, but it was a long time ago. I've moved on and I'm happy. You should too."

I can sympathize to a degree for his grandfather finding him in a situation. The man was not an easy man to like and probably made Hunter feel like shit for days. But that's where my sympathy ends.

"So, Zane is the real deal, then?"

I study him closer. "Real deal?" Grabbing his arm, I force him to look me in the eye. "If you mean do I really love him, then yes, he's the real deal. Did you think I was faking it?"

He puffs an exasperated breath. "A guy can hope."

We didn't part on good terms, but over time, my heart let Hunter go. I knew he wasn't the right one for me. If I had even remotely thought he still carried a flame, no matter how small, I'd never have told Blaze about him.

"Will you be able to do this roping thing? Because we were a damn good team roping. You can still have that. We'll always have that, Hunter."

His game face slides back on, and he spits his toothpick on the ground before looping his rope and letting it hang from his arm. The mutton busting is almost finished and the kids line up for treat bags and a victory lap around the ring. It's almost time for us to do our thing.

"Yeah, I can do it. I promised Jacob, after all."

"Hunter…" There's still this weird vibe between us and I wish there wasn't. We were fine until he got in my face about Zane. He stops and turns. "There was no ulterior motive behind inviting you here. Blaze didn't know. I'm sorry."

He hangs his head. "It's fine, Alec. I know I missed out." Our names are called out over the loudspeaker. "Let's do this."

We mount our waiting horses and, as instructed, ride into the ring, waving at the fans who have never seen a real rodeo event in person. Jacob wanted to draw it out as much as possible, so we follow along and demonstrate before actually doing anything.

It's not even close to a real rodeo. But by the grace of god, none of the people here complain. It's a gorgeous early summer afternoon, and it's hard to complain when the promise of summer nights lies right around the corner.

Jake explains to the crowd that Hunter and I work together as a team. Hunter is the header and he's going to rope the steer preferably by the horns. He then turns the steer to the left so I can rope the back legs as the heeler. When he's run through his spiel and we've hammed it up a little for the spectators, I'm happy to see Hunter with a real smile on his face. He may think he still loves me, but he always loved rodeo more. He still does.

We don't have the regulation breakaway line in front of the horses or steer. Nor do we have an official timer. We're just playing around, and when Blaze holds up his phone as the official timer, the crowd laughs.

"I need to remind everyone that Alec hasn't actively practiced rodeo for many years, but Hunter is still on the circuit." Jacob laughs at me and I shake my head. "Cut him some slack if he makes a mistake."

The man in the chute shouts as he releases the brown spotted steer. It takes off with Hunter and me in hot pursuit. Hunter releases his lasso and… misses. Domino immediately slows and cuts hard to return to the chutes. A young boy opens the gate at the other end of the ring for the steer to run into.

"Oh well, I guess even the pros have a bad day now and then. Everyone cheer him on for round two." The crowd grows loud and I ride closer to Hunter. "Even the mighty sometimes have a down day."

"It's literally my job, Alec. I shouldn't miss." Same competitive streak even for a charity event. Some things will never change, I guess. "He's lining up the little black one next. I have a good feeling about him."

We take our positions again and once the little dude goes running, so do we. This time Hunter's rope is fast and true, catching the steer over the horns. He pulls his horse to the left, opening a clear path for me to rope the back legs. I'm a tad slow on my release and only catch one leg. It's a five second penalty. If this were a real competition, I just put us out of finishing with money.

"Wow, I feel like twelve seconds was a really long time for this? What's a winning time you two used to make?" Jacob grins as we ride back to the start and Hunter answers. "Our best time ever was 4.3 seconds. It was a record then."

Lining up again, I look over at Hunter. "Let's make this one count, yeah? Just like in Morris." That's the rodeo where we set the 4.3 second record. It was a highlight of both our careers. A small smile flits on his lips.

The next steer bolts into the ring and we take off after it. Hunter lets his rope go almost immediately, and as soon as the rope is around the steer's horns, I release my lasso to the spot I hope his legs will land. My gamble pays off and this time both back legs are caught. Hunter already has his horse turned to face me, and Domino knows she needs to pull the rope taught.

It isn't record time but it's pretty dang good, and I nod my head to him across the ring.

God bless the people of Bloomburg on their feet cheering like we'd just slayed a dragon. I quickly untie the little guy and let him trot back to the others and Hunter grins down at me.

"Just like riding a bike, eh?"

"Except my bike has a flat tire and the wheels are out of alignment."

He laughs, and it's a real one. Booming laughter sounds from his gut and it makes me happy to hear.

We decide to do one more round for the crowd since we've found our groove, and I have to admit it's a rush to be in the ring again. Hunter exits the arena and after a quick introduction from Jake, I only do one tie-down with a calf. It's almost perfect execution and the crowd roars it's approval as I kneel next to the calf and tie two wraps and a hooey, securing it's three legs.

It's a struggle to catch my breath as I mount Domino and I may regret this tonight when my hip screams at me.

I'd not want to go back to this life, though. I like my quiet, comfortable place on the ranch, but this has been amazing.

Because there's something I got to experience today that I never had before.

I find him in the crowd. Jumping and shouting with the damn cotton candy, and when he points at me, I can read his lips.

'That's my man, so don't be getting any ideas.'

Zane finally notices me watching, and I wave to him. His beaming smile as he hollers and claps is the icing on this retired rodeo cowboy's cake. I always wanted to have someone rooting for me in the stands. Someone shouting and full of pride for something I did. Someone who makes my heart sing and sets my life aflame with a simple smile.

Little does he know, Hunter made my dream come true. Working alongside your love interest isn't quite the same as seeing them in the stands cheering you on. Especially when your partner isn't out and public affection of any kind is not an option.

People leave the stands now that the event is over, and I gesture for Zane to come down to the ring. He smashes his remaining cotton candy into Sasha's hands and bounces down the steps, weaving his way through the crowd until he's standing at the edge of the fence.

I slide off Domino and meet him there.

"You were amazing. I don't think I can put into words how hot it was to see you on Domino like that. With the rope and all the..." He gestures to me, "All the cowboy-ness. Did I mention the rope?" He laughs and his green eyes sparkle like I've never seen before.

"You mentioned it twice. C'mere."

He leans over the fence, and I remove my hat to kiss him. He returns it with an eagerness I don't know if I'll ever get used to.

"How much cotton candy did you eat? You're all sticky and you taste like pure sugar."

"Lots." he laughs again and his joy, his freedom, his being so open and comfortable with me crushes me with profound happiness.

"I need to get Domino trailer'd after she cools down. Walk with me?"

He hops over the fence and takes my hand while I lead her out of the ring and into the small field in the back. Removing her saddle and gear, I load it in the horse trailer while Zane takes hold of the reins and I return with a lead rope. Domino grazes and drinks. I'm just content to be here with Zane.

"Sorry to interrupt, but I just wanted to say goodbye. I'm gonna head out right away." Hunter stands near my horse trailer and my heart breaks for him.

Walking over, I hold out my hand. "I'm really glad you came. It was great to do this with you one more time. Zane got to see it in person and I'm grateful for that."

Zane hangs back, but I motion him forward.

Hunter clears his throat, stuffing his hands in his pockets after a very quick handshake.

"It was nice to give it one last go round."

"You sure you don't want to stay for the after party at the brewery?" Zane asks. "It's just for the volunteers and a few close people to say thank you."

Hunter shakes his head with a sad smile. "No, I think it's best I get going. Easier to just head out now. But Zane, you ah, you have a great man there. Take care of him, okay?"

"He's the best, and I will."

The awkwardness grows until finally Hunter tips his hat and leaves without another word.

"He was hoping you two still had something, wasn't he?"

"Yeah, he read more into the invite and I feel bad about that. I honestly didn't think he still had feelings for me." Sighing, I take Zane's hand again and we lean up on the fence, watching Domino.

"You think he'll be okay?"

"Probably. He's had some hard times with family and they likely aren't over, but I think he realized he messed up. He always put rodeo first-even after we had our final blow up-but I think he sees now that hiding things isn't always the best choice."

Zane pulls me around and wraps his arms around my waist.

"You're a good person. Anyone who turned their back on you is bound to regret it some day Alec. He's wishing things were different and even though he was an asshole, I can't fault him for wishing he hadn't let you get away."

He presses his lips to mine and I'm starting to like his sugar-filled kisses.

"Want to take Domino home, then get to the wrap up party?"

"Our first official public date as a couple. Let's go."

He pats my ass and motions for me to get Domino.

"If I knew anything about horses, I'd do it for you. So…just do the stuff and I'll wait."

"If you're going to be involved with a cowboy, you'll need to learn about horses some day."

"I will. You have forever to teach me."

And I like the sound of that.

CHAPTER 26

ZANE

"**D**id you have enough to eat? Do you need anything else?"

Finally finding a moment to sit, I pull up an empty chair near Sasha. He's been in the corner most of the night, which doesn't seem like him at all. Not that I know him that well, but the little that I do know, he's usually very effervescent.

"I did, thank you. You make great food here. Did you create all the recipes?"

At least his smile is genuine.

Maybe he just wants to sit and not be 'switched on' tonight. I can only imagine how taxing it must be to always be in the public eye. To be aware of every word out of your mouth and every move you make.

"Most of them are mine, yes. The brewery takes great pride in sourcing local ingredients. Meat, cheese, eggs, vegetables, anything produced nearby we partner with the farmers to purchase from. We even grow our own hops and barley in the fields out back. We buy extra when we need it. From locals, of course."

Supporting community agriculture had been on our agenda since day one. Nothing tastes better than eggs laid that very morning or carrots three days out of the ground to the table. It's a no-brainer for me. Food is life, and paired with small, batch-made beer in our craft brewery? Match made in tastebud heaven.

"Wow, that's really impressive. I knew you guys supported the community, but I didn't realize how much until I came here."

Sasha pushes the coaster around the table, the smile dropping from his face.

"Is everything okay? I thought you'd be socializing and, sorry if I overstep, but flirting with everyone. You've been sitting here alone most of the night. As far I've seen, you only spoke to Heath and your own friends."

The frown on his face breaks my heart. I reach for his good hand and halt the aimless coaster pushing.

"What happened, Sasha?"

He squeezes my hand, acknowledging the gesture, but there's still no smile in sight on his usually cheerful face.

"My agent called, as I expected. I broke a clause in the contract. I lost a lucrative gig, and he's letting me go."

"What!? Is that, like, a common thing?"

He's a model, for god's sake. What kind of clause would be broken?

"It's a long story, but my agent is...not nice. I was young and stupid and trusted the wrong person. I have a clause that says I can't take part in any activity that might damage my face or body. A broken arm is enough to invoke it." He shakes his head with a sad smile. "I could fight it, but honestly, it's likely a blessing. His ethics are questionable and while he got me started in this business, I can go on without him. Assuming he doesn't get me blacklisted."

There's something off about his story, but I don't want to pry. We've only just become unlikely friends. And I'm glad we did. He's not the overly flirty guy he first presented as. He's funny, loves animals, and has a degree from a prestigious business school. He's beauty and brains, and once you get to know him behind all his sequined bravado, he's just a guy who wants to make real connections.

While Alec signed autographs after the auction, Sasha apologized if he'd made me uncomfortable and told me how wonderful Alec and Mike had been when he broke his arm. He'd never had strangers step up for him like that before, and that sort of made me want to hug him extra tight. Which I did, and we instantly bonded. Then he talked my ear off.

"So, what will you do now?"

He shrugs. "I have money. I don't have to worry about it right away. Heath said he's been learning about being a travel agent. He seems nice, so I told him to book something where I could get away and learn to be me again. Unplug and step back kind of thing. I need to take some time and think about what I want to do."

I can appreciate how he needs time to think. After all, I spent most of the last few months questioning if my relationship with Alec might not be what I thought it was.

Before I turn my head, I know Alec is close by. It's like I have an uncanny connection to his whereabouts, a tractor beam tug, drawing me to him without even trying. Alec works his way through the crowd towards us, cowboy hat in place, and those damn blue eyes smiling. My lips curve into a smile and the weird fluttery thing builds in my gut when he smiles back.

"How long did it take you to realize it?" Sasha murmurs when Alec gets stopped by a well-wisher.

I don't even need to ask him to clarify his question. I know what he means because I've answered it countless times over the last few days.

"That I loved him? Too long. But we have the rest of our lives to make up for it."

Alec nods along with the man speaking to him, but his gaze finds mine and I know he's not present in the conversation. He excuses himself and resumes his mission to get to me. God, my belly swoops and my skin tingles just watching him walk this way. Those well-worn jeans know his body better than I do, and I have to admit, the belt buckle is starting to grow on me.

"Hey, sweetheart." Alec pulls a chair over and snuggles next to me. He presses his thigh against mine and, without hesitation, I lean over to place a lingering kiss on his lips.

"Hey, cowboy. Are you enjoying yourself?"

"I am now. Where have you been all night? I was hoping you could be next to christen a spot in the brewery with a quickie. All your co-owners have. I don't want you to feel left out."

"Uh, hello." Sasha interjects and pushes his chair away. "I'm right here and have ears. But I'll leave you two alone. See you tomorrow morning for the horseback ride still, Alec?"

Sasha waves at Roman and gathers his jacket from the chair.

"Of course. Be at the ranch for 9:30 AM and we'll take you out. Zane will come, too. He's new at it and needs to learn."

Alec challenges me with his eyes, and I squeeze his thigh. I'm not turning down a horseback ride with this man. Not now. Not ever.

"Have a good night, you two." Sasha leans down to whisper next to my ear. "My vote is to lock the door in the office and bend over a desk."

He leaves us with a wink and Alec leans in closer. "I'm not opposed to that idea. I've never been over a desk before."

"Dylan and Travis use the office. I have a better idea."

Grabbing his hand, I pull him along through the door leading us through past the brewing vats and out to the garage where the delivery vans are parked.

"Are we gonna make out in a van, Z? Is that your idea? Cuz I'm one million percent on board with that."

Laughing, I shove him up against the van and slant my lips over his. "I've never made out in a car. I think it's hot. Maybe a fantasy of mine."

Alec's hands squeeze my ass as he pulls me tighter against his body.

"Is that your belt buckle or are you liking the idea just as much as me?"

His lips curve against mine with a soft laugh and with two hands confirm it's not just his belt buckle.

"I think you have the—" his breath hitches as my hand slides through his fly under the fabric to grip his cock. He jolts back, bumping his head against the van. "Fuck, Zane. Is this thing open?" His hand smacks around behind him for the handle as he dips his head to bite my neck. "If it's not unlocked, I hope you have a Plan B."

"Nope. I never have a plan; you should know that by now. But," I reach around and pop the passenger side door of the van open. "It's unlocked. I would've improvised if it wasn't."

Alec eyes the bucket seat of the delivery van. "Okay, so will I."

He hops in and slides the seat as far back as possible before pushing his pants and underwear to his knees. "Your turn." He grins and a laugh bubbles out of me.

"I have no idea how to work this without taking off my pants."

"Get in here. We'll figure it out. That's part of the fun, isn't it?"

Somehow, amongst passionate kisses and tangled clothing with limited space, I straddle over Alec, and moan when my dick slides next to his. God, that's what I want. Just to rub on him like a cat until we both come.

Alec's arms flex as he reaches behind him to grip the back of the seat and I swivel my hips over him.

"I like it when you use me to get off. You're hot like this, Z. So damn hot."

He lifts his head to meet my lips, and the heat enveloping my body threatens to ignite my clothing. Awkward front seat sex shouldn't be this amazing. But even lost in this reckless need to be with Alec, I also have to state how I feel.

"I would never use you, Alec. I don't like that word. You're not something I'd ever just use as a means to an end." Curling my fingers in his hair, I tug on the short strands. "You mean too much to me for that." I crush my lips to his and he gasps when I bite his lower lip. "Everything I do with you means something. Everything."

He releases his grip on the seat and cups his hands around my face.

"You make the sun rise for me every day, Z." He pants when I increase the speed of our slide. "You're my world. Never, ever do you mean anything less than the whole world to me."

I know it's time to drop the semantics. Thery're just words after all, and I know he didn't mean that I was in any way treating him less than what he deserves, but sometimes I get hung up on those things and I have to tell him what they mean in the moment.

Words get stuck in my throat and our noses smash together when I press my forehead to his. He brings his hands to my ass, urging me closer, to continue the sweet drag across his cock. The van's seat creaks with every rock forward and we steal kisses in between gasps and mumbles of how good it is. How fucking right it is.

Alec's fingers creep in between my ass cheeks. When he swipes them down my sensitive part, a shudder races up my spine.

"God...I'm almost there. Do that again."

When his fingertips brush down again, this time lingering with pressure at my hole, I bite his shoulder with a moan as my orgasm smashes through me. I'm barely aware of Alec's convulsions as he comes with me because I think my brain left my body, along with my spunk.

"God damn, Zane." Alec mutters before releasing his grip on my ass. His chest heaves and his lips curve with the satisfaction only a great orgasm brings. I know because the same smile is on my lips.

"Wow, we fogged up the windows real good."

Alec laughs and I twist behind me for the glove-box, hoping like hell there's still napkins in there from takeout lunches. Relieved nobody cleaned it out yet, I remove a handful and turn around to wipe up some of the mess off of Alec.

He watches under his thick eyelashes as I mostly smear the stuff across his abdomen because takeout napkins have zero absorbency, and I tug his shirt back down. We'll have to get out, or I will at least, to pull our pants up. But I like being here with him like this–hair all messed up from my hands, his softening cock laying against his thigh. The easy, content smile as he focuses on me.

Absently, his hand rubs at his hip.

"Was today hard on you?" I smooth my palm across his hip bone.

"Yeah. I took some pain meds a few hours ago."

His eyes search mine and the click of his swallow echoes in the small space.

"The clinic texted me they have a spot next week. The procedure in the clinic with the needles."

"Oh, Alec, that's great. You sure though? You can still do the one under anaesthetic if you'd prefer."

"You'll be there with me, right?"

"Of course. If they let me go in and hold your hand, I'd do that too. I'm here. For all of it."

His throat bobs with another swallow.

"I love you, you know. More than I think you know. Sometimes I feel like this is a parallel reality and there's no way you're here with me in every way I've always wanted."

His thumb brushes over my lip, and I take his hand in mine.

"I feel like that, too. Except I never thought what I wanted in life was something I could find in one of my best friends. Sometimes it's surreal to me too, but I've never felt this...this connection. This instant zip when I see or think of you."

Leaning down, my lips caress his and I'll never, ever have enough of kissing him.

"We should probably think about going home," He whispers against my lips with a small laugh.

I reluctantly agree, and once outside the van, we put our clothes into place. Alec cleans out the tissues from the van and dumps them in the can near the door. I pull him along to the small bathroom at the back of the brewery and we wash up before returning to the party.

When we step back inside, most of the guests have left and staff scurry around cleaning up. Dan and Martin sit at a table near the bar with a deck of cards in a tense game of Crazy Eights.

Martin lays down his card with a grin. "I'm changing it to hearts."

Dan scowls at his hand, and I hold back my laugh. He'd make a horrible poker player.

Dan picks up a card, shaking his head. "I've got nothing."

"Miss a turn." Martin lays a card, then another. "Pick up two." He knocks on the table. "Last card."

Dan shoots a withering glance at Martin before drawing his cards and studying his hand. He has at least fifteen cards in his hand, and I didn't know he was so competitive at a kids' card game.

"If I fold right now, you win. If I play a card, you win. There's really no way out of this. I'm going to lose no matter what."

Martin's whole expression changes, and he waits for Dan to look up from his cards.

"What?"

"Is it losing if you can call me husband?"

Dan scrunches his brow together. "What are you talking about?"

Martin reaches across the table and takes the cards from Dan's hand, placing them to the side. He folds his hands on the table with a breath and I hold my own. He's finally doing it.

"There seems no better moment than now to ask you what I've been thinking about for months. Dan, will you put up with my closet full of suits, my grumpy attitude before coffee, and my dislike for muddy farm yards to be my husband?"

Dan's lips part and his mouth moves without sound.

"This isn't a joke, is it Marty? Not some weird way to ease the sting of a stupid card game?"

He shakes his head and reaches into his pocket, where I know he still has the ring. Opening the box on the table, he launches into more words as Alec bumps up against me.

"Is he proposing?" He whispers in my ear, and I nod. Alec's arm around my waist pulls me closer, and he kisses my temple.

Whatever Martin says makes Dan cry, and he's launching out of his chair, pulling him into his arms while Martin tries to push the ring on Dan's finger.

"He said, yes! We're getting married!"

I've never seen Martin so emotional and happy as he peppers kisses on his fiancé's face. He deserves this and they're a wonderful couple. Two of the best people I know.

"Do you think that might be us someday?" Alec asks.

Turning to him, I gaze into the soft blue eyes that changed my life.

"I've never thought about it, but would you...would you want that? Marriage? Kids? How do I not know this about you?"

"I've never thought about it much. I never thought it would be attainable for me, so I didn't allow myself to hope for it." He brushes his knuckles down my neck and kisses me softly. "But I might think about it now. With you."

Nervous, happy laughter sneaks out and I take his face in my hands, planting a giant kiss on his lips.

"Okay. We'll talk about it then. Let's congratulate our friends first."

When Martin hugs me and the happiness of catching Dan off guard bubbles out of him, my heart soars for my friend. For both of them.

Martin clings to me a little longer than usual and whispers in my ear, "I wish I hadn't waited so long to ask him, Z. Don't waste time. If you want it, go get it."

Glancing over at Alec and Dan in their back slapping hugs, I know Martin is right.

"Trust me Marty, I'm not wasting anymore time."

CHAPTER 27

ALEC

Four Months Later

After listing his house for sale and combining our belongings in my farmhouse, Zane was now in my bed every night. And we could enjoy morning coffee together every day. It's such a simple pleasure to wake up with a coffee and the face of the person who means more than the world to you.

Before we became a couple, Zane coloured my life. He touched his eternal happiness to my grayness and provided a watercolour I could survive with. I accepted there could be nothing more. But now, with him in my home and across from me in our bed every morning? It's like I live in a damn rainbow. Everything is bright and vibrant. Even when he leaves his dirty clothes on the floor next to the hamper and not inside it.

Two weeks after he began the move, I had my hip surgery. While the procedure went as expected, I suffered a reaction to the painkiller they gave me. I wasn't near death, but it was bad enough for them to admit me as a precaution. When I woke up, Zane was asleep next to me in a shitty plastic hospital chair. He held his head up with one hand, and he wore the same clothes as when he dropped me off for the procedure.

That's the exact moment I knew.

He blinked open his blood-shot eyes while I laid in bed staring at him and immediately burst into tears. Reaching for my hand, he rambled on about how he couldn't lose me so soon, and how much he loved me.

For him to lament that he almost lost me weighed heavy on my heart. I was never near death, but to him, I was suffering and it troubled him. But I understood how he felt because if the roles were reversed, I'd be beside myself too.

"Good morning, cowboy."

Zane presses up behind me as I finish setting up the coffee maker.

"Good morning, sweetheart."

Turning within his arms, I press my lips to his like I do every morning. He hums and leans his warm body into me.

"Are you ready for the chaos that's about to ensue today?"

Laughing, I pull him close.

"It's not chaos. It'll be fun. You know I love your sister."

"But you've not been with my sister and Dylan at the same time. They tease each other so badly until one of them finally snaps. I swear they're more like siblings than she and I are."

The coffeepot chugs and gurgles and I already know Dylan and Zen will be on their best behaviour. Zane doesn't know that yet, though.

"Then we just ignore them. It'll be a great fall day picking apples in the orchard. We're making pies and applesauce and whatever else your brain comes up with. Some cider. A wagon ride. It'll be great."

"You're probably right. Hard to not be happy today. I get to spend it with you."

He squeezes my ass, and I push him away with a smile.

"Sit at the table. I'll get your breakfast."

Zane gropes me a little more, and we get sidetracked with wandering hands. When the coffee maker beeps, I tear myself away and steer Zane to the table. I have a plan to stick to.

Taking the Froot Loops and his favourite cereal bowl out of the cupboard, I sneak the black box inside the bowl and cover it with his favourite cereal. Before I bring the bowl over, I fix our coffees first.

"How would you feel about getting another plant?"

Zane sips his coffee, and I shake my head.

"You don't think we have enough?"

"Well, yeah, but we could put one in the bathroom. The violets won't like it there. The spider plant might do okay with the sun level from the window, but I think we could get an air plant and try it. They seem cool."

I place the bowl of Froot Loops in front of Zane with a spoon before sitting.

"Sure. We can get one. I don't know much about them, but we can try."

"Are we out of milk?"

"What? Oh, sorry. Yeah, I used it last night when I had a snack. I'm sorry, sweetheart."

We aren't out of milk, but if he'd just inhale the bowl of cereal like he always does, this would go a lot faster.

He shrugs and picks up his spoon, digging in, immediately hitting the box.

He turns his smiling green eyes on me. "Did you hide something in my cereal, cowboy?"

Like the joyful spirit he is, he fishes the box out of the bowl immediately. His smile falls, and he shoves it towards me.

"Aren't you going to open it?"

He shakes his head and heaves a shaky breath.

"What if it's not what I think it is?"

Rather than sounding excited, his voice cracks. Jesus, did I get this all wrong? I thought he'd be laughing and happy. He's pale and looks like he might throw up.

Moving out of my chair, I kneel next to him, and take his hand in mine, kissing the top of his knuckles.

"Zane..." My voice wavers. "It's what you think."

Reaching over, I open the box to display the simple white gold band with 3 small diamonds across the top.

"I knew after my surgery that I didn't want to wait long to be your husband. So, this is me asking you if you'll marry me. We don't need more time to figure it out and all the stuff society says we have to do. You own my heart and every bit of me, from the inside out. I can't give you anymore than all of me. I want to marry you."

Tears stream down his face, and he slides off his chair to meet me on the floor.

"Yes. Yes. A million times, yes, Alec. I'd do it today if we could."

He throws himself on me, and we tumble back together on the kitchen floor. I keep trying to get a word in, but he keeps silencing me with kisses. Not that I mind, but we might have some major plans this afternoon.

"Were you serious about being married today?"

His eyes search my face before he sits back, an incredulous smile on his face.

"What did you do?"

"You can say no. But I thought we were on the same page with nothing big and fancy and to just say I do. I arranged for a justice of the peace at the orchard. She...bent a rule around the wedding licence for me. If you want to, that is. You can pass and we can plan it all together later. I know you like the fall and your sister and Dylan will be here. There are apples and stuff. All good things! Next year feels like forever and —"

"Alec, you're babbling."

"I am."

Biting my lip, I wait for him to decide. I'm not the impulsive one. I plan and organize while Zane leaps into everything, hoping for the best. I want now to be one of those leaps so badly.

"You arranged for us to be married, with my sister and closest friend, at the orchard I love to visit every fall?"

Nodding, I add, "And a few other people who will join us if you say yes. Or we don't do it today and just celebrate being engaged."

"Can I plan the honeymoon?"

His grin spreads and I smile back.

"I think that's only fair. So...are we getting married today?"

"Will you carry me over the threshold when we get home?"

Laughing, I pull his lips back to mine.

"I'll carry you whenever you need me to, Zane. I love you."

"Then I think we have a wedding to get to."

Chapter 28

Epilogue

Alec

One Year Later

The beam of sunshine peeks through the crack in the curtains. Rather than be angry with it, I smile and remember where I am.

At a cabin in northern Québec with the most gorgeous autumn views. One that includes my husband on horseback.

Sometimes it still sounds strange to call him that. My husband. It's incredible how different life is when you have someone to share it with. It's corny, but true.

Zane has been my everything even before our first kiss. He supports me like no one else ever has, and my days mean more knowing he'll be there at the end of each one. He might be watering our plants, making dinner, or just joining me bleary-eyed for coffee. Zane just makes the days happier. Brighter.

And he planned a perfect delayed honeymoon. Fall is a slower time at the ranch, so I'm able to take an extended time away. He found us a secluded cabin to rent with a horse stable a short drive away. We've spent our days either on horseback exploring the woods or in bed exploring each other.

Enough time has passed that we should be familiar with our sexual preferences, but Zane has an insatiable curiosity and sex drive. Always willing to try new things, he's comfortable asking me, and I've not turned him down yet. So far, his favourite is still being tied up, and I'm excited for us to take the class on shibari soon.

"Knock, knock. Is the patient awake?"

"Your husband is awake. I don't know about a patient."

"Oh. Maybe I have the wrong cabin then?"

Smiling, I open my eyes when I don't hear him come any closer and my mouth drops open. When I had my hip surgery last year, I had joked about Zane being my nurse, and while under the influence of anti-anxiety meds, he says I confessed my dirty nurse fantasy to him.

I never believed that I said all that. Now I take it back.

Zane stands in the doorway to the bedroom wearing a lacy nurse's dress, not much different from the slutty Halloween costumes you always see. It barely covers his ass, and if I really voiced my hidden fantasy, he should have a pair of red satin panties underneath. He's even wearing an old-fashioned nurse's cap.

"You have the right cabin," I croak, and his smile says it all. He knows he has my attention and I'm in no hurry to get it back.

"Is your husband okay with you being here alone?" He walks to the side of the bed and bends over, a purposeful show only for me, and I groan. He has red satin panties underneath. With his pale skin, red is such a good colour on him.

He's beautiful.

And he's all mine.

"My husband wants me to be healthy, so I think it's okay."

I have to give props to Zane. I didn't think he'd actually role play. I just wanted to see his ass in red satin.

"Oh, I assure you he wants you healthy."

He pulls the blanket back and his lips tilt in a sex-filled grin.

"How long have you been hard for? That looks like it might be painful."

"Since you walked in looking hotter than the fantasy in my head. Get over here."

He straddles my lap, and I shiver with the texture of the satin against my dick.

"If I knew it would get you this hot, I wouldn't have waited until the honeymoon." Zane shifts and gyrates over my cock and my eyes roll back.

"I didn't think I'd like it this much to be fair."

"Me neither." He breathes as he leans down to kiss me. "Do you want a good nurse or a bad nurse today?"

"Both. I think you've been hiding things from me." I whisper and lick his throat. "Maybe I should tie you up?"

"Oh god, Alec. I won't last thirty seconds if you do."

"That's a lie." I flip us over, pinning him under me, and reach for the rope still on the nightstand from yesterday.

"This is a honeymoon surprise for you. Do you know how h-hard it is to get men's lingerie in a small town without you finding out?"

Pausing my knots around the headboard, I bend to plant a kiss on his lips.

"Oh, I'm surprised, Z. I appreciate every fucking second of thought you put into it, too. But this is for both of us now. So enjoy the ride."

I wink and his breath catches. I finish my knot work, and tie his arms down so he's spread out. Without a footboard, we tried to find something to work for his legs in the cabin, but nothing worked. So we're improvising like the champions we are.

Zane loves it when I tell him what to do, and I love watching him struggle because he wants to pull my hair or run his hands over my back.

"I'm going to drive you crazy with my mouth over this satin. Then I'm going to cum all over you while I ride you." I flick my tongue over his nipple. "Hard and fast until you come inside me."

"Oh, god…" His whimpers and moans are a symphony. Breathless sighs and low moans are the perfect soundtrack. Mouthing his cock through the satin and nuzzling his balls has him straining hard against the rope. His chest heaves and he digs his heels into the mattress.

"Please," he huffs, letting his head rest back on the pillow. "Please, cowboy. Stop making me wait. I want to be in you."

"I love it when you tell me what you want, sweetheart."

As much as I'd love for him to wear these panties longer, I'd rather give him what he wants. He raises his hips and I drag them down his legs.

"Damn, these are really nice. I'm gonna keep those close."

Zane strains against the ropes again as I slick him with lube. "F-fuck…"

I'll never tire of the way Zane responds to me.

Once seated with his cock buried deep, I adjust, and Zane's green eyes focus on my cock in my hand before snapping to my face.

"Where do you want it?"

His mouth drops open, but no sound comes out, and I rock back on his dick with a guttural moan.

"Ah…Alec!"

His cock pulses, and the warm gush in my ass is perfect. I ride him hard and come with a yell, spurting all over his chest.

"Well, that's a hell of a way to start a morning."

I place a tender kiss on his lips before releasing his ties and removing the ropes. I massage out his wrists and kiss each fingertip.

"I guess the satin was a hit then?"

"It is on you."

After I clean us both up, I open the curtains covering the picture window, and we snuggle back under the covers to watch the sun rise over the treetops. Our cabin sits in a valley at the edge of a lake and these mornings waiting for the sun's rays to find us are peaceful. I think we should make plans to come here every year for the serenity it provides alone.

We both drift in and out of sleep and there's no hurry to start the day. Laziness rules. Like Blaze said, when you have someone to share things with, you look at life differently. When an empty place in your heart is filled, even lazy days in bed mean more.

Zane's phone chimes with a ring tone I know well. *Barbie Girl* by *Aqua* and I laugh.

"Why is Sasha calling? He knows we're away, right?"

Ever since Sasha and his friends came to the rodeo and cowboy auction last year, he and Zane have become close friends. They keep in touch mostly through video chats and text. One weekend, Zane flew to New York to help him pack up his apartment before he moved.

"Hey Sasha. You know I'm away, right? Alec is giving me the side eye right now."

Zane puts him on speakerphone.

"Hey…Solomon. Why are you interrupting my honeymoon?"

"Aww, hey Alec. I just missed Zane and wanted to check in."

"We're fine Sash. We have more horseback riding this afternoon and I told you I'd take pictures of that lodge. Although you should just go back and see it yourself."

"Please don't, Z. I'm sorry I interrupted you lovebirds. I just wanted to hear your voice. Tell me about it when you get back. I should plan a visit soon. I miss you both."

"You can always call when you need Sasha." I add. "You're always welcome to."

"I know. Have fun. Love you both."

Zane ends the call, a thoughtful look on his face.

"I wish he'd just let someone in. He's such a good guy. You know he wants me to take pics of the lodge Heath sent him to. That's what we're doing today. I'm supposed to maybe, accidentally on purpose, get a photo of the hot lumberjack who owns the place."

"He will when he's ready. Look at you. You, of all people, should understand his hesitance."

Zane tosses his phone on the stand and rolls over, blanketing his body over mine.

"I do, but I also know the reward can be great when you take the risk."

He kisses me. Lips pressing and tongue sliding through my lips. His heart is in tune with every beat of mine because he's an extension of me.

Zane wears my heart everywhere he goes. He always has. Only now he knows it.

"Did you ever think we'd be here like this?" he whispers across my lips between kisses. "Friends, lovers...husbands."

"You know I never did. That was a dream I kept in my heart."

His green eyes stare into mine and they're so deep I feel like I could drown in them.

"Every day I thank anyone who will listen for giving me the courage to reach out to you. Every day, Alec. And I'm so fucking happy you kept that dream alive so we could live it."

"Are you trying to make me cry on purpose?"

"No. Just trying to tell you I love you."

"I love you, too. Always."

"Wanna go ride some horses?"

"Wanna kiss me one last time before we go?"

He presses his lips to mine with a smile.

"Always."

Curious about Sasha?

His story, Beauty and the Beard, starts a new series!

Or you can read about Blaze!

Acknowledgements

Dear reader, I owe you an immense thank you.

It was a long time to wait for these two, especially if you're a Zane fan. I'm so grateful you stuck it out and waited for him and Alec.

These two are an emotional pair, and I love them dearly. I love all my characters, but these two have a little extra special something. I hope you felt it too. And I'm so grateful you're still here!

Special mention to Kim Michener, a member of my Facebook reader group who suggested The Burgatory as a name for the restaurant in the book. And to Jenn for naming the peacock Jeff. Thank you both for the input!

I never make it a secret that I have a team of people behind me supporting me with every book. My editor, Jenn, thank you so much for your support and encouragement. Your enthusiasm and honesty is appreciated more than you know... all 3000 comments worth, lol.

Cilla, thank you for your very in-depth feedback, LOL. Your comments make me laugh and I value the time you put in to offer help.

My street team! Thank you so much for picking up where I often flounder and help spread the word about Alec. You're truly angels for your help.

I can't forget my lovely early readers. Reading time can be scarce and I'm so honoured you give my books some of your time. Thank you for always coming through for me.

Finally, for my friends who lift me when imposter syndrome strikes or help me talk through plot issues – I appreciate you so much. You know who are and I'm so lucky to call you all friends.

I hope to see you all again with Sasha's story in the next series. It's full of lumberjacks and hurt/comfort vibes, and of course some laughs! Did I mention lumberjacks? LOL

Watch for the Maple Mountain Lodge series to begin early 2024.

Until we meet in the next chapter,

RM

About the Author

RM Neill lives in Ontario, Canada with her husband who never stops providing character inspiration, her daughter who loves to help name those characters and an adorable cat named Moon. Moon provides comic relief.

Her goal is always to make you swoon and snort laugh, but most importantly, to illustrate love comes in all kinds of packages for everyone. She likes to create worlds where nobody cares who you kiss, as long as you're happy doing it.

When she's not writing, she's in the garden nurturing lavender (IYKYK) or on the golf course inventing cuss words.

She loves answering reader email. You can contact her at rm@rmneillauthor.com

Or find her in reader group on facebook sharing dad jokes.

ALSO BY

Find all my books by scanning the code!